PRAISE FOR REBECCA RAISIN

'Absolutely fantastic book, had me hooked from the first page'

'I absolutely loved everything to do with this book'

'Rebecca Raisin has a way of writing that is so evocative, it brings each and every scene to life'

'Romantic, emotional, hilarious in places but most of all beautiful'

'Full of anticipation, a real page turner. Loved it!'

'A good holiday read'

'Be whisked away on a beautiful adventure and pick up a copy today!'

REBECCA RAISIN is a true bibliophile. This love of books morphed into the desire to write them. Rebecca aims to write characters you can see yourself being friends with. People with big hearts who care about relationships, and most importantly, believe in true, once-in-a-lifetime love.

Rosie's Travelling Tea Shop

REBECCA RAISIN

ONE PLACE. MANY STORIES

HQ
An imprint of HarperCollins*Publishers* Ltd
1 London Bridge Street
London SE1 9GF

This paperback edition 2019

24 25 26 27 28 LBC 6 5 4 3 2
First published in Great Britain by
HQ, an imprint of HarperCollins*Publishers* Ltd 2019

ISBN: 9780008414207

Typeset by Palimpsest Book Production Ltd, Falkirk, Stirlingshire

Printed and bound in the United States

For the hero in my very own love story.
This one is for you Ashley.

CHAPTER ONE

'You're just not spontaneous enough, Rosie...'

I've misheard, surely. Fatigue sends my brain to mush at the best of times but after twenty hours on my feet, words sound fuzzy, and I struggle to untangle what he's getting at.

It's just gone 2 a.m. on Saturday 2nd February and that means I'm officially 32 years old. By my schedule I should be in the land of nod, but I'd stayed late at work to spontaneously bake a salted caramel tart to share with Callum, hoping he'd actually remember my birthday this year.

He's never been a details man – we're opposites in that respect – so I try not to take it to heart, but part of me hopes this is all a prelude to a fabulous birthday surprise and not the brewing of a row.

'Sorry, Callum, what did you say?' I try to keep my voice light and swig a little too heartily on the cheap red wine I found in the back of the cupboard after Callum told me we needed to have a chat. Surreptitiously, I glance to the table beside me hoping to see a prettily wrapped box but find it bare, bar a stack of cookbooks. Really, I don't need gifts, do I? Love can be shown in other ways, perhaps he'll make me a delicious breakfast when we wake up...

1

My eyes slip closed. With midnight long gone, my feet ache, and I'm weary right down to my bones. Bed is calling to me in the most seductive way; *come hither and sleep, Rosie*, it says. Even the thought of a slice of luscious ooey-gooey birthday tart can't keep me awake and *compos mentis*. But I know I must focus, he's trying to tell me something…

'Are you asleep?' The whine in his voice startles me awake. 'Rosie, please, don't make this any harder than it has to be,' he says, as if I'm being deliberately obtuse.

Make what harder – what have I missed? I shake my head, hoping the fog will clear. 'How am I not spontaneous? What do you even *mean* by that?' Perhaps he's nervous because he's about to brandish two airline tickets to the Bahamas. *Happy Birthday, Rosie, time to pack your bags!*

He lets out a long, weary sigh like I'm dense and it strikes me as strange that he's speaking in riddles at this time of the morning when I have to be at the fishmonger in precisely five hours.

'Look…' He runs a hand through his thinning red hair. 'I think we both know it's over, don't we?'

'Over?' My mouth falls open. Just exactly how long did my power nap last for? 'What… *us*?' My incredulity thickens the air. This does not sound *anything* like a birthday celebration, not even close.

'Yes, us,' he confirms, averting his eyes.

'Over because I'm not—', I make air quotes with my fingers, '—*spontaneous* enough?' Has he polished off the cooking sherry?

My husband still won't look at me.

'You're too staid. You plan your days with military precision from when you wake to when you sleep, and everything in between has a time limit attached to it. There's no room for fun or frivolity, or god forbid having sex on a day you haven't sched-uled it.'

So I'm a planner? It's essential in my line of work as a sous-chef in esteemed Michelin-starred London restaurant Époque, and he should know that, having the exact same position in another restaurant (one with no Michelin stars, sadly). If I didn't schedule our time together we'd never see each other! And I wouldn't get the multitude of things done that need doing every single hour of every day. High pressure is an understatement.

'I... I...' I don't know how to respond.

'See?' He stares me down as if I'm a recalcitrant child. 'You don't even care! I'd get more affection from a pot plant! You *can* be a bit of a cold fish, Rosie.'

His accusation makes me reel, as if I've been slapped. 'That's harsh, Callum, honestly, what a thing to say!' Truth be told I'm not one for big shows of affection. If you want my love, you'll get it when I serve you a plate of something I've laboured over. That's how I express myself, when I cook.

It dawns on me, thick and fast. 'There's someone else.'

He has the grace to blush.

A feeling of utter despair descends while my stomach churns. How *could* he?

'Well?' I urge him again. Since he's dropping truth bombs left, right and centre, he can at least admit his part in this... this break-up. Hurt crushes my heart. I hope I'm asleep and having a nightmare.

'Well, yes, there is, but it's not exactly a surprise, surely? We're like ships that pass in the night. If only you were more—'

'Don't you dare say spontaneous.'

'—if only you were *less* staid.' He manages a grin. A *grin*. Do I even know this man who thinks stomping over my heart is perfectly acceptable?

He continues reluctantly, his face reddening as if he's embarrassed. 'It's just... you're so predictable, Rosie. I can see into your future, *our* future because it's planned to the last microsecond! You'll *always* be a sous-chef, and you'll *always* schedule your days from sun up to sun down. You'll keep everyone at arm's length. Even when I leave, you'll continue on the exact same trajectory.'

He shakes his head as though he's disappointed in me but his voice softens. 'I'm sorry, Rosie, I really am, but I can see it playing out – you'll stay resolutely single and grow the most cost-effective herb garden this side of the Thames. I hope you don't, though. I truly hope you find someone who sets your world on fire. But it's not me, Rosie.'

What in the world? Not only is he dumping me, he's planning my spinsterhood too? Jinxing me to a lonely life where my only companion is my tarragon plant? Well, not on my watch! I might be sleep-deprived but I'm nobody's fool. The love I have for him pulses, but I remember the other woman and it firms my resolve.

He sighs and gives me a pitying smile. 'I hate to say it, Rosie. But you're turning into your dad. Not wanting to leave the...'

'Get out,' I say. He is a monster.

'What?'

Cold fish, eh? 'OUT!' I muster the loudest voice I can.

'But I thought we'd sort who gets what first?'

'Out and I mean it, Callum.' I will not give him the satisfaction of walking all over me just because he thinks he can.

'Fine, but I'm keeping this apartment. You can—'

'NOW!' The roar startles even me. *You want to see me warm up?* 'LEAVE!'

He jumps from the couch and dashes to the hallway, where I see a small bag he's left in readiness, knowing the outcome of our 'quick chat' long before I did. With one last guilty look over his shoulder, he leaves with a bang of the door. He's gone just like that.

As though I'm someone so easy to walk away from.

Laying down on the sofa, I clutch a cushion to my chest and wait for the pain to subside. How has it all gone so wrong? There's someone else in his life? When did he find time to romance anyone?

Sure, I don't go out much, other than for work purposes, but that's because there's no bloody time *to* go out! I'm not like my dad, am I? No, Callum is using that as ammunition, knowing how sensitive I am to such a comparison.

The sting of his words burns and doubt creeps in. Am I not spontaneous enough? Am I far too predictable?

Admittedly I'd been feeling hemmed in, ennui creeping into everything, even my menu. Each day bleeding into the next with no discernible change except the *plat de jour*. Sure, my professional life is on track but lately even my enthusiasm for that has waned. I've had enough of tweezing micro herbs to last a lifetime. Of plating minuscule food at macro prices. Of the constant bickering in the kitchen. The noise, the bluster, the backstabbing. Of never seeing blue skies or the sun setting. Of not being able to sit beside my husband on the couch at a reasonable hour and keep my eyes open at the same time.

Is this my fault? Am I a cold fish? I like routine and order so I know where I fit in the world. Everything is controlled and organised. There's no clutter, mess, or fuss, or any chance I'll lose control of any facet of my life. That need to keep life contained is a relic of my childhood. Is my marriage now a casualty of that?

But he'd promised he'd love me for better or worse.

Am I supposed to hope he comes to his senses or to beg him to come back?

Sighing, I place a hand on my heart, trying to ease the ache. I could never trust him again. I'm a stickler for rules, always have been, and cheating, well… I can't forgive that.

But bloody hell, our lives had been all mapped out. Our first child was scheduled for conception in 2021. The second in 2023. And he's just blithely walking away from his children like that! Didn't he understand I would have given up my career for our future family? The career I'd worked so hard for! And I would have done it gladly, too.

Now this?

The gossip will spread like wildfire around the foodie world. My name embroiled in a scandal not of my choosing. It's taken me fifteen years to get to where I am in my career, and that's meant sacrificing a few things along the way, like a social life, and free time, real friendships. But that was all part of the bigger picture, the tapestry of our lives.

It hurts behind my eyes just thinking about it all.

And I mean to cry and wail and torment myself about the 'other woman', or force myself up off the couch and throw my lovingly baked birthday tart at the wall, or eat it all in one go as tears stream down my face – something dramatic and movie-esque – but I don't. Instead, I fall into a deep sleep, only waking when my alarm shrills at stupid o'clock the next day, and with it comes the overwhelming knowledge that I must leave London. At 32, this could be my rebirth, couldn't it?

Not spontaneous enough? Cold fish? Spinster? Like my dad? *I'll show you.*

CHAPTER TWO

At Billingsgate Market the briny smell of seafood hardly registers. I dash to the fishmonger, rattle off my order, too distracted to make the usual small talk. John, the guy with the freshest seafood this side of Cornwall, notices my jittery state.

'What's up, Rosie? There's something different about you today.' He gives me a once-over as if trying to pinpoint the change.

'Oh,' I say, mind scuttling. 'I haven't had any tea.' My other great love. Making hand-blended teas for various moods. Wake-me-ups. Wind-me-downs. And everything in between. If I ever leave my job, I have a backup plan at least… tea merchant!

John cocks his head. 'You don't look like you need it though, Rosie. You look alive.' He shrugs. 'And utterly different from this fella.' He points to a dead flounder whose glassy eye stares up at me as John lets out his trademark haw, while I flinch slightly at being compared to deceased marine life. He bags my order, promising to courier it on ice to Époque immediately.

Do I look alive?

As I make my way to the butcher to confirm my weekly order, it occurs to me. Shouldn't I be puffy-faced, red-eyed, fuzzy-headed from tossing and turning all night? Instead, I feel this sort of frenetic energy because I realise that I'm about to do something very out of character, bold and brave, and completely unexpected – what that entails, I'm still not quite sure, but the desire is there and I'm about to implement a huge change. *Shriek.*

I'm steadfast Rosie, I don't *do* change.

I'm going to prove to the world that I'm not staid. Not stuck in a rut. I'm going to surprise even Callum, by doing the opposite of what he expects because I know if I don't move on fast, I never will.

Being predictable has its disadvantages, and it's time I shook things up a bit. Jumped, as it were, into a new reality.

What that is though exactly, remains to be seen…

When I think of my once heart-melting, lovely, red-headed husband my lungs constrict, so I push him from my mind as quickly as possible. As I walk, I repeat the mantra *do not fall apart, hold yourself together,* and promise myself I can wail in privacy later.

I visit the butcher at Borough Market, then the French boulangerie, and finally our fresh produce supplier before all my jobs are done and I'm ready to prepare for lunch service.

When I arrive at Époque, I find the restaurant manager crunching numbers, a steaming espresso in front of her untouched. I've always liked Sally; she's a sassy, funny Glaswegian, who chain smokes and is fantastic at her job.

'Coffee?' she says absently, fiddling with paperwork.

'And a chat,' I say, dumping my bag on the bench and joining her at the table.

'That sounds ominous.' Her eyes dart to me before she bustles to the coffee machine, which spits and hisses under her hand.

A headache looms. Am I about to make a huge mistake? I've been yearning for change for such a long time, but it's hard to tell if it's a lie I'm selling myself. Callum might have pushed me to act, but I'm not being impetuous, am I?

As worry gnaws away at me, outwardly I remain calm and busy, unwinding my scarf and taking in the restaurant. It's not often that I'm front of house. When I first started at Époque the décor was art nouveau, then it went on to have various makeovers, and right now it's industrial chic. Any successful London establishment must move with the times, so the *in* crowd doesn't become the *out* crowd.

And the kitchen is no different. I'm always looking for the next foodie sensation, the dish that will blow patrons' minds, get us write-ups and reservations booked solid for the next six months.

You name it, I've tried it. Molecular gastronomy, sensory gastronomy, *multi*-sensory gastronomy. While it's all very theatrical, and a feast for mind, body and spirit, there's times I just want to cook up a big, hearty bowl of comfort food without any flourishes – real, honest meals that will fill your belly and warm your heart. Alas, that's never going to happen in a Michelin-starred establishment like Époque.

Sally returns and places my tiny cup down. 'So, talk,' she says, staring me down. It's her no-nonsense attitude I love. She doesn't mince words, and you always know where you stand with her. Do her right, and you'll have a friend for life. Cross her and forget working in London again. Sally's been around forever and knows everyone there is to know in the industry. We get on well because she accepts me for who I am, a cookery nerd. That, and she's partial to my twice-cooked fromage soufflé.

'I'm officially handing in my notice,' I say, surprised by the confidence in my tone. With that sort of voice, I could almost fool myself into believing I know what I'm doing! What the hell *am* I doing?

Handing in my notice?

I hope my brain will catch up with my mouth, sooner rather than later.

Sally purses her lips and nods. 'And you don't think this is a knee-jerk reaction to what that despicable excuse for a husband has done to you?'

'You've heard *already*?' That's got to be a record, even for the likes of the London cookery establishment.

With an airy shrug, she tries to downplay it. 'You know what it's like. There were whispers about him a while back, but I didn't think they had any substance, hence why I never said anything.'

Just how long has the affair been going on? Were they having mad, passionate, *unscheduled* sex, while I worked? My heart bongoes painfully inside my chest as though it's preparing for an attack. I will myself not to give into it. He doesn't deserve that. The rat. The pig. The cheating no-good husband. But oh, how it hurts.

'So who is she?' I hate asking but I need to know who he's replaced me with.

Sally takes a cigarette from her purse and lights up, despite the restaurant being a strictly non-smoking venue and the fact there's enough smoke alarms installed to have half of the London Fire Brigade here within minutes if they're set off.

When she doesn't answer I urge her on. 'It's OK, Sally, honestly.'

With a tut, she says, 'I want to wring his scrawny neck! The things that guy has put you through.'

I'm not a fan of wandering down memory lane. What point does looking back serve? Sally's never been keen on Callum; she's of the opinion he rides on my coat-tails. And I suppose for a while he did. And once, early on before we were married, he did sort of try to steal my job from under me and Sally hasn't forgotten that. I had until this very moment. Clearly I've used poor judgement in the whole choosing my husband department. Back then I had love hearts for eyes, and the world was a wondrous place.

'Who is she?' I prod.

'Khloe,' she says, with a reluctant sigh.

I shake my head. 'Why is it *always* the chef de partie? What a cliché. And Khloe with a K, for god's sake.' I'd met the exotic-eyed vixen at an industry party, and she actually introduced herself as 'Khloe with a K'. Who does that? Kardashians and husband-stealers, that's who.

That means Khloe worked *under* him, literally and figuratively. The thought leaves a bad taste in my mouth so I sip the bitter coffee to wash it away.

Sally leans closer, surveying me, as if waiting for me to cry, for one solitary tear to fall, or my bottom lip to wobble, something – anything – that shows her I'm not a robot, but I use all my willpower to remain calm and keep telling myself he does not warrant such histrionics. I'm a professional, dammit, and I won't be a sobbing mess at work. I suppose this control is what makes people think I'm aloof, steely, strange, when in fact it's the opposite, it's purely a protective instinct.

Inside my heart twists and shrinks, this pain probably doing me lifelong damage. Will my heart shrivel up altogether, leaving me as predicted – a lonely old spinster? Is rebound sex the answer? No, I will fall in love, not lust.

Hearing about Khloe firms my resolve. London is too toxic for me right now. I need to put some space between me and the city I've loved for so long.

Sally rubs my arm affectionately. 'The whispers will die down, you just need to keep focused, keep working and ride out the storm. Don't give up your career because of that snake in the grass. Please. You've worked harder than anyone I know. Don't let that go to waste.'

I take a moment to decipher my feelings. Eventually I say, 'It's not just him, Sally. It's everything. I've had this nagging feeling life is passing me by for a while now. I've been slogging it out here since I was seventeen. I'm in the prime of my life, and if I don't look up, I'll miss it. What Callum did might have been the catalyst, but it's not the entire reason. I promise I'm not making this decision lightly or *just* because of him.' As the words rolls off my tongue, I feel the truth in them. I've been unhappy for such a long time but put it down to overwork, life fatigue, the daily grind.

'Listen, you're giving me four weeks' notice, right?'

11

I nod.

'Take that time to think it over. I mean, *really* consider it. Instead of interviewing for a replacement straight away, Jacques can hold the fort alone for a month while you decide.'

Jacques is the celebrity chef de cuisine and won't like having to wait in limbo for my decision. He's an ogre to work under. In actual fact, I do his job so he can sashay about front of house before returning to the line and barking orders and cursing. As his star rose, I worked my way up behind him, and we have a sort of grudging respect for one another. While he has an ego the size of the Titanic, he lets me control the menu and I have complete freedom in the kitchen, even if he does take the credit.

'Thanks, Sally. I appreciate that. But I'm quite sure, so you can start interviewing.' No point pretending. They'll need a sous-chef so things run smoothly, and while I'm not super friendly with Jacques, I do like the other staff and would hate for them to have to carry the extra weight of my absence.

After one of Sally's breath-stealing hugs, I leave her and go to the kitchen to shuffle the fresh produce around and prepare the day's menus, hoping the kitchen staff won't pry, even though I bet they've woken up to gossipy text messages about me and Callum.

That's the culinary scene for you.

CHAPTER THREE

After a strangely quiet Sunday shift, I'm home earlier than usual, giving me time to mull over whether I've taken leave of my senses. Who quits their job on a whim like that?

My phone beeps constantly with messages like:

Darling, that swine didn't, did he? Text me back. Kimmy x

I wrack my mind wondering who Kimmy might be and come up blank. There's another from Leroy who I vaguely recall works with Callum.

So are ya leaving then? If y'are can you put in a good word with Jacques for me?

The rest are of a similar ilk; people wanting the inside scoop. No one actually offers to help me drown my sorrows or bring cake over so I can eat my feelings. And seeing as they're all chefs, it hurts.

They want the gossip or my job. The vultures.

I don't dwell on it much – just every hour, on the hour, or so. Still, if there's one thing I'm good at it, it's making a plan. New life scenarios. What *not* to do, kind of thing. I write down various possibilities – stopping just before *what if the sky falls down* – and realise for once in my life I have absolutely no idea what to do, or where to go when my notice is up.

It's a scary thought. Yet somehow liberating.

No one gives up a sous-chef position at Époque unless they've married royalty or won the lottery, and that's exactly why I'm relishing the thought. No one, absolutely no one, including my husband (do I call him ex at this juncture?), thinks I'll react.

The whispers in the kitchen were that I'd work even longer hours and virtually chain myself to the line with some kind of mad zeal, avenging myself by doing the job of three until one day when I'm a lonely old crone someone has to drag me kicking and screaming out of the kitchen. So nothing new there then.

The wine helps clear my mind and I drink steadily, delighting in the rich Shiraz, a gift from Sally, thrust into my hands at the end of my shift with the words: *enjoy your day off tomorrow, but think things through…*

Inexplicably the bottle empties, so I open one of my cheap quaffers as I skim through various blogs online, hoping to find an idea, or something to give me perspective. Those uplifting, let-the-breeze-blow-you-here, change-your-life type of blogs.

As I sip, I read so many wonderful stories of transformation, of risking it all. Families who've wrenched their kids from school to live life on the road. Single women (just like me now!) who've thrown their spatulas down and taken the reins and live by their own rules. People with pop-up food vans. Campervan pottery shops. Musicians who play from tiny homes. Artisans who make jewellery by the sea, sell their wares and follow the sun. I shake my head. There's a whole community of people out there *living their best life…*

Could I be that person? Probably not.

So it can't hurt to look at campervan prices, can it? I'm only *looking*, I'm not buying. Even if I were to go out on a limb and envisage a totally new way of life, I'd have to commit to months of research to see if it's viable. Then there's the flat to consider. My possessions. Money. I'm stuck, really, aren't I? It strikes me that we humans build these lives for ourselves that have the tendency to trap us. I guzzle more wine and wonder how I can fix the mess I've found myself in...

***

The next day, I wake up with a screaming headache. The pounding in my head is in staccato with the buzzing of the doorbell. My one and only day off from the restaurant, and my most relished lie-in has been ruined. By me, and the copious amounts of wine I'd put away, and by whoever deems it acceptable to visit at – I scan the clock – barely eight o'clock. It should be a criminal offence. I silently berate myself for drinking so much red on an empty stomach. But cooking for one, well, I'm not used to it.

The buzzing continues and it dawns on me. It's Callum come to his senses and seen the error of his ways. He'll wear that apologetic gap-toothed smile of his, his too-long red hair hanging over one eye, so he can hide behind his mistake. And I shall relish telling him to spin on his heel and go back the way he came!

I dash out of bed, as the world spins on its axis. Bloody hell, just how much *did* I drink last night? Don't tell me I'm going to be one those tragics who drink their life away and use the empty wine bottle as a microphone for an impromptu concert? A memory forms; did I karaoke the night away strutting my stuff for my own reflection in the window? As alarming as the thought is, the doorbell buzzing makes my hangover worse so I hurry along to answer it.

Hand on wall, I steady myself and wish I'd brushed my teeth and had some painkillers on hand. Urgh. Quickly, I pat down my bed hair and open the door with a grimace.

It's not Callum.

15

And suddenly it occurs to me I'm braless in a teeny tiny singlet wearing a pair of Callum's old tracksuit bottoms, so big they gape at the front. So not appropriate. With a wild grin that I hope masks my discomfort, I grasp desperately at the coat rail to my right, while pondering who this stranger is, as my fingers finally make contact with my jacket and I fling it on.

'Sorry,' I say. 'I wasn't expecting anyone.'

Confusion dashes across the elderly man's face. He's dressed in a worn duffel, denim jeans and has a kind smile. He doesn't look like a Londoner, somehow – his features are too soft, too amiable, his face too open, like a doting grandparent. 'Erm,' he says scratching the back of his neck. 'You said you'd pay extra if I got here early.'

Oh bloody hell. Pay extra? Is he some kind of gigolo? He looks a bit too old for that caper. Not that I've had any experience with such a thing, but still. Was I so inebriated last night I thought *that* was the answer? I'm losing my damned mind!

'Excuse me, sorry, it's been such a long day…' Oh, hell, it's only 8 a.m. 'I mean, a long night—', I cough loudly, '—the night before, I mean. As in last night.' *Stop talking!*

He nods, but worry flashes in his eyes. 'Well, do you want to come and have a look at her?'

Relief washes over me. *Her?* I've bought a puppy? Or even better a 10-year-old rescue hound who needs some love after too long in the shelter! Forget my 2021 child, I've adopted a fur baby who'll cuddle me better than Callum ever did. It makes sense. There are so many animals out there that need adopting and I mentally give myself a pat on the back for being so forward-thinking.

'Ah, sure,' I say and tighten the coat around me, holding the voluminous pants with my other hand. Note to self: wear own pyjamas in this time of drastic change.

I stumble down the steps after him, thinking just how perfect an animal companion will be. Snoopy can snuggle with me at night, be my best friend, my most faithful…

'Here she is.' He points but nothing jumps out at me. There's a great big fuchsia pink van parked on the side of the road blocking my view. I scan parked cars up the length of the street, expecting to see a furry face peeking out, a wet nose fogging up the glass but don't see a single animal.

Just when I'm about to question him he hands over a set of keys. 'The credit card payment has been approved so she's all yours. Let me show you around.'

The credit card.

The what?

What the hell have I done!

The con artist and stealer of my money opens the pink campervan door to reveal a very tidy tiny home complete with small kitchen, doll-sized sink, an electric hotplate and oven. A wave of claustrophobia runs down the length of me. It's so compact, how anyone could live in such a space is beyond me. However, there's a faint aroma of cinnamon sugar in the air that makes me smile, as if whoever cooked here last, made comfort food.

'This here's the dining room,' he says, pride in his voice as he motions to a fold-down plank of wood with two padded bench seats on each side, which he lifts to reveal deep storage cavities. Everything seems to have a double function.

Next to the dining area is a one-person sofa with pink storage nooks above. I spy a bedroom off at the back and take a peek in. The bed is made up with fine linen and one rose cushion sits lovingly in the centre of the bed. It makes my heart tug for some reason I can't pinpoint.

A gauzy floral chiffon curtain separates the living and sleeping quarters. There's a bathroom, which is so narrow I have to crab walk in sideways, but it's neat and sparkling clean. Of course, the tiles are pink, and they slowly grow on me as I understand the need for décor to match. There's no excess, everything here serves a purpose. It's not chintzy, it's homely, as if someone put a lot of care into making things pretty and comfortable for long, slow journeys.

But I don't do things on a whim. I most certainly don't buy campervans for... the full weight of winter runs right through me from my head down to my toes.

'Excuse me, how much was erm... the approval?'

He frowns. 'Five thousand pounds like we agreed and an extra five hundred to get her here by 8 a.m. I drove through the night.'

Flip. Fluck. Fugger.

What the hell am I supposed to do with such a thing? Live in it? Is it even roadworthy? Can I drive such a big, long, hulking thing? And pray tell, where the bloody buggery am I meant to be going in... *her*. Urgh. How do I know I even spoke to this guy? He could be one of those internet stalker, hacker types. Really, this is very out of character for me.

A scream echoes through my brain.

'I'm sorry about Callum,' he says. 'But you're doing the right thing. Leaving the big city toxicity behind and heading out on the open road. You'll find yourself there, Rosie.'

Oh god. I did buy this fuchsia pink monstrosity. I'm never drinking again.

'Yes, well, I'm lost quite a lot of the time,' I say, swallowing back panic. 'So finding myself will be a real bonus.'

He waxes lyrical about hidden storage, and petrol mileage, permits, parking and a bunch of other stuff, I stop listening, as I find it hard to catch my breath. Five thousand five hundred pounds! That's almost the entirety of my savings. I'll have to repay my credit card. I'll have to sell this on. I'll have to...

'The trailer hitches on very simply, and inside that are all your tables and chairs, and even a little fire grate for those cold days, customers just love milling about that, warm cocoa in hand.'

'Customers?'

He gives me that same look as if he's worried I'm unhinged

18

which I clearly am. 'Yes, your pop-up tea shop customers, remember?'

'Erm…'

'You want to go back to making comfort food, big portions made with love, not a micro herb in sight. Served up with steaming pots of gourmet hand-blended tea. Cream tea Sundays. You *are* Rosie, aren't you?' Uneasiness lines his face.

'Yes, yes, I'm Rosie. And yes, my very own pop-up tea shop, of course I remember. I haven't had any tea yet myself you see, that's all.' My calming blend would go down a treat right about now, there's not much that marshmallow leaves, camomile, and mint can't fix. Well, except making big life decisions while under the influence of Shiraz. I haven't blended a tea to fix that just yet.

I glance once more at the van and a murky idea takes shape. A pop-up tea van could work. Hadn't I wanted to go back to my roots, cooking big batches of cookies, apple crumbles, and layer cakes laced with rum? Scones with lashings of home-made jam and thick luscious cream. Rib-stickers, nourishing food that warmed you from the inside out like big bowls of hearty stew, and rich rustic soups. Or cinnamon rice porridge, dishes that filled your belly and kept you warm on those cold wintry nights.

Coupled with my hand-blended exotic teas, maybe inebriated me had a plan and I just had to remember it. *Rosie's travelling tea shop…*

'So…' The man takes some paperwork from his bag. 'We just need to fill these out and Poppy is all yours.'

'The van's name is Poppy?' I think of the pink cushion, proudly sitting on the bed, like it should mean something to me, but what? Why?

He laughs and his cheeks pink. 'My wife chose it. We ran Poppy round for some time before she was taken ill.'

'I hope she's feeling better.' As soon as I say the words I understand, but it's too late to snatch them back.

He thrusts his hands in his pockets and his eyes cloud. 'Sadly she passed, but you know, Rosie, she was an eccentric like you…'

An eccentric? I'd been called worse.

'… and I think she'd be very happy that Poppy is going to be in such…' He blushes and mumbles something incoherent before recovering and saying, 'in such good hands.'

I forgive him for stumbling on the words. I'd be a little dubious handing over Poppy to me too, with all those memories attached from the trips they must have undertaken together.

The poor man, you can see the loss in the lines of his face once you know. 'I'm incredibly sorry to hear about your wife. I promise I'll take good care of Poppy.' Curiously, I feel a bond with this elderly fellow. With Poppy. As if his wife left me clues to say: follow your heart!

'We're going to have a lot of adventures.' As I drive straight into a town called Losing-My-Damn-Mind – Population: One.

His face softens, and he swipes at his glassy eyes. 'Rosie, take it from me – life is so fleeting. Being on the road is full of challenges but nothing comes close to the simple joy you'll find in some remote corner of the globe. Keep safe, and keep your mind open to possibilities…'

My spine tingles with recognition and a slow smile settles across my face. Who says I'm not spontaneous? Poppy and I are going to embark on an epic journey, one long overdue… But how to afford it? And where to go?

CHAPTER FOUR

A couple of weeks later, after a dizzyingly long shift at Époque I realise leaving really is the best course of action, no matter how much it scares me. Work has been a nightmare with the rumours, gossip and constant whispering behind hands and I want out.

But first I need to formulate a plan. I have Poppy and now I just need figure out what to do with her. Back in the flat, after a healthy and nutritious meal of a packet of salt and vinegar crisps, I fire up the laptop and do a bit of investigating.

OK, I go straight to Khloe Parker's Facebook page, and see she's updated the masses already: *Khloe Parker is in a relationship.* She's tagged Callum in the post and collectively, they've had seventy-two comments. I can't help myself and I click them open, hoping they're not all congratulations.

Does anyone remember he is in fact married? Even though it's like a stab to the heart, I read each comment, from the inane '*wow*' to the more heartbreaking, '*Congrats guys, glad it's finally out in the open!*'

In the gloomy evening, in the quiet of night, I realise I was the last to know, and the thought pains me so much I can barely swallow my tears. Our mutual acquaintances had known and no one bothered to tell me. Instead they've sent the happy couple their best wishes… What kind of life have I been living here?

I click over to Callum's page, and find photos of the pair, selfies taken up close, their bright eyes and wide smiles taking up the frame. I quickly close Facebook down, and resolve never to check their pages again. Not my best idea, was it? It makes me feel lower than low, as if I don't matter to anyone.

Is it just because I'm leaving and will have no relevance anymore, because I won't be Rosie Lewis, Michelin-starred sous-chef…? Or more truthfully is it because I was always on the periphery anyway, never quite fitting in and not knowing how to do anything well, except cook. With my legs well and truly kicked from under me, I forge ahead, trying to push it from my mind.

Mindlessly I scroll the internet, looking for something to distract me. Funny cat videos work until I picture my future with a furry companion and a very healthy herb garden, and quickly move on. Hours later I stumble on a website that catches my eye.

Van Lifers: Living the dream on the open road

As I click through the site, marvelling at the exotic pictures of these strangers' travels, I find a forum, and request to join. I plan to lurk and read their live conversations, but as soon as I'm approved, a message pops up from another member, so I don't have the chance.

Hello there Rosie! I'm Charlotte, one of the moderators. If you have any questions, do let me know.

Golly, I thought I'd sneak in and read their posts before actually having to chat to anyone!

Thanks, Charlotte. I'm just going to have a peruse.

She sends me a thumbs-up emoji and I shut the chat window down and spend the next little while trying to make sense of all the different threads, and the plethora of advice from nomads.

Dare I try to live such an unstructured life?

Just the thought of it almost makes me break out in hives. Every day would be different, and I'd have to learn to let go of my obsession with planning every minute, and factoring in variables. Could I do such an audacious thing?

I shut the computer with a bang. Doubtful. But their profile pictures stick in my mind, some with islands and cerulean water in the background, others with rugged mountains, forests, or verdant fields, but they all shared one trait: huge smiles that threatened to swallow them whole. Not the fake selfie smile, the forced rigor mortis of social media pictures, but real joy emanating from these strangers as if they've found the pot of gold at the end of the rainbow.

That's what I want. To feel joyful. But are some people predisposed to joy and others to worry? It would be an experiment then, right? To shed my old self, and see who hides beneath. Despite my self-enforced alcohol ban, I pour a glass of white wine, and think about where I'd go, and what I'd sell to be able to afford the lifestyle, and mostly how I'd manage to reinvent myself if only I took the first leap.

Logging back on, I click the chat button and find Charlotte's name and type:

Charlotte, do pop-up food vans make enough money to fund travel, or do most people have a safety net of savings?

I send it before I can overthink it, cringing at how desperate I must sound. How do I, planner extraordinaire, not have enough savings? After buying Poppy I wiped out most of what I had; coupled with the cost of living in London, there's not much left to save even if I wanted to.

Ellipses appear as she writes a reply, and finally:

Everyone is different and it depends on what sort of lifestyle you want to maintain, but generally speaking, pop-up food vans do exceptionally well – everyone needs to eat, right? Not only do they sell to the public at various festivals, and fairs, they also sell to the other nomads, so if that's your speciality, what are you waiting for!

Hmm, she has a point, everyone does need to eat, and who doesn't like a freshly brewed pot of exotic tea alongside scones with jam and cream. I could keep my menu simple to start with, and see how things go. Poppy can't sit on the side of the road forever.

Thanks, Charlotte. What am I waiting for indeed! I'll mull it over J

***

A few days later, a rough idea takes shape, and even though it's daunting, it somehow feels right. But I need more information so I head back to the forum to find Charlotte. Her name isn't on the chat window but before I can ask anyone another person pops up.

Hey Rosie! I'm Oliver. Welcome to VL. What's your location?

Blimey, why does he need to know? I can't just give out my location willy-nilly, can I? There's a lot to be said for remaining anonymous. Why did I use my real name? An amateur move!

Is this part of my problem though, being so reserved with people? Always holding back, keeping everything bottled up. Slowly but surely becoming an outcast in my own life? Still, he could be anyone! I can't just trust strangers, *especially* names on a screen. I compromise, and reply, albeit guardedly. Really he can't be any worse than my real-life acquaintances, who've all kept quiet despite my heartbreak.

Hi, Oliver. I haven't started my journey yet. Just getting the lay of the land, so to speak. I'm looking for Charlotte, if she's around?

I scroll to the top of the current thread and read. It's an online forum for anyone who needs advice or help when it comes to travelling in a caravan or campervan. Born2Travel asks about the best travel insurance, while WanderlustWendall shares an anecdote about an altercation she had with a national park inspector near the Welsh border. They seem so vibrant, so happy; even when WanderlustWendall shares that she copped a fifty-pound fine, she says she learned her lesson and is generous enough to share the tip so others don't make the same mistake. TravelBug1978 discusses the money saving merits of a 5:2 fasting diet, while NomadbyNight scoffs at the idea.

Charlotte won't be back for a few weeks, she's guiding a cycle tour in the Peak District and will be out of range.

Are they all so adventurous? I couldn't imagine being on a bike for a day, let alone for weeks at a time. Wouldn't that provoke some sort of injury, all that sitting on a teeny tiny seat?

Thanks, anyway.

I blow out a breath, having psyched myself up to speak openly to Charlotte I feel somewhat deflated.

No worries, so when do you plan to leave?

I want to chat away, and share all my hopes and dreams, but I'm not that person. And for some reason, I felt more comfortable talking to Charlotte, perhaps it's a female thing. It gave me hope that if there were a bunch of other women travelling the globe alone, then I could do it too.

Soon.

What else can I say? Even if I don't meander from place to place, I'll be driving Poppy somewhere, even if it's only a caravan park where I spend the remainder of my life hiding... No, no I will make the effort, I will adapt, dammit. So Charlotte is currently burning her thigh muscles cycling up and down hills, that doesn't mean I can't ask Oliver the same questions.

As I dillydally with how to begin, he asks:

Do you blog?

While I love reading blogs, I'd never write one. My creativity is in the kitchen, and I don't pretend otherwise.

No, sorry, I don't.

Another person joins the site, so I'm betting he'll welcome them and I'll be able to read through the amazing threads with eye opening titles like: How I quit my corporate job and now live on fifteen pounds a day and couldn't be happier. Or: Life after Loss, on the open road. And: My pop-up Pimms van, and how I make money to fund travel. So many stories, so many different versions of life, ones I'd never ever considered. Goose bumps prickle my skin, as if my body knows this is the next course of action for me too. Taking Poppy on an adventure like I promised, and making money along the way, enough to keep me going, until I work out exactly what I'm searching for...

Don't apologise! A lot of VLs blog about their journey, almost like an online diary to keep track, that's all. It's a great way to follow along with those you connect with.

I contemplate his theory. It would be nice to keep a record, keep track of where I go. But I know myself, and I'm more of a reader. Maybe I can keep my own online diary for myself.

Do you blog, Oliver?

His blog might shed light on exactly how this Van Lifers movement works and who he is.

Yes, my blog is <u>oliverstravels.co.uk</u> *I mainly post pictures because I'm a photographer. Check it out if you have a mo.*

I click the link. *Wow.* His pictures are truly breathtaking. Stunning snowscapes. And lush green fields. Black and white wedding portraits. I find his 'About' page and read his bio. I stop short when I see his profile picture. Oliver is jaw-droppingly handsome. One of those boy-next-door types who grows into his looks and suddenly becomes a heart-stopper. He has brown wavy locks, a trustworthy clear-eyed gaze, and his lips curve into a perfect sweet smile that conjures the idea of romance. Seeing the man behind the words, I feel less suspect about him, and more willing to talk, before I realise how shallow I'm being. While he doesn't look like a serial killer, that doesn't mean he isn't!

Your photography is stunning.

My hands hover over the keyboard. Should I say more? Less? I am clueless with these sorts of interactions and I don't want him to get the wrong idea.

Thank you. It keeps me on the road so I'm grateful for that.

I scroll further through his blog, trying to get a handle on where he is, how long he's been doing this for. There's not a lot of writing, like he said, it's mainly photos. I can't see any other information, no travel route, no other clues as to where he might be. So he must work as he goes, taking photographs for people before moving to the next place. While the idea of no fixed abode terrifies me, I can also see the romanticism in it. The absolute freedom.

Where are you now?

I'm only asking out of politeness. Not because Oliver is a bit of alright.

Ireland...

I've always wanted to visit Ireland. In this new strange life of mine, maybe I can go. Really, what's stopping me from ditching the material possessions and living a simpler life, like all these Van Lifers are doing?

Oliver and I chat for a while longer about this and that before he tells me all about various camp sites where I can stay for next to nothing, stock up on cheap supplies and meet likeminded nomads. I make notes about the locations to research later.

He makes it all sound so *easy*, as if it's as simple as readying the van and filling up with fuel.

When I finally sign off we agree to chat again soon and I give myself an imaginary pat on the back for being so social and open when it feels so alien.

After doing a few hours of research myself, Bristol seems like the most logical place to travel to first. It's just far enough to blow the cobwebs out of Poppy, and not too far to turn back if I chicken out.

When my notice is up at Époque, I'll pack and get the hell out of here and see where the breeze blows me.

Look at me, making friends and being *spontaneous*. I blithely ignore the shake in my hands by circling them around a nice steaming cup of passionflower tea, a blend of florals made specifically to calm nerves, promote calm, and induce sleep. Just the ticket for my spinning mind...

***

Before long my notice is up and it's time to leave my job. My career. My safety net. I say my goodbyes at Époque, getting teary when I hug Sally. It's impossible to imagine not waking with the birds and rushing around London in the morning, just like I've done for the last fifteen years. Or coming home after dinner service with heavy legs, and a dull throb in my head. Who will I be, if I'm not a sous-chef at Époque?

Suddenly I feel anchorless. Like those solid walls I built around me are caving in.

Back home, I begin to pack, knowing I've only got a few more weeks' grace, as per our divorce stipulations. The divorce itself won't settle for aeons, but we'd set out the terms and conditions, and as much as it hurts I will stand by what I promised. I'll be out of London by April. Callum wanted me to move sooner, offering me a payout at settlement, but I held firm. Their little love nest will have to wait. I need these next few weeks to plan, to come to terms with whatever it is I'm going to do.

I brew a pot of comforting raspberry and thyme tea, hoping it will perk me up. While it steeps, I fire up the laptop and decide to email Oliver for advice.

Hi Oliver,

If one was to set out on a journey, where would I likely go? Are there certain routes for novices, or is it more of an organic thing? I've been toying up seriously with the idea of a pop-up tea van...

Thanks for your time.

Rosie

With that done, I sip my tea, and spend an age staring out the window at the relentless March rain. I should be enjoying this time, strolling through Covent Garden, wandering through Hyde Park, eating out at all those new restaurants that have cropped up over the years that I haven't had a chance to try, but I don't leave my flat, except to go to the local Marks and Spencer's and stock up on ready-made meals that I eat half-heartedly.

I don't have the inclination to cook for myself – it hardly seems worth it – and I realise this is probably the first time in my life that my appetite has waned. Food tastes bland, and I only hope this is a phase. Instead, I sit in front of the TV like a zombie, too disheartened to leave the flat for anything other than wine. I hear the echo of Callum's recriminations: *You're just like your dad.* I'm not. I'm just taking some *me* time.

I check my email and am surprised to find a response from Oliver already.

Hi Rosie,

It depends on where you want to go, and what your time-line is. The Hay Festival begins in May, and is one of the best, in terms of crowds and length of time. Ten days long, it tends to be a good money spinner for those starting their journey over the summer. If that suits you, you can stock up in Bristol and camp there beforehand, it's close to the Welsh border.

It seems like a sign that he's suggested the very same place I'd had my eye on.

That's where a lot of the festival nomads meet and find travel partners, someone to journey along with on the open road. Worth thinking about. Then you can choose a route (check the attachment for ideas). Along the way you'll find fairs, and markets and all sorts that tie into the festivals so there's plenty of work to be had – or not, depending on what your motivations are.

If you have any other questions, shoot them over. But in the meantime, check out the attachment.

Oliver

I click on the attachment and find more information about Wales, and various travel routes depending on what you sell or what kind of journey you're undertaking. There's ones for those with a literary bent, itineraries for sporty types who love climbing mountains (nope) and one that grabs my attention: the foodie/festival route. I lose the next few hours imagining a brave new life, and wondering if I have the courage to live it.

When I stumble on a picture of a suspension bridge high above a tea-coloured Avon Gorge, I make a mental note to avoid it all costs… These nomads sure like to live on the edge. I'm risk averse, and picture myself instead picking wild flowers, and baking up a storm on flat, solid ground.

I take my tea and walk to the window. Rain lashes down and grey skies hover over me like a heavy sigh. I take it as a sign. There's nothing for me here now, and the only bright spot in my life is Poppy, with her *interminable* pinkness. The thought makes me smile. It's time to pack up my things, sell what I can, and donate the rest. I can't take much with me, and that's a freedom in itself. Luckily, I live a very uncluttered life, so it doesn't take long to sort my belongings into piles of keep, sell, donate, or leave for Callum as per our agreement.

I'll have to wash Poppy thoroughly once more, and make sure she's all kitted out.

Hi Oliver,
Thank you for your advice. Bristol looks just the ticket. I checked out that link you sent, and I do really like the idea of following that set route like so many others do. At least I'll know tentatively where I'm going and that's enough for me.
Thanks so much,
Rosie

CHAPTER FIVE

Am I off to an unlucky start choosing April Fool's day as the beginning of my journey? Fools rush in, right? With my forehead pressed against the living room window I watch as rain lashes down on poor Poppy. Her windscreen is frosty and opaque, the wipers half-mast like eyes closed for sleep. So much for a sunny-skied spring – although the weather does match my mood.

Drenched Poppy, copping bucket loads of rain, seems solemn somehow. I know it's the first sign of madness having affection for an inanimate thing, but I feel an affinity with her, perhaps because she is finally going to ferry me away from here, hopefully onto better, brighter things.

In the time since this whirlwind happened, Callum hasn't called or visited once. All our discussions have been handled through lawyers. *Lawyers.* Grave and dull men with no spark in their eyes. They handle our case, the two opposing sides, as succinctly as possible. There's a sterility to it all, and I can't help marvel that life can change so devastatingly fast.

He's agreed to buy out my share of the apartment, which comes to almost nothing since we're still paying the interest on the debt and not much else, and I gave myself until today to embark on my new adventure.

As I gaze around our once happy home, the same old feelings claw at me. How could he discard me so quickly, so easily, as if I were rubbish? I don't want to be alone, to be unsocial, to push people away, but I struggle making friends because there was never the time or the inclination.

This loneliness is deafening.

Getting away will broaden my horizons, give me some much-needed life experience, and I'll find my place in the world. I'm aware of my downfalls. That need to retreat usually trumps everything else, and I can't let it.

Hefting the last box from the tiny little south London flat Callum and I have shared for the last seven years, my heart shrinks once more.

With a lump in my throat, I shut the door and try my best not to think of my replacement – Khloe, a younger, perkier version of myself – moving in as soon as I move out.

As I walk to Poppy I feel boneless, like I'm going to fall, and no one will be there to catch me.

For the first time in fifteen years I won't have to be at Époque this coming Friday ready for the three busiest days in the restaurant. This feels so alien, so foreign to me that of course I'm bound to feel a little jelly-legged.

'Ready, Poppy?' My voice breaks. I tap the side of the van before stowing a box inside and hopping up into the front seat. I freeze. What the hell am I doing, leaving London, leaving all I know?

I sit there catatonic for so long that one of my neighbours, old Mrs Jones, raps on the window, her face pinched, and asks if I'm waiting for the RAC.

A flush of embarrassment flares. I shake my head, and say, 'Oh no, nothing like that. I'm just…' *Summoning courage, wondering if you can die from a shattered heart, the usual.* 'Waiting for the right time to leave.'

Old Mrs Jones shakes her head in that supercilious way of

hers. She's never liked me – doesn't like the hours I keep, the way I stack the recycling, the fact I lock my letterbox, trivial things that leave me bamboozled. But over the years I've learned she's like that with everyone, a little judgemental, a lot dramatic.

'Well, off you go!' she harries. 'My daughter is on her way, and she could use this parking space. She has a *baby*, you know.'

I hold in a sigh. Everyone has a baby these days. Probably Khloe will have a baby that she and old Mrs Jones can bond over, cooing and speaking baby language. Best not to think of it.

'Right,' I say and start the engine, wondering if old Mrs Jones *will* make friends with Khloe. They can gossip together, just like she's tried and failed with me, because I don't care if the single guy in apartment four *'plays those fecking video games with all the guns and the shooting at midnight!'* And I especially don't care if the twenty-something in six wears *'those trashy boots that go all the way up to her derrière as if she's a lady of the night!'* Their lives have nothing to do with me. Perhaps she, Khloe and Callum can dine together at her infamous Monday night supper clubs, and whisper gleefully that they're grateful I'm gone. Tears sting the back of my eyes and it feels like I might implode – I have to get out of here.

But my imagination runs wild and I visualise Mrs Jones sniping, *'She's an odd one that Rosie; always darting away from people like she's got something to hide.'*

I won't miss old Mrs Jones.

With a deep breath, I pull out and tackle the traffic, ignoring a blast of horn and the wide-eyed look of a pedestrian who edged a little too close for comfort. How many hours of this do I have ahead?

I drive, well, *sputter* along in Poppy, clamping the steering wheel so tightly my knuckles turn white. London is difficult to navigate on foot at the best of times, but in Poppy it's downright terrifying. My first rendezvous point is the camp in Bristol so I set my mind to achieving the goal of arriving there, not dead.

With grim determination, I manage to concentrate and also to ignore the sound of my pulse thrumming my ears by turning the music up. Like people, Poppy has her quirks: she backfires when she's disgruntled as if she's telling me off, and pulls sharply to the left if senses me veering this way and that.

It's a learning curve, and we simply must get to know each other better. When I have a moment of panic, just the usual, *WHAT THE BLOODY HELL WAS I THINKING*, she drives straight and true as if she knows she must take control while I briefly lose my mind. Before long, I find my groove, and Poppy belches and squeaks as if urging me on.

Goodbye, London, hello… brand new, exciting life! I crank the music and a slow smile settles over my face. I've done it, I've really done it and a sort of pride creeps over me.

CHAPTER SIX

Five hours later, well over schedule, I reach the camp in Bristol, accidentally accelerating when I mean to brake, and career out of control towards a beautiful red-headed girl who wears a look of abject horror because I'm about to run her down!

I stamp hard on the brakes, Poppy fishtails wildly as airborne pebbles shoot into the poor unsuspecting girl like bullets, the sound *pow, pow, pow* ricocheting off her tiny frame but before long she's shrouded in a mist of dust. I come to a screaming halt, the smell of burnt rubber permeating the air. Have I hit her? Stiff as a toy solider I manage to fall out of Poppy and land directly into a pile of mud with squelch as I miscue my exit from such a high perch. I turn onto my back, my bones creaking with effort. While my body may have the appearance of someone in the first stages of rigor mortis, I feel strangely euphoric.

I survived!

Poppy survived! London is long gone and I can finally breathe fresh air, and… and then I remember *the girl*! As the dust settles, I see she's frozen on the spot, her mouth opening and closing but no words fall out. I'm hoping it's on account of the dust she's swallowed and not because a pebble punctured her lung or something. Just as I'm about to call for help, she chokes out, 'That was some entrance!'

Still supine, relief washes through me as I stare up into her face, her coppery hair falling over her cheeks. She seems calm enough considering I almost killed her. Well, to be fair, *Poppy* almost killed her. Bloody hell, we're going to have to practise when it comes to parking and dismount.

When I don't respond she says, 'Are you OK?' Concern ekes from her voice. She's one of those effortlessly pretty girls whose natural good looks don't need adornment. Her bright hazel eyes are framed by lustrous black lashes sans mascara. Her hair is the colour of fire, and flashes in the soft sunlight and I feel drab in comparison.

I've taken too long to respond, and her eyes dart about looking for help. I get that look a lot.

'I'm… great,' I say with what I hope is a convincing smile that belies my inner turmoil. Just the *where am I, why did I buy a van under the influence of Shiraz, how am I meant to wash this mud off me,* kind of thing.

But there's no need to panic, it's all going on the to-do list, things I can improve on, a list of people *not* to run over, that kind of thing.

A frown appears between her thick, perfectly symmetrical eyebrows. How are girls achieving eyebrows so thick they need their own postcode? Tentatively I touch mine, wondering how you can add body to such a thing. There's a whole world out there that I haven't had a moment to consider while I've been cooped up in a commercial kitchen.

'You don't look great, to be honest.' She's noticed my eyebrows, and their rather spartan lustre, dammit. 'You look like you've just escaped the jungle, or something.' She grins.

I laugh for the first time in aeons but by the look on her face the sound is more maniacal than I intend. *The jungle*, that's one way to describe it. 'I have. I've just come from London. The urban jungle.'

The unreality of my situation hits me and I just feel so... disconnected from my old life, my old self, and while it's strange, it also produces a feeling of wild jubilation. From this very moment on, I can be whoever I choose to be!

She holds out a hand to help me up. I pray my legs carry me after being ramrod in Poppy for so long. 'Let's get you cleaned up.'

I follow the girl to a bathroom and jump in fright when I see my reflection in the mirror. There's no way she could have been judging my eyebrows or any of my face for that matter, because she can't have seen it under all the caked-on grime from the muddy puddle and who knows what else. Bloody hell! I look like I've just participated in a mud wrestling competition, and even my hair sticks out at odd angles, probably because I spent the better part of the drive pulling at it.

'Did you sleep rough?' she asks, concern on her face.

'No, gosh no. The mud is the culprit. It's amazing that I can find the only puddle from here to the never-never, but there you go.' After I've cleaned up as best I can, we head back outside. Poppy makes the strangest hissing sound and I give her a quick once-over to determine where the noise is coming from.

'The tyre!' Air slowly leaks from the front tyre and Poppy droops to the right, as if she's exhausted. 'It's OK,' I say more to myself than anyone. 'I'm sure I can...' I realise I've never changed a tyre in my life, and wouldn't have the foggiest how to go about it.

Bloody hell, who goes travelling around the countryside without knowing how to change a tyre? It defies belief that I could have overlooked such a thing. Me, methodical to a fault, queen of contingency plans.

'Don't panic,' the girl says. 'I can help you change it. Do you have a spare?'

Oh golly. 'I'm sure I must do. I guess van maintenance slipped my mind.'

'I can also give you some pointers on the mechanical side of things. I'm a gun at oil changes and whatnot now, anything to save money, right? I'm Aria, by the way,' she says, holding out a hand, which I find endearing since my own hands are stained black after my ordeal.

'Great. I'm Rosie.' We shake and she gives me a wide smile as if my presence has brightened her day.

'How'd you find us here?'

'I stumbled across the Van Lifers online forum and got chatting to a guy called Oliver who told me this was a good starting point, close enough to Wales to stock up and get my bearings.'

You mad, mad thing.

My body aches in strange places, and I'd found the drive as hard as being in command of a busy kitchen. A different sort of hard.

'I'm glad you're here,' she says, flashing bright white teeth.

'Me too,' I say, and find myself meaning it.

'The Van Lifers forum is great. Lots of tips on there, maps, market and festival info, that kind of thing. Plenty of people offering support.'

I nod, overwhelmed by the environment. It's like I've fallen through a trapdoor and arrived in a parallel universe. Checked shirts are obviously a prerequisite. A group of bearded hipsters sit around a campfire, as a gorgeous brunette strums a guitar and sings a haunting song. A few play cards on fold-out tables, some hang washing under their awnings, while others bustle about packing their vans in readiness to leave. A handful give me a wave as I walk past, and I smile tentatively back.

I'm not like them. I sense it already. They exude this sort of worldly air, a certain grace as if they're comfortable in their own skin, with their open faces and wise eyes that sparkle with all they've seen. But I'm determined to sink into this lifestyle and find the ease they all wear in their ready, lazy smiles.

Aria pulls me from my reverie. 'I'll make you a brew and we can chat.'

She opens the door to her little van and I gasp as the inside comes to life under flickering candlelight. It's a utopia for bibliophiles. Rickety bookshelves line the sides of the van, filled to the brim with chaotically stacked books. On the floor, cane baskets cradle bundles of vintage Mills and Boon books, bound together with string. Every nook and cranny is bursting with novels, candles, cushions or rugs and the scent of recently brewed coffee lingers in the air.

While I understand how this would appear like a nirvana for most, for me it produces a sense of unease. This kind of clutter all begins innocently enough. A few things here, then there. Then everywhere.

'You have a travelling bookshop?' I say and then mentally slap my forehead.

'The Little Bookshop of Happy Ever After. I sell romance novels. Word nerd at your service.' She salutes and I can't help but laugh.

'Word nerd has a nice ring to it.'

The dim space is perfumed by posies of fresh wild flowers, and scented candles. Coupled with the aroma of old books, there's a musty dustiness that hints of times gone by. An old, wrinkled, leather high-back chair sits squished against the side of the van and I bet it's where Aria spends most of her days.

There's a bunch of ruched velvet ruby cushions stacked in a pile, textured woolly throw rugs drape from hooks. I imagine whiling away time in the Little Bookshop of Happy Ever After would appeal to bookworms everywhere, but another thing concerns me, and I grapple with whether I should speak up or not.

It's usually these little truth bombs that tend to detonate in my face, but it's actually a matter of life or death – so I decide to be honest and figure out a subtle way to broach the subject.

I clear my throat. '*Should* you leave burning candles unattended?' I ask in the nicest possible way, when really I mean, 'you most certainly should *not* leave burning candles unattended, especially with so many books laying haphazardly around'. While Aria rescued me from the depths of a muddy puddle, her entire livelihood could have gone up in flames – it's only fair I should warn her. It's what I imagine a good friend would do.

She laughs, a big haw that startles me coming from such a wisp of a thing. 'They're all part of the ambiance, they add to the romance! People wander in when I'm not here so I want them to feel at home. Feel comforted. And what better way to do that than with the scent of old books and sweet-smelling candles?'

My eyebrows shoot up. 'You let people come in here without you being present?' What if they go through her things? Read her diary. Nap on her bed? Or worse, steal books?

'Sure I do! They leave a note if they borrow a book, or money in the kitty over there if they buy something.' Aria points to an unassuming pastel green *unlocked* cash box. I know it's unlocked because the padlock sits next to it, rusted open as if it's spent the better part of its life in the sea. Surely strangers would take advantage?

'But…' Words fails me.

'Sit down,' she says. 'I'll make a pot of tea.'

I move to the wrinkly leather chair and it sighs as I sink into its weathered embrace. I fight the urge to tidy, to right fallen books, to fold the rugs. *Be cool, Rosie.*

'So,' I say, squaring my shoulders. 'Is everyone this erm… lax with their vans?' I could always go back to London, it's not too late. Get my old job back. Live in some bedsit I'll jokingly refer to as the crack den. Start over. Adopt a rescue dog. Buy one of those lint brushes to remove pet fur from my clothing. Invest in some quality sneakers for all the *walkies* I'll take Rover on. I picture myself, getting dragged along by a slobbery French mastiff, my life literally going around in circles. But where's the fun in that? No, I must stay resolute and wait for my shiny, sparkly brand new life to take off. I desperately want to live outside of ordinary.

No change comes easy, right? I'm sure everyone feels like this when they upend their life, their hopes and dreams scattered about like so many escaped marbles!

She laughs again, that same boom that reverberates around the van. 'Not everyone is so lax. Why, Rosie, does it bother you?'

'A little,' I admit, scrunching my nose.

'It's fine, really,' she says. 'I've never run into any trouble doing things this way. Most people are honest and if I lose a book or two that's nothing in the scheme of things for the freedom I have, right? If I loan a book out I never get back, who cares? I can come and go as I please, and at the end of the day, there's a little money in the kitty for the next adventure.'

I doubt I can ever be like Aria. I'd have a nervous breakdown. But in reality we have two very different businesses and I'll have to be at my post – after all, the tea won't brew itself. I don't have to be *exactly* like her to fit in, do I? My tables and chairs will be outside, so no one has to traipse through my van unless I invite them to.

'What made you pack up and leave?' she asks, switching the subject while she fills a glass teapot.

'Oh,' I say, dropping my gaze. 'Nothing really, I just felt like a change was in order.' Who wants to be thought of as the dumped desperado, fleeing in disgrace? Not me.

She doesn't probe further, but I can tell from the question in her eyes, she wants to. I detect Aria has a story too, from the way she looks knowingly at me – a likeminded soul, perhaps? But she lets the moment pass, balances a pot of tea on a stack of books between us and hunts in a cupboard for cups, finally producing two mismatched mugs, one that reads: *Bookworms do it better*. The tea is a fragrant blend of vanilla and jasmine and I go to ask her where she procured it from, when she interjects.

'Do you have a rough plan, or will you take each day as it comes?' she asks, her voice muffled as she reaches in to an overhead cupboard before brandishing a dusty biscuit tin.

Once the tea has steeped, I pour and the scent of jasmine fills the air. I'm eager to get started on blending a new range of teas for my pop-up shop, imagining the heady fragrance of fresh floral bouquets, or spicy nutty blends. Back in the present, I say, 'I haven't got an exact itinerary in place, but I thought I'd follow one of the festival circuits, so I have more opportunities for the tea shop.'

Her eyes twinkle. 'You're opening a tea shop?'

'Rosie's Travelling Tea Shop! I want to go back to my roots making old-fashioned comfort food served with big pots of house-made tea blends. I can't wait to get started. I just hope Poppy's tiny kitchen can handle it.' Even though I'm muddled with this new version of me, of what I'm supposed be and feel, I know being in my happy place, the kitchen, will help centre me and ease those doubts, when I'm doing what I love.

'Whatever cake and tea can't fix, the open road can.' A shutter comes down over her face. It's so slight, I don't think anyone else would notice it, but it's as though what she's saying doesn't actually ring true for her. I see it, because I know that feeling well. Suddenly, she's staring into her tea, her shoulders stiffening slightly. I have an inkling that asking her might cross that fine line between being nosy and potentially ruining a burgeoning friendship. I mustn't say the first thing that pops into my mind, I've learned that the hard way.

'Yes,' I say, realising she is waiting for a response. 'The open road... the possibilities are endless.'

'It can be daunting doing that first big trek if you're alone,' she says, staring over the edge of her mug at me.

Poppy could break down at night, the very moment a guy with a hair fetish escapes from a prison up the road and lops off my white blonde locks. I could bake scones and buy fresh cream from a local farm and have not one customer. I could get robbed. My petrol siphoned. Get eaten by bedbugs. Go weeks without speaking to a real person.

I glance at my watch, wondering if there's enough daylight left to announce I've left the oven on in London, and I'll be back... never! Note to self: stop reading true crime books for the foreseeable future.

'This might be presumptuous,' Aria says, blowing her hair from her eyes. 'But why don't we stick together? Not to live in each other's pockets or anything, but books and tea are a match made in heaven, and I think we could do well side by side.'

Oliver told me Bristol was the meet-up place, and safety in numbers and all that. A ripple of happiness runs through me. Despite turning up looking like I slept on the streets – dirty, grimy, muddy, and a little lost – Aria has managed to ignore all of that and has taken a shine to me.

Have I made a friend, so easily? I begin to doubt her motivations. She's known me for all of five minutes. There must be something wrong with her. But what? Is she on the run from police? She doesn't look like a criminal. Maybe she's someone famous in hiding. Or is she lonely amid all these people? That, I can understand well. Does she sense I'm lost? She's a little lost too, despite her apparent popularity, despite being surrounded by people of the same ilk to her. I see it in her eyes, the way they cloud over.

'Stick together?' I say.

'Think about it,' she says, gazing past me as if she is picturing us in the future. 'We follow the festival route. Set up next to each other. Join our tables and chairs out the front for our customers, but best of all we have someone close by to hang out with in those lulls. To drive with on the long hauls.'

It couldn't hurt. And as independent as I like to think I am, I'm terrified of driving Poppy through the lonely hours of night-time.

'It could work,' I say, trying to play it cool. 'So you don't have a set route?' I ask. 'Or follow any schedule?' I like knowing where I'm going and where I'll be. The festival route is a nice, orderly clear-cut circuit, with set dates and schedules.

She laughs. 'I'm more a *fly by the seat of my pants* type of gal. I move whenever I get the urge to, and that's how I've always been, but there's plenty to see on route as we follow the festival circuit, and I'm happy to stick to that for business, and we'll only run off course for adventures.'

Adventures? 'OK…' Does it really matter if we go off course every once in a while? Planning my old life down to the minute didn't work out so well, after all.

'Let's do it,' I say before I can change my mind.

We are opposites, that much is certain, but don't they say opposites attract? Aria's effusive, bubbly, and definitely popular, going by the number of waves and *hey yous* thrown at her as we'd walked past clusters of nomads outside. That's what I aspire to be like, to have that ability to blend in easily, to not be the person on the sidelines all the damn time. I want adventure, a new purpose, to really grab life by the shoulders and shake it up!

'Brilliant,' she says, smiling. 'And I get how you're feeling, Rosie. At first it's a little intimidating. Getting off the beaten track, following roads to nowhere, sleeping under different patches of sky every week, but you will learn to love it. And eventually you'll look for the hidden places, ones empty of footprints and hope that real life never comes calling again.'

'OK, I guess I have a lot to learn.' A place with no footprints sounds a little too deserted for my liking, but Aria will be there (safety in numbers). Even so, it's not like we're going to be attached at the hip. We're basically just travelling at the same time and setting up next to each other, in order to promote our pop-up vans.

'You can learn as you go. All we need to do is make enough money for our adventures.'

'Our adventures are what exactly?' I picture myself skydiving, or parachuting, and my belly somersaults with panic. I'm more of a feet-firmly-on-the-earth type.

'This and that.'

'I'm not really fond of—'

She holds up a hand. 'Outdoor adventures, Rosie – running, climbing, swimming in the most beautiful places you'll ever see. Eating at fancy places, or holes in walls. Paying exorbitant prices at tourist traps, or eating fruit from a tree in the middle of nowhere, it's all part of the fun! But first you have to give your-self some time to get acclimatised.'

I guess I hadn't thought of exploring as much as I had about escaping. What would I see? Life changing sunsets, a galaxy of stars, water that runs backwards. I pinch myself to make sure I'm not dreaming.

'Let's head off to Wales on Monday?' I say, deciding that will give me enough time to consult my maps, speak to Oliver from the online forum for advice and double check I've done everything I can in terms of van maintenance.

'Perfect. The Hay Festival is next month and in the interim there's other local fairs we could set up shop at.'

My strength is my love of fragrant tea and hearty food and the absolute joy I find in making it. How can anyone resist my baking when I pour my heart and soul into what I do? Or taking a big sip of a spicy nutty tea blend that invokes a place yet travelled? This has the potential to be life changing for me.

And now I have a travelling companion. A feat in itself.

'Wales it is.' A place I've never seen.

What is this new world? The lost part of me shimmies with anticipation.

Later that day, I sit on my bed and email Oliver to double check I haven't missed anything. I'm mindful not to bother Aria with every single thought that pops into my head, so I figure friendly Oliver can field some of my questions. His reply beeps back almost instantly.

> Hi Rosie,
> You've ticked all the boxes as far as I can see. Just make sure you double check with the council before 'popping up' anywhere. Some councils require certain approvals and health checks since you're selling food. Let me know if you run into trouble and I should be able to point you in the right direction at least. Safe travels.
> Oliver

The paperwork side of things is a lot more time consuming than I'd imagined, but that's what spreadsheets are made for, right? I make a list of possible fairs and places to 'pop up' around Wales and enter all the relevant info into an excel spreadsheet so I'll have it on hand when we need it. I send Oliver a thank you email and fall into bed wondering what Callum is doing right now. Does he miss me? I fall asleep with him on my mind.

***

By Sunday I'm as ready as I can be. A map is taped to the wall, and coloured thumb tacks mark our route. I've allowed for weather delays, car troubles, and sourced where to get fresh produce and supplies to cook with as we go from place to place. I've watched countless YouTube videos about car maintenance and feel confident I will at least know the basics if I break down. Aria's showed me how to do an oil change in return for some basic cooking classes so she can learn how to switch off the pan one step before charcoal, which is probably more a life-preserving measure than anything. I've never seen anyone burn so much food before!

I feel strong, capable, and enjoy learning more skills, even on the go.

We plan to set off early the next day, and I'm jittery with anticipation.

But I'm prepared this time. I have engine oil, the flat tyre has been fixed and refitted and a wheel alignment done on Poppy. There's an extra car jack, a spare canister of petrol, oil, water and a maintenance kit. All our permits and insurances are sorted thanks to Aria, who it turns out is a dab hand at all that mind-numbingly tedious legal side of things, completed online without much angst by her. Council approval is a headache but Aria knows how to apply quickly and efficiently and which places to avoid that have fussier rules and regulations and are likely to decline us.

As I check my bank balance, which has taken a hit from all the extras for Poppy, my email beeps. I open it to find a message from Oliver.

Briefly, I worry he's going to ask me to sign up or join, and my funds will take another beating. He's been handy when I've had lots of little incidental queries crop up that I didn't want to keep bothering Aria about. So I suppose it's fair if he expects to recoup financially from all my questions.

Hi Rosie,
   Just checking in to see how you're enjoying Bristol? I've been busy with work, I had two weddings to shoot over the weekend and now I'm editing the pics which is the most time-consuming aspect of it all.

I wait for his sales pitch, join today and get the fee fifty percent off! I keep reading.

   After that I'm going to hike Llanberis Path, to the summit of Snowdon, which I've always wanted to do. It's meant to be

like a little lost Eden. I get cabin fever if I'm cooped up in the
van too long, so this should do the trick.
   Safe travels,
   Oliver

No sales pitch. No join now. No sign up for this or that promotion. Maybe Oliver is just interested in other people's journeys? But what is it about all these nomads who want to climb the summit of rocky outcrops, and see the world from the highest perch? Perhaps I've spent too long in the kitchen on my feet. In my opinion, the best method of relaxation is of the horizontal-on-the-couch-kind. I grab at my muffin-top (a mere side effect of being a chef!) and wonder if I need to partake of a bit of one-foot-in-front-of-the-other action?

I type Llanberis Path, Snowdon into a search engine and my enthusiasm flees. It's a six-hour return hike for a 14.6 kilometre trek to 3300 feet. It's practically Everest in my opinion. And I couldn't imagine myself taking on such an arduous climb.

Hi Oliver,
   Haven't seen much of Bristol yet (besides the hardware shop!) but Aria mentioned something about visiting town later for a wander. Getting my head around all of the logistics of travel and all that entails. Aria has been an enormous help. We leave Monday for Wales. Can't believe I'm doing this but here I am!
   Good luck with the hike, sounds like an epic journey.
   Rosie

After I've sent the email and tidied the tiny space I use for a desk I head outside to find Aria. Her van door is wide open and she's in her usual repose, feet up, nose in book, half cups of tea circling her as though she's incanting a spell with them. A pot of baked beans bubbles on the stove so I go and give it a stir, not surprised to find them sticking to the bottom already.

'The bookworm in her natural habitat,' I say, envying her ability to immerse herself in reading the way she does. For some reason I always feel this strange guilt if I read for too long, as if I should be doing something more constructive with my time. It eventually gets the better of me and I pack the book away and clean and tidy, sort my things, whereas Aria can lose an entire day between the pages of a book. I make a note to schedule some time expressly for reading, no interruptions, no excuses.

She yawns and stretches herself languorously, before setting her book down.

'This bookworm needs a bit of fresh air. Want to go to Clifton Village?'

'What about your erm… lunch?' The congealed mess doesn't look very appetising to me but Aria doesn't seem to mind that sort of thing.

'I've burnt it again, haven't I?'

'Yes.'

She laughs. 'Let's go out instead.'

I settle in the passenger seat of the little bookshop and find it comforting that Aria's van belches and backfires just as much as Poppy does. Maybe these old vans all have their quirks and it's just a matter of translating their meanings.

As we chug along, I relax into the seat, watching the world flick by, so different to the vista I had in London. A silence falls between us, and I debate whether to fill it with something inane or just let it be. Aria doesn't seem the type to mind either way, so instead of mumbling and bumbling I keep quiet and enjoy the scenery. As I look up my breath catches, the sky is a riot of colour.

'Look!' I say, pointing to the bevy of hot air balloons that float gracefully in the air.

'Aren't they beautiful?' she says. 'You know there's an actual hot air balloon fiesta in August? Balloonatics come from all over the world to fly right here in Bristol. Hundreds of them.'

'Wow, the sky awash with floating barometers.'

She giggles. 'That's what they look like from here, right? Gosh, Rosie you have to go on one. Looking straight up from the basket into the belly of the balloon is like starting into a kaleidoscope with the different layers of colour and the lick of flames. A spectacular sight.'

'I'll stick with watching them from ground level. Hell will freeze over before I risk life and limb to ride in a hot air balloon.'

She lets out a cackle. 'Rosie, you're not super adventurous, are you?'

'The exact opposite.'

'That'll all change, mark my words.'

I shoot her a look that says, *not on my watch*.

When we come to Clifton Village, Aria pulls into a carpark and I'm immediately assailed with the vinegary scent of fresh fish and chips.

'A girl's gotta eat, right?' She arches a brow.

'You know the way to my heart, obviously.'

We order beer-battered fish and chips and munch away, lightly debating about whether minted mushy peas adds or subtracts to the meal. 'But how can you *not* have mushy peas?' I ask, bewildered.

She grins. 'I'm as British as they come, but you know, I really don't like them. They remind me of baby food! And I don't think they pair with fish and chips. They just don't.'

My mouth falls open. 'I'll have to take this under consideration. I'm fairly sure that's treasonous and I don't know if we can be friends.'

'Take your time, think about it. I promise it's my only foodie qualm.'

'Pass your peas over then.'

She screws up her face, handing the offending side over.

'So, after this shall we wander over the bridge? I've heard the vaults are pretty spectacular. We can do a tour through them.'

'Sure.'

Half an hour later when I see the bridge up close I have second thoughts, remembering now the picture Oliver sent of this very same bridge. A *suspension* bridge. 'Is it just me or is that bridge *swaying*?' Holy moly, the bridge seems so high, the dark tea river running perilously fast way, way underneath. Of course I've crossed many a bridge in my time but not one of such epic proportions as this. And on foot.

Aria's machine-gun cackle startles me. 'Yeah, apparently the bridge deck moves and everything! Sometimes they have to close the bridge to traffic when it's too squally.'

'You say that like it's a good thing.'

'It is! It's almost like a living being, bending and blowing about like it's got something to say.'

'And it's saying "*Stay the hell away*", I believe.'

Before I can make excuses, she grabs my hands and propels me forward and just like that I'm on the walkway of the bridge. As cars whoosh past, I feel the ground move under my feet. It's so damn high, it takes my breath away.

'You big tough Londoner, you!' Wind whips at our faces and Aria calls out, 'Doesn't it make you feel *alive*?'

'Well, yes, only because I'm picturing my imminent *death*…' but my words are whipped away by the gale. 'Which does make me appreciate being here, right now, alive and well and on a crazy adventure with the first British person I've met who doesn't like mushy peas!'

'I'm so glad you're here, Rosie.' She lets out a laugh and then pauses before speaking with a nervous lilt. 'A couple of days ago I had this silly idea that I'd cross this bridge for the last time.' She averts her gaze. 'Not Thelma and Louise it off or anything, just say goodbye, pack up and head home back to my parents. Give up on this whole van life. Back to the grind of nine-to-five, you know?'

Shock must register on my face because she shrugs, and gives me the ghost of a smile and continues. 'Things haven't been great, and I sort of made this deal with the universe, to send me a sign, give me some sort of reassurance to stay and at that very moment you tore into the parking lot, nearly ran me over, and then opened the door and fell straight into the mud. I knew instantly, that you had come tearing into my life for a reason.'

I'm lost for words, but scramble for some. 'Were you really going to give up the van life for good?' I can't picture Aria doing anything nine-to-five, she's too ephemeral, too different to live such a mundane, regulated life.

'Yep, incredible, right?'

'Why though?' What would make her consider such a thing? If Aria can't handle van life, how can I?

She grabs my elbow and carries me along, tucking her chin against my arm. With a long sigh she says, 'I felt like there was no sunshine anymore, you know? Like I was trudging through interminable darkness. Have you ever considered why you're here, Rosie? Like right here, right now? This moment.'

I had, only mere moments ago, and it strikes me it's because of Aria that already I've jumped far, far out of my comfort zone and relished it, even though it scares me. 'Meaning of life type of scenario?' I ask.

She nods.

'Oh, Aria I am probably the worst person you can ask. My life imploded in London and I spend almost every second of every day wondering what the hell I'm doing. I shift between abject terror, and horror, with occasional bouts of hysteria. But already, you, with your gutsy attitude and go-getting vibe, have opened my eyes. I wish I could say the right thing to make you realise how wonderful you are, how I aspire to be a girl just like you, but I'm not good with words. I'm not good really at anything except cooking.'

'You undersell yourself, Rosie. You just happened to show up right when I needed you most. And now look, we're walking across this bridge, instead of me packing up and going home to a bleak, boring life, and I wonder how I ever thought that was a good idea.' A stray tear welds its way down her cheek, and I know there's more to her story. Much more, but I don't push her for details. Whatever the reason, for once in my life I feel as though I'm exactly where I'm meant to be, if that means being here for Aria. I look at the water rushing beneath and squeeze her hand tightly. 'So you're staying?'

'I can't argue with the universe when they send me my very own Rosie, now, can I?'

CHAPTER SEVEN

We leave in convoy, if a convoy can be a group of two that is. Aria is ahead in her little bookshop van and I trail behind. Poppy occasionally backfires and hiccups as if warning me to take it steady. With deep centring breaths, I tell myself to relax, to take in the scenery, to be at one with the world, but driving such a big rig still doesn't come naturally and I stiffen over the steering wheel and concentrate hard.

Will it ever get easier driving Poppy? I picture a future me, hair blowing sideways in the wind, the open road ahead, sunglasses reflecting prisms of sunlight, as I warble some folky song into the ether...

Instead, with jaw clenched tight I force my mind to wander to my new menu, hoping that will be distraction enough to loosen up. It's enough to keep me grounded and eventually we arrive at Hay-on-Wye, colloquially known as the 'town of books' and home to the literary Hay Festival at the tail end of May.

Until the ten-day festival begins we plan to pop up in nearby towns where Aria has found various fetes and markets, leaving us plenty of time to explore what's around too. I park next to Aria, and jump from Poppy, managing this time to keep myself upright and avoid any puddles. Mother Nature hasn't exactly got the memo that spring has arrived, and while it's not bucketing down, it's not exactly sunny either.

Pride creeps over me. Sure, every now and then I still think about going home, but I'm learning how to live in the moment. It's sinking in more that I might even deserve to. There're times I feel regret that I've spurned a great career for living frivolously, chasing an idea so foggy, even I don't truly know what I'm doing, but then there are times like this, where I look up at the view and think – you know what? Life doesn't have to be so ordered, so rigorously planned. It can just be enjoying the groan of Poppy's door as I bang it shut as if she's saying, *don't leave me!*

I stare in wonderment at the new sights before me. Hay-on-Wye is the prettiest of places with its grassy green fields, thatched-roof cottages and abundance of bright pretty flowers climbing crumbling stone walls. The place is fairy tale-esque, like a story book come to life.

'You have to see this.' Aria motions for me to follow her. She leads me down a hidden laneway and we come to identical twin cottages with a big stone wall half secluding their facade from the public. Just their windows peek above, like eyes, but that's not the most extraordinary part. In front of the walls are rickety wooden shelves packed with hardback books and a sign advertising them for a pound apiece. The books are weathered and warped from the elements, but sit enticingly, some upended whose pages flutter in the breeze as if whispering a foreign language, a code I can't decipher but Aria surely can. Her eyes widen and her whole faces changes, as she gazes on enraptured.

It seems utterly romantic that any stranger wandering by has a book so close at hand. A bookworm's paradise right here in a secret little laneway.

'We've got to buy a few,' I say, inexplicably compelled to adopt my very own even though I have a rule about only owning so many of each particular item, but these are special, and I internally make a deal with myself that I can always donate some of the books I have to Aria.

'A few? We need to buy them all! Aren't they just beautiful?' She goes to the first shelf, pulls down a once cobalt blue hardback – its cover now ravaged and faded with time – and she takes a great big sniff, before she turns to me, her eyes bright as though she's just discovered the meaning of life. 'That is the best scent in the world, better than any perfume, any flower. It's the smell of lives lived, the weight of words…'

'Well, I guess I never quite thought of books that way before.' Sure, they could transport you to another place, be there for you when no one else was, but I hadn't quite pictured secondhand books as having lived their own important lives, being ferried from one person to the next, imparting a little magic along the way.

A doddering old woman wanders out from the cottage on the left, her progress slow as she leans heavily on a cane. She must sense a likeminded soul in Aria, and says, 'Ah, you've found the Heart Seeker edition, I was wondering when it might find a new home. Romance books are on the left.'

'Consider them sold.' Aria beams at her.

'You're a little early for the festival,' the elderly woman laments as she bags books as quick as Aria can hand them to her. How does she know we're here for that?

As if reading my mind she says, 'I can always sniff out a fellow bookworm.' She taps her ruddy nose, 'They have a particular smell, don't you know?'

The woman, with her crepey skin and wrinkled brow, seems suddenly youthful when she's talking in riddles. 'What do they smell like?' I ask, interested.

'Tequila!' she cackles.

'Tequila?' I'm not sure if she's joking or if she's bonkers but I laugh along with her and, subtle as anything, I take a step closer to Aria and sniff her. Young tequila has an almost agave scent to it, and I realise the old woman is right; Aria does smell a touch sweet, a little citrusy, a lot like forgotten hopes and lost dreams.

'See?' The old woman raises a brow.

'I do indeed,' I say.

Are all bookworms this... mystical? The pair seem to be communicating by glances alone – an eyebrow raise here, a slight tilt of the head there – as Aria makes her way along the shelves handing over books that catch her attention.

'That should do it,' Aria says, handing her one last novel. In her handbag, Aria roots around for her coin purse and hands the woman some money.

'Thank you, dears. Now, there's a foodie fair starting up in a few days, you'd both do well to set up there. It's over by...' She goes on to explain how we get to the next village, and what we'll need to do in order to get our permit. 'I'll be seeing you again this time next year,' she says, knowingly.

We wave her off and Aria hands me a book: *Romeo and Juliet*.

'Really?' I ask.

Hand on heart, Aria says, 'Star-crossed lovers, gets me every time.'

'A classic. Maybe I should make a *Romeo and Juliet* inspired tea, a love potion?'

'It's romantic! If only they could have escaped together!' At that her voice catches and I deduce she must really love Shakespeare. Maybe she's a little in love with Romeo herself? Bookworms do that a lot, fall for the hero in their latest read and get terribly down about the fact they're fictional.

'A *Romeo and Juliet* love potion might be just the thing,' I say and then snap my fingers as the most sensational idea hits me. 'What about a whole *range* of literary inspired teas! *Alice in Wonderland* for those looking for adventure, *Romeo and Juliet* for star-crossed lovers, *Little Women* for friendship, what else...?'

'Oh my gosh, Rosie, this is possibly the best idea I've ever heard!'

'Even better if we collaborate. If you happen to have the matching books to sell we can use it to send customers from one side to the other?'

'You're a genius!' Aria's face shines with excitement. 'Let's make a list of what you need and get started, then I can order in the correlating books. You marketing whiz, you!'

We head back to Poppy, brimming with ideas. 'What about packaging, branding? Or do I keep it simple, rustic, handwritten labels with tea in environmentally friendly bags?'

'Always keep it simple, Rosie.'

We spend the afternoon brainstorming ideas and just what we want the tea to conjure, with the perfect book as an accompaniment.

Later that evening there's an email from Oliver and I ask Aria if she had a moderator from the Van Lifers forum keep tabs on her when she first started out. I've had a number of emails from Oliver, usually at the tail end of the day, checking how I'm going, just shooting the breeze as it were.

She raises a brow. 'Not a one. Zilch, zip, zero. So what does that lead you to believe?'

'He's bored.'

She cocks her head and gives me a strange look I can't decipher. 'What?' I ask.

With a harrumph she says, 'There's more chance that Oliver is a little taken with our Rosie, than wanting to remind you to check the pressure in your tyres or whatever excuse he used this time…'

I blush to the roots of my hair and interject, 'I hardly think it's that, Aria! And I'm more worried there's something wrong with him, maybe he's—'

'—maybe he likes you and is trying to get to know you by pretending to be interested in every squeak and whine of Poppy's. Why do you constantly sell yourself short like that, Rosie? You do it *all* the time.'

'It's not that at all.'

Her glossy mane shimmies as she shakes her head. 'You do, you dream up these crazy scenarios, axe murderers, robbers, prisoners on the run, instead of admitting the guy probably has a crush on you. Or else he's a lonely nomad just like the rest of us.'

I give her an awkward smile. 'So you *don't* think he's an axe murderer?'

With a sigh, she lobs a cushion at me. 'No but I might be if you keep that up.'

'Eeep! But seriously Oliver is just a name on a screen as I am to him as well. Surely you can't have even a twinge of a feeling for someone through a few emails?'

'You're doing it again, you're overthinking.' She grins at me.

'Well, *Miss Know It All*,' I say, 'I find it hard to grasp the notion of falling for someone in cyberspace, that's all. It seems desperate, or silly, or just not safe.'

'Not safe? In this day and age it's how everyone meets! You can't knock it until you've tried it.'

I cluck my tongue.

'I went out with a guy I met online and he wasn't a knife-wielding maniac, far from it.'

'So what happened?'

She scrunches up her nose. 'The poor man could not kiss to save his life. I mean, not at all!'

'What do you mean? He had lips, didn't he? How can someone not kiss at all?'

'He had lovely lips, and a big sultry smile, but he was a messy kisser, urgh. I felt like I was being swallowed up whole. And it quite put me off.'

'So you broke up with him?'

She nods. 'Online.'

'You broke up with him by email?'

'Facebook message.'

My jaw drops open. 'Mean!'

She laughs. 'I know, but I couldn't face him. Anyway, that was a million years ago. I've matured since then.' She dons a serious look.

'Yeah, right.'

'What about you, Rosie? Do you have any dating horror stories?'

I think back to boyfriends past, and cringe at the memory of being young and in love wearing blinkers. 'Well, I did once date this guy in secondary school only to find out that he had the worst breath ever. I'd take a messy kiss any day over that.'

'No!' She covers her mouth and laughs. 'So what did you do?'

'I shook his hand.'

A frown appears between her perfectly-groomed eyebrows. 'What?'

In retrospect, it does seem hilarious. 'I took to shaking his hand, instead of kissing him, and I kept our relationship *strictly* platonic.'

She lets out a howl of laughter. 'Oh, Rosie, you are the limit. And then what happened?'

'We broke up, not surprisingly and then he spent the rest of school going from one girl to another, until one day he came to school sucking mints and he was never without one again. Someone, I don't know who, must've given him the bad news.'

'Did he have a long-term relationship after that? Poor guy.'

'I don't know, I left. To London for my glittering career as chef, which meant I was in charge of *mise en place* for four years before eventually being trusted to assist with the garnish on entrées.'

'Sounds like you had to bide your time longer than most.'

I nod. 'It's the culinary industry; there's a pecking order and it's all about patience.' At the thought of all I've given up, my stomach clenches. Fifteen years at Époque, starting so low I wasn't even on the bottom rung of the ladder, let alone climbing it.

'And now you're here, and *you're* in charge.'

She always seems to know what to say to pull me from panic. 'Yes,' I give her a small smile. 'I'm the captain…'

CHAPTER EIGHT

A few weeks later, it's time for the Hay Festival. Staring out into a field chock-a-block with caravans and campervans, the usual signs of intimidation edge in. That same fear that always holds me at arm's length from people. The worry that I'll say something wrong, or react the wrong way. That I'll be a laughing stock because I appear almost robotic when I'm nervous. I shut off and go blank eyed, or worse, say the very first thing that comes to mind, which is usually not appropriate. If these festival pilgrims don't take to me, what then?

In the weeks leading up to today, we'd 'popped up' at some small fairs, swap meets, and church fetes, but nothing on this scale, for this length of time, or with this many people! As my chest tightens with every *what if*, I brush myself down, marvelling that somehow I'm always just that little bit dusty these days.

'Come on, Rosie!' Aria's pretty face appears beside me. 'We've got work to do!'

Her smile is infectious and as I join her in the field, a cacophony of sounds greets me. Laughter, chatter, doors slamming, people hefting tables, chairs, strumming instruments, the sound checking of a microphone. It's absolute and utter mayhem. Festival vendors unpack their wares, set up shelves, visit other campers with coffee cups in hand.

'It's so bloody noisy and busy, and there's people everywhere!'

Aria shakes her head as if I'm a hoot. 'And it will be even louder tomorrow when it opens to the public. Wait until we get to a music festival, *then* you'll know what loud is.'

'Fluck.'

She cocks her head. 'Fluck?'

'Exactly.'

'Clearly, Gordon Ramsay you are not!' She cackles and says, 'You should get a bit of business from the other Van Lifers tonight once everyone is set up for tomorrow. So get cracking and shout out if you need a hand. Make sure you get your literary teas on display, I know they're going to be popular amongst the bookworms so now's your chance to get the word out to the vendors – news travels along the grapevine.'

I nod. 'OK. I need to get moving, I have so much to do.' The thought of baking away in Poppy calms me. I'm mentally prepared, and know once I begin, all worry will fall away as I get into the baking zone.

By late afternoon, things are looking brighter. In Poppy's tiny kitchen, I'm in control. Cooking is the place I can be myself, where I can pour my heart and soul into it and be as expressive as I like.

My ice cream churns away, ready for my knickerbocker glories; the old-fashioned sundae made with vanilla bean ice cream, meringue, Chantilly cream, fresh fruit and nuts and of course, the obligatory cherry on top. Really, who wouldn't indulge? It's enough to conjure your childhood right before your very eyes.

Finally, I'm doing things my way! My future patrons can expect generous portions and a full belly if they come to the travelling tea shop. Not a teeny tiny degustation serve in sight! Not a micro herb to be found.

Fresh scones bake away in the oven, and my blueberry jam bubbles on the stove while I finish making scotch eggs. A rush of happiness encircles me, making these old-fashioned favourites, an homage to my English roots, and so different to the contemporary French cuisine I've been making for too long.

I relish using my hands, plating tweezers long forgotten. I do worry I'm overcatering, but it's hard to gauge exactly how much I'll need. And while I don't want to waste food, I don't want to miss an opportunity to sell and add some much needed money to the coffers.

Even cooking in larger quantities, things gel. I've found my holy grail inside Poppy's minuscule kitchen and not even her slight idiosyncrasies are enough to put me off. So the oven is a little slow to heat up, and the stove top is ancient… I can make do. Fridge space is at a premium, storage is an issue, bench space is sparse but not so much that I can't deal with it.

There's a lot to be said for taking my time, and being solitary, no yelling from the line, no Jacques bellowing, his face turning heirloom-tomato red. Just me and Poppy, who I talk to as I work. Which I hope isn't another sign of madness!

Once I'm done, I wash the dishes and get to blending another batch of my *Romeo and Juliet* love potion, completely tickled at the idea behind it.

The handwritten cards read: *Forbidden fruit, rose and thorns, a love so great.*

In actual fact, it's a mix of rose petals, strawberry, raspberry and cinnamon. Even in its dried state it smells divine, just like the first flush of new love, where the world is sunshine and roses, and sweeter than honey.

It reminds me of Callum, and when we first dated, how effortless it all was, how I couldn't wipe the smile from my face for months, amazed that, for the first time ever, someone recognised something special in me.

'Knock, knock!' Aria enters the van, her face alight. 'Oh, my god, Rosie what is that smell? Something sugary and buttery and just divine.'

'That's treacle tart. Help yourself. There's a knife in the block there, and plates are in the cupboard above you. There's a fresh beaker of cream in the fridge, be generous. And tell me what you think. Patisserie quality, it is not. These dishes are rustic and so utterly different to the delicate desserts I oversaw at Époque for years but are honest and humble and what good food should be. I hope?'

'What do you mean you hope? I will always give thanks for the day I found you in the mud.' She puts her hands up in prayer and looks to the ceiling as if giving thanks to god.

She helps herself to a slice, and then stops suddenly, her eyes widening at something outside.

'Ooh, Rosie, it looks like you've got yourself your first customer of the day and, *phwoar*, would you check him out? That must be Nola's son, the one I keep hearing about. He could be Jason Momoa's twin!'

'Jason... who?' I wrack my brain trying to think of all the people Aria has introduced me to over the past few days and can't remember meeting any Jason Momoas.

Aria goes puce, actually *puce*-coloured. 'You have spent thirty-two years on this planet without clapping eyes on the *god* that is Jason Mamoa? He's an actor; a very hot, buff, fierce-looking hulk of a man, much like that specimen right out there.'

'Oh Aria, I don't have time for movies or television!'

'Well, add Game of Thrones marathon to our girls' night list. You, my little innocent, are going to get an education!' she stage whispers to me as the guy edges closer to read the menu board.

My so called 'education' is soon forgotten as panic sets in. This is my first real customer at a *proper* festival – I can't mess up. I must appear casual, friendly and most of all, non-robotic.

I'm used to being at the back of house, but now I must be

front, back and everything in between! I can do this. *But do not act like a parody of everyone else!*

With a toothy grin in place, I approach the fold-down serving counter. 'Hello there. Can I help you?' I tilt my head invitingly as if I am a dab hand at this serving caper. How different it is from being invisible back of house!

He frowns.

I can't think why he's frowning.

I surreptitiously pat myself down. Clothes, check, apron check.

The silence drags on. I can't even hear Aria breathing, it's like she's holding her breath in anticipation too.

Just when I'm about to ask if he's OK, he says in a beguiling deep velvety voice, 'You're in my spot. And it looks like you've camped for the duration.' He points to our tables and chairs, which I note Aria has decorated with lovely vases full of fresh wild daisies. Our A-frame signs are up advertising our wares. We're connected to the electricity; our cables are taped down to avoid being a tripping hazard.

'Sorry, Mr…?'

'Max.'

'Mr Max—'

'It's just Max.' He has a hint of an American accent. Of course he does. He couldn't just be a regular guy. There's something about the man that sends a tingle up my spine. He's all bulging muscles, taut, and tanned, and powerful somehow. Quite the spectacle of a man. He has a presence. And if I was in the market for a bad guy, he would be the one. But I'm not, I remind myself.

'Max, I'm sorry for the confusion but we've been given this allotment. You must be mistaken. Now if you don't mind…' *Look at me go!*

He folds his arms, and those biceps of his actually bulge. There's fire in his feline eyes, and he's quite disarming if you're into the fierce, primal, rugged type. He looks like the type of guy who spends his life running up hills with his pride of lions. I guess

I'm used to Londoners – executive, business-suit-clad men, not the likes of... Max.

'This is my spot.'

'No, it isn't.'

'It is.'

Witty repartee aside, I begin to have doubts. Am I in the wrong spot? I exchange a look with Aria and she shrugs breezily, continuing to stare unabashedly as she forks treacle tart into her mouth.

'Let me check our paperwork.' I dash off to the space that I call my office but is in fact a chair with a tiny pull down shelf. Space is at a premium in Poppy. Finally, I find the festival permit and check the numbers. Dammit. I am in the wrong spot, but I'm not far off.

I race back – well, walk the four paces at speed – to see he's still got his huge arms folded, his muscles bursting out all over the place. He is an actual man mountain. I'm quite flustered. It's that animal magnetism of his, and really it's so hot all of sudden with the oven going and pots on the stove... I shake my shirt to try and circulate some air.

'You're right,' I say, willing myself to speak with authority. 'I'm supposed to be on the other side of Aria's bookshop. It's not that big of a deal, though? You can go there, and I'll stay here?'

He lifts a shoulder and its only then I notice how long his locks are, dark at the roots but golden blonde at the tips like he spends a lot of time outdoors. He's almost leonine. I bet he roars, too.

'Would you like some spotted dick, as a thank you?' I ask, hoping there's no hard feelings.

'What?' He throws me a look that suggests I'm handling this all wrong. Am I that bad at communicating? I'm offering the proverbial olive branch, and he's reeling back as if I'm offering him poison.

People are so complicated.

'Spotted dick? A nice big...'

Before I can finish he bursts out laughing, shakes his head and saunters away.

I turn to Aria, puzzled only to find her doubled over as tears begin to stream down her cheeks. 'What?' I say, bamboozled.

'You…' She struggles to control herself. 'You…'

At this rate we'll be here all day.

'You are *hilarious*, Rosie! His face!' She falls about laughing, for no reason I can fathom.

And then it dawns on me. 'Oh god. He's American so he probably doesn't know that spotted dick is a pudding, right?'

I give her credit, she tries very hard to compose herself and hold in another bout of laughter but eventually it spews out of her in a loud cackle that *boings* around the van. What a faux pas! Already!

'Right!'

'What should I do? I don't want word to spread that the travelling tea shop is offering… offering, well something untoward!'

'Nothing.' She goes back to forking cake into her mouth.

'But…' How to explain to Aria? From the weeks I've spent with her I know she's one of those people who fit in in any group, assimilates easily, doesn't second guess herself. If it had been her, Max probably would have taken the spotted dick just because it was her doing the offering. 'I think I need to explain to him in case he thinks I'm weird.'

'Or is it because he's gorgeous?'

My mouth opens and closes, and I find myself flummoxed. This is a crazy conversation to be having. How far my life has drifted off course, and so quickly. 'He might be gorgeous to some, but I'm not interested in that kind of man.'

Oliver's profile pic flashes in my mind. In comparison to Max he seems so safe. So normal. In his last email he sent pictures of himself at the top of various mountains, triumphant boy-next-door smile in place. Whereas Max is this hulking, superhero type, so out of the ordinary in the real world.

And anyway, why am I even comparing the men! Love is definitely on the menu, but not with Max. I have to be sure my next relationship is with someone solid and dependable, and not judging a book by its cover or anything, but Max doesn't seem like that kind. OK, so I am judging him, but only because I have to protect my bruised heart.

Next I try a wheedling tone, 'Can you take him some spotted dick and explain? Maybe *you* can exchange numbers while you there?' I ask in a sugary-sweet voice.

She shakes her coppery head. 'No, I'm not interested in him,' she says. 'But I swear I saw sparks coming off you both. I bet he's following the same festival route as us, so we should get to clap our eyes on him a lot!'

'Have you been drinking again?' Aria is partial to a tipple whenever the mood strikes, and I wouldn't put it past her. Lots of the Van Lifers sit around and drink bottles of plonk and play cards, any time of the day. Time isn't regulated like it is in the real world. Everyone is on the go at different times of the day, so the routine is: there is no routine. They'll have wine for lunch and tea before bed, it doesn't matter.

'Not this time. But Rosie, are you quite sure you didn't feel a thing for him?'

'Quite,' I say primly and fold my arms.

She raises a brow. 'Is there a man in your life back in London?'

'There was.'

'And…?' Did she really need to know the whole sorry story? I'd managed to keep it under wraps so far, despite our many girlie nights talking under the stars and musing about life and all its intricacies.

'It ended.'

'Why, though?'

'The usual reasons. What about you, Aria?' My new ploy, answer every question with a question.

'What about me?'

I narrow my eyes. Was *she* answering every question with a question?

'Have you got a significant other?'

Laughter barrels out of her. 'A significant other?'

'Well?' I used the same stare down tactic she tried with me.

'Nope. And I'm not looking for one either.' Her words sound bruised somehow, like there's a layer of hurt just below.

My gaze drops to her left hand, a small gold band on her wedding ring finger. How had I not noticed it before? Is she on the run from him? Is she in witness protection? No, because if so she'd take the ring off surely? Is it a ruse to stop men from pestering her? I sense from the sudden stiffness in her shoulders that the topic is off limits and give myself a big pat on the back for noticing. Usually I suffer foot-in-mouth disease, not picking up cues from people because I'm simply not listening hard enough, my mind always on the next thing. Here, I guess I'm already learning to slow down and take note.

Is this when I should step up, be a good friend? It's so hard to know when my closest friend in London was my Thai basil plant – and how well it grew from our late night conversations! 'Erm, so why not? You're young, gorgeous, free-spirited. What's stopping you?'

'Been there, done that, got the bookmark and now I'm going to spend the rest of my life with the dashing heroes in my romance novels.' Her smile stretches as though it pains her to do so. Is it a need for privacy? If so, I get that. Telling me won't really help her, will it? It will just bring all those feelings up again and feelings are best left locked up and out of the way. She's probably gone through a messy divorce, and I can relate. While mine is cold and clinical, the end result will be the same. Singledom.

'Right,' I say, deciding I must take my own future in hand. 'I'm going to go give him some spotted dick and see how he likes it.'

Her laughter follows me outside.

As I walk over with a container filled with various sweet treats,

I give myself a pep talk. *Be cool, be calm, and witty if you can.* As I get to his van, he's bent at the waist hoisting something upwards. His jumper rides up and exposes his back, and I promptly freeze. There's something erotic about the flash of skin, as innocent as it is. His muscles flex as he moves and it's captivating.

Before I can think he turns and catches me staring. 'I wasn't staring.' *Gah!*

'That so?' He lifts one eyebrow and it's all I can do not to turn and run. I know his type, I can tell by the ways his eyes flash that every woman is fair game to him. Well, not me. He looks like the love 'em and leave 'em type and I want no part in that.

This guy, this veritable wild man, has heartbreak written all over him and I feel for the girls who'll lose their minds over what will never be. Call me presumptuous but he doesn't look like the settle down sort.

He's giving me a hard stare and I wonder briefly if I've spoken my private thoughts out loud. It wouldn't be the first time. 'So,' I cough. 'You rushed away so fast I didn't get to give you a peace offering for parking in your spot. I've got some treacle tart, and some erm spotted…'

He holds up a beast-sized hand, which is when I see tribal-like tattoos snaking up his arm like the ultimate bad boy. 'Thanks, but no thanks. I don't eat refined sugar.'

'What?' *All bad boys eat refined sugar!* 'And why is that?'

'Do you really want to know?' His feline eyes flash. Just how does one get their eyes to flash like that? I'm sure mine don't do anything of the sort. They're just your average deep blue but sort of dull eyes, not opalescent like Max's are. Really, it's quite unfair.

'Well, yes, I'd love to know why you'd deprive yourself, but I'm guessing I know the reason – your body is your temple, right? But life is about more than…'

He does that same laugh, and shakes his head, the rest of my sentence freezes on my tongue.

'Sugar has zero benefit for the body.'

'It does! A side effect is happiness, *that's* beneficial. Like a big plate of pancakes with ooey gooey chocolate sauce…'

'I don't eat processed carbs; they turn to sugar in your body too.'

My mouth falls open. 'Next minute you'll be saying pork chops are unhealthy!'

'Well, any animal product is. I'm vegan,' he says, and my heart literally stops beating. For a chef 'vegan' is a problematic word. A complication. A *real* headache.

'Vegan?' I recoil.

He can't be vegan! He's so caveman-esque! I picture him gnawing on a chargrilled turkey leg by the camp fire, or pulling a knife from his leather belt and stabbing a huge T-bone steak drawing it to his mouth, a slick of oil coating his lips…

'Vegan,' he confirms.

It's sacrilege! 'To save the animals?'

'Partly, and the earth, the environment.'

Golly. 'But don't you miss meat? Dairy?'

'Not at all. Don't look so surprised. You can't knock it until you try it.'

Why does everyone keep spouting that line to me, lately? Still, I blanch at the thought of being vegan, as a chef I just couldn't do it for love nor money. 'No, no, not for me. I would die if I couldn't eat a creamy camembert or heap a mound of parmesan on my pasta. Literally die. And then there's milk, I'm partial to the odd milkshake, they're just so comforting…'

'There's cashew cheese, and almond milk, plenty of substitutes—'

I hold up a hand. 'Cashew cheese is *not* cheese.'

He raises a brow as if he knows better. 'Have you *tried* it?'

I go to fold my arms defensively but realise I can't because I'm carrying a container of puddings he's basically calling toxic. 'You know I haven't.'

'Why don't we start with an almond milk smoothie? Your body will thank you for it, trust me.'

74

'My body will thank me for it? What's that supposed to mean?' So I'm a little curvier than most? Is he fat-shaming me or something?

His eyebrows pull together. 'It means you'll feel more energetic, more vibrant ...'

'I'm quite happy with full-cream cow's milk, thank you. How about you stick to your, your… creations—', abominations, more like, '—and I'll stick to mine.' His stare feels laser-like, as though he's trying to hypnotise me. How could you ever cook for a man who's vegan? There could never be crispy crackly sticky Asian pork belly, nor slow braised rosemary and thyme lamb, or…

'You do realise you're speaking out loud?'

Kill me.

He holds his hands up in mock surrender but still wears that amused grin of his that irks me so. 'If you change your mind, you know where to find me.' He points to his van but he practically blocks out sunlight so it's no wonder I didn't see his great big sign advertising *The Lean, Green and Clean Café*. Max is certainly a paradox.

'Thanks but no thanks. Enjoy your day.' I spin on my heel, and head back to Poppy, feeling unbalanced all of a sudden.

'What?' Aria asks as I trip over the step and fall head first into the kitchen.

'That man! He's… he's…'

'He's what?'

I take a deep breath, and let the words pour out of me in one great big stutter. 'He's *vegan!*'

She throws her head back and laughs. 'Wow, plot twist! How does a man with a body like that live entirely on vegetables?' Shaking her head, she stands and puts the kettle on to boil.

'I don't know.' I mean, I really *don't*. 'And… and…'

'What?'

'He doesn't eat refined sugar! Or processed carbs!'

She lets out a haw. 'No sugar? He's probably sweet enough.'

She puts a finger to her chin. 'Actually no, he's not sweet, he's spicy!' Cue the eyebrow waggle.

'It's unfathomable.'

'Why do you *care* so much?' Aria asks, psychologist voice at the ready. 'This is as animated as I've ever seen you.'

I shake my head as if she's obtuse. 'Because I don't understand how anyone can live with restrictions like that! Tell me, is there anything better than when you've had the worst day ever, like missed the bus in a hailstorm bad, and you get home soaking wet and shivering, and practically fall into a bowl of steaming hot, oily, garlicky, parmesan laden pasta with a rich creamy sauce? It actually hurts to think about forgoing that for your entire life! Plus there's—'

She lifts her palm. 'I know, I know. But what I mean is why does him being a sugar-free vegan concern *you* so?' Her eyebrows shimmy, those thick caterpillars dance.

'Well,' I say, suddenly bewildered. 'For the reasons I have just outlined, *obviously*.'

Why *does* it bother me so much? Is it left over from a work life of chest-clutching when a waiter announces two patrons out of a party of four for the ten-course degustation are vegan, and 'is that a problem because they didn't ring ahead'?

Probably.

'Maybe it's the fact that generous serves of béchamel-laden lasagne, or slices of salty crumbly quiche Lorraine are called comfort foods for a reason! They have the ability to shift a mood, to lighten a day; mud cakes with extra frosting, dark chocolate and orange ganache, all these can actually help mend a broken heart. How can he not see that?'

Aria grins and says, 'I think it's because you had this vision of feeding him spoonfuls of luscious crème brulée, licking the vanilla off those kissable lips of his, and now that fantasy is out the window.'

I gasp. '*You* are insane! I knew you were too perfect to be normal!' I mean, licking vanilla off his lips, honestly! Despite the mild weather, I'm uncomfortably warm.

Her spoon clatters to her plate. 'You should see your face! Just admit Max is hot, and you've thought about him in *that* way.'

I shake my head. 'In *that* way! How old are you?' The situation suddenly seems hilarious and my shoulders shake as I laugh along with Aria, feeling flush with a type of happiness I haven't felt in such a long time. The kind that comes with joking and teasing and developing a real friendship.

Even if she *is* way off base with Max. Sure, he might draw the eye and send prickles down the length of me (prickles, *not* tingles), but Oliver is more my type of guy. Poetic, quiet, a thinker, someone who'd blend in, not stand out in a crowd. Aria and all this talk is driving me to distraction.

Before she can retort, another man wanders over and trailing behind him is a glamourous sixty-something woman, wearing a bright purple woolly jacket that falls to her ankles, her white-grey locks blowing out in the breeze behind her.

'Hey,' he says, nodding his head in that slow way these travelling folk have all mastered as if there's no rush and they have all the time in the world. 'Welcome to the circuit. I'm Spencer and this is my wife, Nola.' I take his proffered hand, and Nola edges past and tries to hug me which is difficult with me being inside the van and her outside. Nevertheless, I feel a sort of paternal and maternal warmth from them. There's a calmness to their every move, almost as though they've figured it all out, this messy business called life.

'Hello, nice to meet you. Can I get you something?'

'We'll have two of your knickerbocker glories, please. Haven't had one of those since we were kids, hey Nola?' He turns to the woman who grins.

'Far too many years ago to count.'

'Would you like a serve of scones too, they're not long out of the oven?' Upsell, isn't that the way of the world?

'You could twist my arm,' Nola says, and smiles up at me. There's something familiar about her, but I can't place it.

'Take a seat,' I say. 'And I'll bring your order over.'

Before long the couple is surrounded by a small crowd, hugging and exclaiming over them as if they're celebrities. 'Who are they?' I whisper to Aria as I heap homemade ice cream into tall glasses, adding crushed meringue, fresh fruit, and dolloping a heap of fresh cream, a nice cloudy bed for the cherry on top.

Her smile threatens to swallow her up and she speaks in an almost reverential tone, 'They're Van Lifer royalty. Both in their late seventies and have been on the road since for*ever*. They practically invented the movement, and are just the sweetest people you'll ever stumble across.'

'Late seventies? Wow, they look great.' Especially Nola with her mane of white-grey hair and chic bohemian style. The laugh lines on her face crinkle into stars when she smiles and only add to her appeal. She carries herself with an assured air that only comes with being comfortable in your own skin, a trait I envy and aspire to all at once.

'Doesn't she? Doesn't look a day over sixty. They're popular among the nomads because they're so bloody nice but also because they kind of made this lifestyle popular back in the day, not just travelling from place to place, but they set up their own festivals before they were popular and it made life so much easier for wanderers. They come and go though, travelling from country to country. This is their first year back, they've been in Indonesia for a few years. Before that Canada, America, Australia...'

There is definitely a pulse in the air from the couple. 'Gosh, I hadn't thought about visiting other countries in Poppy.'

Aria leans back and closes her eyes, hands resting on her belly, the early signs of falling into a food coma. 'Yeah, it's the next step. Once you've done the UK, of course. We could go to France, Italy, Spain...'

I cut scones in halves and lather the base with jam before

topping them with cream, but my mind is elsewhere as I think of driving through other countries, sampling different cuisines from rustic cafes to fancy restaurants and everything in between. I've always wanted to broaden my foodie horizons, but there has never been enough time.

When I did have holidays, we went to Cornwall to visit Callum's parents, two stiff-upper-lipped people who I tried very hard to win over, but I never quite succeeded. And even though I yearned to travel elsewhere I thought it a good quality in him that he wanted to see his parents on our holidays – how could I say no?

As I finish plating their scones, I rip some fresh mint from a pot on the sideboard and place it on the side. 'How do they find the money to travel?'

All I can see is Aria's rump as she peruses the mini cake fridge. Where she puts all the food is beyond me, lithe thing she is, but I'm glad I have such an enthusiastic taste-tester.

'Oh,' she says her voice muffled. 'They sell all sorts of whimsy things; Nola's handcrafted dream catchers, woven rugs, that kind of thing. They're both arty and into textiles as their main medium. You should see the batik they imported from Indonesia, it's stunning. I'm sure there were times they've been stone-cold broke and unsure of where their next meal was coming from – but I guess we've all been there, and they prove you can consistently live this type of lifestyle long-term if you really want to.'

What a love story; them on the road side by side for years, watching sunrises together, going on never-ending road trips. Buying, selling, living, loving. 'Yeah, wow. I guess I never thought about living this way for longer than a year… if that. Do you think they miss having a place to call home?'

'No, their van is their home, and even when they travel and leave it parked up, they know they can always come back to it.'

It's a lot to ponder but I can see how home is wherever you park up. Already I'm attached to Poppy, and couldn't imagine selling her even if I decided to leave this nomadic life.

'Oh,' Aria says, almost as a side note, as her voice becomes breezy. 'They're also Max's parents.'

'You minx! You knew it all along!' Of course they are! Nola with those same catlike eyes, and Spencer with a wild woolly mane of hair, thick still at seventy-plus. I should have known! 'But they're not vegan?'

She shrugs. 'Guess not.'

Interesting. Bustling outside, I serve them their scones and sundaes and wait until they're finished before quizzing them about their extraordinary life.

'That knickerbocker glory is manna from heaven,' Nola says, her face shining.

'Thank you. It's my go-to when I need a pick-me-up.'

'I can see why.'

'So... Aria tells me you've been on the road forever.'

She laughs. 'It feels that way, and I guess to you young folk we're pretty ancient.'

Face palm. 'I didn't mean...'

She stops me. 'Sweet pea, we're almost eighty, we *are* ancient.'

Spencer is called away by someone further down the path, so he makes his apologies and leaves.

'We've been on the road since as long as I can remember, I shudder to think of living any other way.'

Nola's accent is decidedly British. 'You're Max's parents but he's got an American accent... Did you spend a lot of time in the States?'

Toying with the handle of her mug, she takes a moment to reply. 'Max has dual citizenship because he was born there – Spencer is American, you see. So my adrenaline junkie son Max got it into his head that being in the armed forces US Military was his calling.' She lets out a plaintive sigh. 'How any son of ours thought that was a good idea is beyond me.' Her words aren't bitter, but full of bafflement nonetheless.

'Why, because of the danger?'

'Well, the danger but also the idea of being armed, it goes against every principle we hold dear. Peace, always, not guns, we *never* promoted guns. And yet he insisted on going when he's such a gentle giant himself.'

'Must've been about more than the guns for him.'

Her face softens and she pats my hand. 'I think there's a part of him that always wants to protect, to be the glue that fixes problems. But there's so many other ways he could have gone about that and probably have done more good in the long run, but what can a mother do, except let him go and hope to god he doesn't come to any harm. Lessons have to be learned the hard way sometimes. I know that for a fact.'

'But he's back now…?'

'Yes, finally I've got my boy back, where he should always have been.'

It strikes me as odd that Max would choose such a profession. A guy who is vegan to save animals and the planet, yet holstered a gun and went to war – it doesn't add up. And that he'd go against his parent's wishes when he seemed so similar to his mum in that love-the-world kind of way.

'How long did he serve for?' I ask.

'Ten years.'

My eyebrows shoot up. 'Wow.' Words fade away as I imagine Max in the US Army but I fail to reconcile the image of him as a soldier. Yes, he has the buff, athletic physique for it, but he just doesn't seem like that sort of man. It goes to show you can never really tell with anyone…

CHAPTER NINE

At Hay-On-Wye I soon learn that bookworms are a happy, patient bunch, who don't seem to mind queuing for tea and cake as they chat to each other about their spoils, which signed books they'd snagged and the authors they'd managed to meet.

Not surprisingly, they are all totally in love with Aria's little bookshop, and many find themselves a perch inside her van, snag a throw rug and, with book in hand, settle in for the duration.

They're all Aria clones, a species in their natural environment; all they need are books, rugs, tea and cake to be content.

It occurs to me life is all about simple pleasures, and for these doe-eyed, ready-smiling girls, it comes in the form of a book. As predicted, together we've been the perfect antidote for their needs and as quick as I bag up my literary tea blends, I sell them, before sending the bookworms to her for the matching book.

Finally, I get to the end of my queue, and serve my very last customer for the day.

After making the customer a takeaway pack of fruit scones, I say goodbye with a smile. My legs ache from the intensity of the long day but it's no different to a long shift at Époque where my feet would be practically numb after a hectic night of covers.

Outside, bookworms read at our tables so I figure they

probably want to take a moment to rest too. There's no need for me to pack everything away. I pull down the awning and place a *Back Soon* sign up, grab my laptop, and flop on my bed to reply to Oliver.

I've been mulling over Aria's opinion that he's probably a little lonely being a solitary traveller, and that's why he checks in on me so often – even electronic communication is better than none. Unlike us, he doesn't follow the festival scene, so lots of his days are spent alone editing his photos, and trying to drum up business and keep going.

> *Hi Oliver,*
>
> *What a hectic time it is at Hay. Mayhem in the best possible way. I see now though why the quiet weeks between festivals are so necessary for body, mind and spirit.*
>
> *The bookworms are utterly lovely. They cuddle their books like newborn babies, chat for hours over tea and cake about their favourite writers, cliffhangers, preferred chapter length, eBooks versus paperbacks and the like!*
>
> *In a way I wish I could have poured my own pot of tea and sat with them like Aria did. You have to envy her 'job' sometimes. It's a great way to live life.*
>
> *Do you know much about travelling abroad? I'm wondering if the language barrier is an issue when trying to pop up in a foreign country. I do like the idea of moving on at the end of the year… if I'm still doing this, that is. I feel a bit like Alice. I've fallen down the rabbit hole into this strange new world, and I must learn how to live in it.*
>
> *Best,*
> *Rosie*

Part of me feels silly talking so openly to this stranger, but the other part feels secure, knowing he'll understand. And is it so bad to open up every now and then? Didn't I say I would try?

I brew a pot of *Romeo and Juliet* love potion; the scent of roses and romance permeates the air. As I go to open my spreadsheet and type in the daily takings and expenditure, a reply from Oliver arrives. Maybe he too is sitting somewhere in the milky twilight musing about roads less travelled.

Dearest Rosie,

I've been on the road a year and a half, which probably sounds like a long time to you, but I'm 'new' according to most Van Lifers I meet. I've met pilgrims who've been doing this for decades, others who've been around the world twice. Some who've never known any other lifestyle. The forum has been great for connecting with people, and I help out with new members when I can because I know how overwhelming taking that first leap can be and I also learn a lot for my own travels.

Once you commit to it – this new, strange, utterly enriching lifestyle – the world opens up in a way it never has before. You'll see.

When I'm sitting in the van as the sun retreats for another day casting an orange glow across the sky, I feel so alive, so filled with this new-found vigour that I wonder why I didn't start this journey years ago. I want to phone every old friend I can find and tell them to chuck in their jobs, pack a bag and ditch suburbia, but of course I don't. I just sit here relishing the fact that this is my reality. How lucky am I?

Would I feel like that too? Once I got out and about and into the wild more as time goes on? With damp earth under my feet and wind in my hair? That kind of stillness scares me, but what if that's only because I haven't tried? I find myself warming to Oliver. Not hard when he has the heart of a nomad, and a romantic soul.

*In terms of travelling abroad, I'd have to do some research
and get back to you. I've never really considered it myself, so
haven't paid much attention when it's been discussed in the
forum. Let me see what I can find.*

Oliver

***

As the festival ramps up, my literary teas fly off the proverbial
shelf. Aria takes to handwriting the description cards so I can
bag more tea whenever I get a chance. As I'm wrapping another
bundle of the Alice in Wonderland blend a customer squeals
when she spots Poppy. Who knew having a bright pink van with
a thick teal stripe down the side would be such an advantage?

'This is the one.' She motions at a gaggle of friends. 'We've
heard about the tea!' she says, beaming up at me. 'Please tell me
you haven't sold out?'

'I've just made another batch!' I blush at their openly friendly
faces staring rapturously at me. Literary tea at the Hay Festival
was a stroke of genius! 'Would you like to taste first?'

'Sure!' I pour them all a cup of tea as if they're wine tasting,
and realise that's something I can promote at future events. Tea
tasting with a dessert plate, pairing sweets to tea.

'*Alice in Wonderland* for me, please,' one of the girls wearing
a red fedora says. I hand her a bag and she reads the label to her
friends: '*Drink me.*' She giggles. 'How perfect is that?'

'It comes with these,' I say, and hand her another little bag
filled with colourful macarons.

'*Eat me,*' she reads.

My two favourite lines in the book, of course, and so relevant
to tea and biscuits. 'Aria at The Little Bookshop of Happy Ever
After has copies of *Alice's Adventures in Wonderland*, and a host
of reimaginings…'

I'm not sure if it's the quality of the tea or the literary aspect these bibliophiles at Hay-on-Wye love, but either way, it bodes well. It's so much fun hearing them discuss each blend as if it's a fine wine, what flavours they discern, which books match with the classics in question. The girls pay and dart off to Aria's van with a backwards wave, chattering ten to the dozen.

Aria visits later that evening, and brings in a man in chef whites. 'Rosie, I've found a chef friend of yours! Come and say hello!'

Not only have there been contemporary fiction authors at Hay, but there has also been a range of non-fiction authors, namely chefs spruiking their cookbooks. Their popularity is on the rise as the celebrity chef cooking show phenomenon has hit around the world. They're the new reality TV stars, and have quite the gaggle of fans following them around the festival when they dare step out for a wander.

Once I recognise him, my stomach flips. Callum's boss, and owner of esteemed Italian restaurant Brodo. How bittersweet to see his ruddy face. Back in the day, when I first moved to London, he'd been a big support to me, someone to go to when Jacques made my life hell. I couldn't face him after Callum left, knowing that he must have been aware of the fling and had never said a word to me. I understand though, who wants to be the bearer of such news?

'Mario,' I say. 'How are you?'

'Good, good, nice set up you've got here.' He rocks on the balls of his feet.

'Thanks.' What does he really see when he glances around the tiny confines of Poppy? I'm sure he thinks I've done a runner to save face, to hide out. But what does it matter? I'm not the one in the wrong, and it dawns on me that even though I did throw away everything in order to escape, it's made me stronger, more alive in a way I haven't felt in years.

He scrutinises the floor, not able to meet my eye. 'Rosie…' He runs a hand through his salt and pepper hair. 'I wanted to tell you, I did, but I didn't know how to. I tried to talk sense into him, but—'

I hold up a hand. 'It's OK, Mario.' I wave it all away, the past, the sadness, the hurt. 'It's not your fault, and you shouldn't have to feel bad about it.' And I find I really mean it.

A blush creeps up his cheeks and I wonder if there's more to it, but I don't press him.

'Would you like some tea?' I ask. Should I ask him about Callum? Would he tell me the truth?

'Ah, no thanks, Rosie. I've got a cooking demo in an hour to help promote the cookbook so I'd better get myself organised for that. Your friend here thought you might like a signed copy,' he says, his voice high with embarrassment.

'Oh, sure, I'd love one.'

He hands me the book like it's on fire and then says, 'Better go. Good luck with… all this, Rosie. You're not missing much in London, that's for sure.' He gives me a big squeeze and says, 'For what it's worth he knows he made a mistake, but it's too late now.'

What does that mean? It is too late for me, at any rate. There's no chance of reconciliation, not on my part.

Once the door bangs behind him, Aria turns to me. 'What the hell was all that about? Who was he?'

'He's my soon-to-be-ex-husband's boss.'

She claps her hands over her face. 'Of all the people I could have dragged here, I chose him! When he introduced himself as a London restaurateur I thought you might have known him, I didn't think it'd be quite in *that* capacity. Sorry, Rosie.'

'It's OK, really, it's fine.'

I flip through the *Brodo* cookbook – a modern glossy hardback, filled with so-called secret family recipes. Each dish has a story behind it, and funny little anecdotes; it's quite heartwarming and relatable for a cookbook.

But a few pages in, I see why Mario did a runner. There's a

two-page spread with Khloe spooning panna cotta into Callum's mouth and a description of their jobs and how they helped make Brodo successful under Mario's tutelage.

I read aloud. 'Listen to this. "All you need is a pinch of desire, a dash of rapture, a splash of passion, season well with love and respect and that's how you'll find *amoré*!" Urgh, cheesy!' I snap the book closed before I can read any more. Did they fall in love when they were posing for these cutesy pics while I was slaving away at Époque?

Aria looks desolate. She pries the book from my fingers. 'I'm going to return this...'

'It's OK, really. Mario's family recipes will definitely be worth flicking through. Maybe you can just rip out the pages they feature in?' I say, trying to crack a smile while inside my heart shatters once again.

'I'll do it so carefully you won't even know the book isn't complete. Shall I make us a G and T? I think under these circumstances it's purely medicinal.'

'No, it's OK,' I say. 'I have to sort the fridges while I've got the chance. And then I might have an early night. I have to be up at stupid o'clock to get the cakes baked.'

In times of high stress, I clean. I clean and I clean once more so I know I'm still in control. I'm capable. I'm not my dad, I'm not falling apart. There's no clutter, no mess.

She nods and by the pitiful look she gives me I know she doesn't believe me, but knows me well enough to gauge I need to be alone.

The end of a marriage is like a grieving process and it keeps coming back to haunt me. I need to move on too, but how?

After a two-hour cleaning frenzy, I tuck myself up in bed with my laptop to see an email from Oliver with all the relevant information for travelling abroad in Poppy. He's put so much effort in and now the idea of travelling abroad seems absurd. Who do I think I am?

Perhaps it was seeing Mario's shocked face as he scanned Poppy, as if he couldn't quite believe I'd gone from Michelin-starred restaurant to pop-up food van.

But does it matter what anyone thinks as long as I'm happy? I guess I'll always have that fear that I gave up my stellar career on a whim but I'd done everything I could at Époque. I couldn't get any higher unless Jacques gave up the helm and there'd been no chance that would ever happen.

Hi Oliver,

Thank you so much. You've been a great help. I do wonder though if I'm cut out for this kind of life. There're times when I think I've made a huge mistake, and run away from my responsibilities when I probably should have been more adult and faced my troubles head on. Haven't I just made it worse, by leaving? How long can one really live like this? Especially a city dweller like myself…

Anyway, I sound ungrateful and I'm truly not. It's probably that there's more time here to ruminate all those sweeping highs and lows…

Rosie

Flipping the bed covers off, I go to Aria's van for a chat. Maybe she can help me untangle these feelings if I open up to her. Then I see her light is off so I retreat the way I came, deciding that sleeping off the pall of sadness is probably the best idea tonight.

CHAPTER TEN

Rosie,

Are you OK? I hope you don't think I'm intruding, it's just I remember so well my first few months on the road and how adrift I felt, how almost every hour I wondered if I'd made the wrong decision to pack up my previous life and leave on what amounted to a whim. Tell me to mind my own business! But if you need a shoulder to lean on, I'm here, virtually at any rate. We've all had that same flash of regret, but trust me, soon you'll move past that and see this is going to be the making of you.

Best,

Oliver

He's right, of course. From the sounds of it, it's an adjustment everyone who suddenly ups and moves goes through. But his words feel more personal, like he knows I'm in need of boosting. I'm not used to having a guy sense moods and feelings so easily, and to do it across email, is even more surprising.

Ollie – I've begun to think of him as an Ollie – is the veritable boy-next-door, the sincere sort, asking me if I'm OK. It's enough to make my eyes glassy. Do I just pour my heart out and hope he's dependable? It goes against all my protective instincts but I'm tired of reining every thought and emotion in so tightly. My ex-husband called me a cold fish because of it, when I'm anything but.

Hi Oliver,

Thank you. I've had a wobbly time of it. One minute I relish the freedom, the next it feels like a jail sentence I'm forcing myself to wait out. All because I've run off from London, sprinting away from a broken heart, and the last vestige of a marriage. Silly, eh?

I hesitate. Is there any point sharing? I mean, really, who hasn't had a broken heart? Lots of people have divorced. Millions. It's not like I'm dead or dying, is it? But still, *share*, I urge myself, *believe he cares.*

So he's a stranger through a screen and I'm confiding in him about my private life. It's not as though it's a secret – half of London knows the sorry story. What's one more person, who will at least hear my side of it?

I worry that I've made a mistake in leaving my job, a career I've built over such a long time, all because of him. Who does that? I'm usually very orderly, organised to a fault, methodical, and here I can't be that person, because every day is different and you never know what will crop up. So far I've lost cakes to cows (don't ask!), had my spare tyre stolen from the back of Poppy, had a customer complain that my cannoli taste like tears (they bloody well did after that!) and that was just Thursday's offerings… sometimes I wish I could click my fingers and go home, back to my husband (pre-cheating), my life, my flat, pre-divorce. Life doesn't work like that though, sadly!

Of course, it's not all bad, I've made a great friend in Aria. And cooking big generous portions of comfort food satisfies me in a way I haven't felt in ages. I love waking with birdsong

and being outside to watch the sun sink behind the mountains,
colouring the sky an Eros pink.
Is this inner turmoil all because I've avoided change in the
past? Well, if so, I'm going to hang on tight, see where this
crazy adventure takes me, and just hope that it's somewhere
beautiful...
Rosie

Before sense kicks in, I hit send with one hand and pour a big glass of red with the other.

Dear Rosie,
You've got what I call the first few months jitters. On paper
this lifestyle sounds utterly divine, but it does take some getting
used to. Trust me, it won't be long before you wake up one
day, stunning view on display from where you lay, and realise
you never want to go back to your old life. It just hits you as
quick and surely as that. All those obstacles along the way will
be forgotten as you grow more confident in the path ahead.
That's the beauty of this, you can be whoever you want to
be. If you don't like the vibe, you can pack up, leave and start
over. Skip to other countries, meet more people. Discover a
wonderland as you inch your way forward. From the sounds
of it, you did the right thing escaping from London, leaving
a man who clearly didn't deserve you, and starting afresh.
We have that in common. I left too because of a break-up.
We'd been married almost seven years when it ended quite
suddenly. I won't bore you with the details, but she was
unfaithful and I just cannot forgive that.

I catch my breath. We have so many things in common. No wonder he's so empathetic about what happened with Callum, he knows exactly how I feel! A shiver of compassion races the length of me.

When I left, angry, confused, lost, I knew it was a knee-jerk reaction, but truthfully, it turned out to be the best damned thing I could have done. What I'm saying is, while you might feel the same now, if you're anything like me (and I think you are) it won't last long. Soon you'll catch yourself laughing more, thinking of the past less, and wondering why you didn't pack up and leave years ago.

Where are you off to next? Maybe we will cross paths?

Ollie x

Cross paths? I shut the laptop and go to find Aria tell her all about Oliver's email. Meeting up, already? Why not?

I grab a hat from the hook by the door. The days are warmer, and spring flowers scent the air.

I knock and enter to find Aria sitting dozily on the leather chair, clasping a gold picture frame to her chest. Her eyes are slightly swollen as if she's been crying. Usually Aria hides her emotions well behind humour but she can't hide the utterly bereft look on her face.

'Do you want to talk about it? I ask gently.

'Thanks, Rosie, but I'm good,' she says. 'Can you hit the light on your way out?'

The air feels heavy, sombre. I want her to confide in me, but she seems too vulnerable right now. It's clear I've intruded on a private moment, so I nod and smile and take my leave. Shutting up shop in the middle of the day is a sure-fire sign things are not OK, but I don't want to overstep the mark.

As I return to Poppy, my steps grow leaden for my friend. We've both chosen this adventure, but is it really making us happy? Under the filmy sunlight, it seems more like we're hiding from reality than anything else…

***

The next day there's a knock on the door; I glance at the clock and find it's barely 6 a.m. I've been awake since five, unable to sleep. Groaning, I wrench the covers from my bed and open the door to find Max there. His skin shines with a luminosity I haven't noticed in a man before, dammit.

'Want to borrow a cup of sugar?' I joke, as a yawn gets the better of me.

'Nope, I need an abseiling partner,' he says, and I wait for him to laugh it off. I wait and wait and yet he stares studiously at me.

Holy mother of tofu. 'I think you've knocked on the wrong door, Max. Do I look like someone who scales mountains to you?'

'Have you ever seen the Brecon Beacons?'

'The what?'

'Get dressed. I'll wait outside.'

'Max I'm not bloody going…' But he's gone, leaving me no choice to but get dressed. What exactly does one wear to the Brecon Beacons? I'm fairly sure it's the big national park that's famous for its many hiking trails and extreme rugged beauty, but I'm more of an indoors person and I do *not* own hiking attire, for very good reason. Still, I dress as comfortably as I can, and wrack my brain for plausible excuses. Leg cramps? Allergies? Acrophobia? Suddenly I picture myself at the peak of a mountain and the room spins. Best not to wish yet another quirk on myself. Sighing, I grab a light scarf and head outside into the dewy morning.

'Let's go,' he says, grabbing my hand and pulling me along.

'Max,' I say stiffly. 'I'm not your average nomad who relishes hiking, or extreme sports, plunging up, down or around cliff faces, so I'm not sure why'd you'd choose me.'

'Your light was on.'

'That's why?' I deflate a little.

'Yep.'

'Will I hold the rope at the foot of the mountain or something as you climb?' I'll probably drop him, he'll be dead at my feet.

With a scoff, he throws me an incredulous look as if I'm joking. 'I'll harness you up myself. You'll be fine.'

I harrumph as true fear takes hold squishing the breath from my lungs. 'I'm built for baking not abseiling! I could fall, plummet to my death! What if the buckle comes undone, what if—'

'Relax your shoulders and stop worrying.' He grins, he *actually* grins. 'Get in.'

Is this considered kidnapping? With heavy legs, I get into his van and after a long drive holding myself as still as a statue we arrive at the Brecon Beacons.

The sun slowly rises, casting the mountains a canola yellow so vivid my breath catches. The light that bathes the world is different here, almost tangible, as if the *air* itself is colour. You'd never capture it on film, it's one of those marvels you have to see for yourself. I'm completely mesmerised. Without Max, I wouldn't have come here, I wouldn't be bathing in this incandescent light that feels almost like it has healing powers.

'Wow.'

'Right?' he says, grinning. In the pureness of the morning, the sweet smell of spring hangs between us. I feel this sudden sense of rapture staring at Max with his suntanned skin and bright smile.

When it's just us, away from the noise, the crowds, he's different somehow. Maybe it's the look of peace that settles across his features, as if he's more at home here than when he's surrounded by people. While he makes me feel safe, I'm still concerned about scaling anything higher than the bank of a muddy puddle.

'Max, I'm too scared to climb.'

'I'll be with you.'

'But what if I fall?'

'Rosie, I'd never let you fall. And in the unlikely event that you did, I would *always* catch you.' My heart tugs, as I read too much into his words, as if they aren't about abseiling but a metaphor for our lives. Maybe it's the air, the altitude sending me batty, but for one lonely minute I want to believe.

That same old fear thumps inside of me but as I look at the limestone belt and up to the peak, I realise I can't turn back now. The only way I'll find out how magnificent it is up there is by trusting Max. Normally I'd quiz him, check the equipment, research the correct climbing technique, but I don't want to be negative Nelly, anxious Annie all the damn time. Maybe this is what living in the moment is all about?

'OK.' I blow out my cheeks and try to release all the fear in one breath. 'I trust you.'

'Wait here.' Max jogs back to his truck and takes out a pack full of gear. As I glance around I notice it's not the tallest peak, so there's that at least. In fact, it's quite small compared to the surrounding peaks.

He takes my hand, and with it I feel his energy, the warmth radiating from him, as he spins me and helps me into some sort of leg harness. His fingertips brush the inside of my thighs and I will the wooziness away as an inexplicable flash of longing rushes through me.

Look at me go in this crazy thing called life!

'Slip these on,' he says, handing me a brand new pair of shoes.

'I'm no fashionista,' I say, slipping on the bendy, mouldable footwear, 'but these are the ugliest shoes I've ever seen.'

He throws his head back and laughs, his shiny white teeth catching the sunlight. 'But they'll do the job, you'll see.'

It occurs to me he's bought them especially for me, as I rip the price tag off. Why would he do that? So he didn't pick me only because my light was on? I double check everything is buckled up and tight while I wait for him to prepare his kit.

'The pink helmet is for you.'

'Aww, you shouldn't have,' I joke and clip it on.

'Ready?' he says, giving my gloved hand a squeeze.

'I was born ready,' I say, letting the lie float away in the breeze.

My legs tremble but I figure I can fake it until they're trembling for real from exertion. Holy moly, what am I doing! My heart bongoes so hard I'm sure it's going to give out.

Max gives me a lesson on abseiling and before I know it I'm doing the unthinkable, scaling the mountain. My breathing is ragged, my legs feel like jelly, and my pulse is thundering, but I have never felt so free. It's part adrenaline, part terror, but its liberating! Some of the rocks are mossy so I avoid those, and try and get a toehold before inching my way up.

The fresh air hits me like a balm. Is this why people are adrenaline junkies, because of all the beauty found in these remote parts of the globe?

'Woo-hoo!'

Max turns to me and grins. 'I knew you'd like it.'

Amazement crashes into every fibre of me. Jeez, have I been missing out on living because I've let my fear drive every single choice I've ever made?

The early morning fog makes my skin dewy as we ascend and I'm grateful we have gloves so our hands aren't slippery.

When Max hits the peak he turns to help me and a huge grin splits my face. On top of the mountain, we look out to the valley cast below and it's like something from a storybook. Foggy wispy cloud cover opens up to luscious green valleys as far as the eye can see. Max points out the six main peaks of the Brecon Beacons and I finally understand why people love hiking or abseiling for the view they're rewarded with. My emotions jump all over the place, and they're all from trying something new and being here with Max, who's taken a chance with me. I take some clear, thin-aired breaths.

'Wow.' It's all I can think to say again. Words don't do the view justice. It's a full five minutes before I can wrench my eyes away.

'Milady.' He adopts an old-fashioned twang, and rests his head over my shoulder. 'Can I interest you in a spot of breakfast?'

I take a moment to enjoy his proximity, before I turn to see he's set up a checked picnic blanket and a range of small containers line the edge.

'I'd be delighted,' I say, staying in character, as I take his proffered hand and we sit next to each other on the rug. If I have to eat cashew cheese or some other vegan substitute, then I'll gladly do it now that Max has opened my eyes up to being more adventurous.

He gives me that same sweet grin. 'I took the liberty of making you a smorgasbord because we all know—' he lowers his voice as if imparting a secret '—how fussy the carnivores amongst us are.'

At the sight of his high-browed, mock-outraged face, I let out a howl of laughter. I'd never thought of myself as a carnivore before. 'The carnivorous amongst us thank you for your efforts. So what's what here?'

'These—' he points to what looks like some kind of nutty muesli bar '—are smoky quinoa and cacao bars. Full of all the good fats for energy and high in protein to keep you fuller for longer.'

'See,' I say, holding a finger up. 'That's where we differ. I don't want to feel fuller for longer, because then I have to wait ages to eat again. I like eating.'

'I do too, so I see your point.'

'And this?' I ask. 'Pancakes, obviously, but made without eggs or milk?' How, then? They look suspiciously like the real thing.

Shaking his mane of hair he says, 'Don't baulk, they're made with soymilk and nut butter. But let me plate them up first. Prepare to be amazed.' He opens another container full of fresh luscious red strawberries and tops the pancakes with them, and then adds lashings of maple syrup.

'Now we're talking!'

'And if you don't like either of those I also have chickpea wraps, stuffed with cashew cheese, English spinach and guacamole. One of the Lean, Green and Clean Café's biggest sellers, I'll have you know…'

Brow knitted, I fork a bite of pancake into my mouth, and I'm surprised at the fluffy texture considering I'm a food snob and have rigid ideas about the natural order of things. 'Wow.'

'You say that a lot.'

I feel my face crinkle into a smile, and realise he's right. 'They're OK,' I say and try to hold back my grin. 'Considering.'

It's his turn to stare me down. 'Try the cacao bars.'

'OK.' They're a taste explosion, the nuts adding a textural element, while the cacao is so rich, and chocolatey I want to take another bite, and another. I come to the chickpea wraps, and know I have to try the cashew cheese or I'll never hear the end of it.

I take an un-ladylike bite to prove that I'm game and wait for the inevitable reflex of disgust as I try a 'cheese' that goes against every principle about dairy I hold dear.

Damn it.

'Go on, say it.'

I chew slowly, ignoring him.

He puts a finger in my rib, which I *can't* ignore, my tickle reflex is so weak. I laugh and once I manage to compose myself, he leans up close and whispers, 'Say it.'

I clench my jaw, but it spills out regardless. 'Wow. There are you happy? Wow, wow, WOW!'

He falls back on the rug and lifts his hands to sky triumphantly. 'My job here is done.'

Truthfully, I'm amazed he's managed to fill the dishes with such flavour using substitute ingredients. I've been conditioned to think that butter, milk, sugar, and flour are the bones of real cooking.

I fall beside him and we turn to face each other. I can't remember a time when I felt so free, and happy. He moves closer and we lay there for an eternity. The air sparks with chemistry and I don't trust myself to speak. It feels delicious and unnerving all at once.

Usually I'd jump up and hightail it out of there to avoid awkwardness at all costs but there's nowhere to go but down, and in this moment of spontaneity I enjoy the thrill of staring into his opaline eyes, and delight in the way my heart pumps a little faster.

Because today is all about living in the moment, I inch closer, reading desire on his face. I'm going to kiss him and to hell with overthinking everything! Just as I close my eyes, I hear the most unearthly sound, and turn suddenly to see the cutest little pony hawing at us curiously as if he can't quite understand what we're doing here.

Max groans. 'Bloody Welsh mountain ponies!'

'But look at his little face!'

The spell is broken – I know that without even glancing at Max – but I laugh anyway, as the pony brays for attention, and nuzzles the open containers of food. 'Maybe he's vegan too?'

Max lets out a hoot and gives the mountain pony a pat.

CHAPTER ELEVEN

The Hay festival all too quickly comes to an end and I find myself fluctuating between happiness that I managed to survive the manic ten days, and sadness that it's over. As I dress, I note that my reflection in the mirror is mostly the same – an ordinary girl with straight blonde hair, unassuming face with a faltering smile – but I feel different, as though I've peeled a layer of protective coating off, and with it unearthed a slightly altered version of myself. A better version.

I feel a strange sort of contentment knowing if things veer off course, I can handle it. If I mess up, which I do regularly – with people, with orders, with putting my foot in my mouth – I laugh it off. I'm still the new kid on the block and because of that I'm forgiven for my foibles. These nomads are big-hearted people who almost revere eccentrics like me, a refreshing change that allows me to open up and find out who I really am.

I'm still bubbling over the almost-kiss with Max, but push it from my mind because while I've been floating on a bit of a bubble, Aria has retreated. I've hardly seen her since the day she was hugging the photo frame to her chest. The little bookshop has been open but Aria nowhere to be found. I don't know how to broach the subject with her, sensing that for all her exuberance, all her effervescence, there's this melancholy in her that she holds close and doesn't want to talk about.

I'm supposed to be packing, ready to leave by nine as I promised Aria, but instead I wander outside, relishing the early morning spring sunshine and cast about hoping to catch Nola and ask her advice on how to approach Aria about her sudden absence.

Nola is in the field opposite collecting wild flowers, so I jog over to talk to the elderly woman who resembles a delicate forest nymph rather than someone approaching 80.

'Hey, Nola!' I say breathless from the run. After scaling a mountain I'd have expected my fitness to be a darn sight better, but I grimly guess that it doesn't happen instantly (dammit!) – quite like dieting, which is why I've never bothered with that either.

'Rosie.' She gives me a wide smile. 'Don't you look pretty with some colour in your cheeks!'

I'm probably beetroot red from stumbling the length of the field. Maybe I should start trekking with the nomads? Or join the swim group who throw themselves into the closest water source at sun up? Then again, maybe not. My body is built for comfort not calisthenics.

'Er, thanks,' I say, every thought flying out of my head. Her mannerisms remind me so much of Max that I get tongue tied.

'What's up?'

'Well…' I tuck a tendril of escaped hair back. 'It's Aria.'

Nola nods and I sense she knows the secret that snatches the smile from Aria's lips and dulls the shine in her eyes. 'Like always, there's whispers,' she says. 'By the sounds of it, Aria's had a hard time of it.'

Being travelling royalty, of course she knows the ins and outs of everyone in the camp. While people wander near and far, it really is a tight-knit community, those friendships tightened by social media where friends are only a click away.

'I'd figured that but she hasn't confided in me. We haven't

known each other very long, and I'm a private person myself. Should I push her to open up to me? Or would that make it worse?'

Nola inhales like she's some kind of yogi and contemplates. After an age, she replies, 'She's lucky to have a friend like you.'

'Oh.' I wave her away. 'She's got a million friends.'

Nola drops and plucks a flower from a grassy patch. 'Aria may have a way with people, they flock to her because of her gregarious personality, but what you see isn't always what you get. Aria is a great actress. I'd say you came into each other's lives for a reason, at just the right time. She could use a *real* friend, someone she can share her sadness and joy with. *You*, Rosie.'

I mull over her words, wondering how she knows for sure. I've had friendships disintegrate far too quickly because of the way I am, because of my OCD tendencies, my need for extreme clean. I worry I'll lose Aria if I'm not who she needs me to be. 'Thanks, Nola. I'll give it some thought. We're off now,' I give her a loose hug, she smells like patchouli. 'See you soon. You... erm, haven't seen Max have you?'

'Yes, darling, he left about thirty minutes ago...'

He didn't stop to say goodbye? Did I ruin our friendship by leaning in to kiss him? I dash back to Poppy, mind spinning. I didn't *actually* kiss him but I guess my intentions were clear and his reaction is to pack up and leave without even a wave?

I'm running late and still have to wash Poppy and tidy up. Our electrical cords have a thick coating of mud that needs to be cleaned. There's a fine layer of dust inside the van and I have to scrub the outside before I can go any further. There's work to be done so I fill a bucket with soapy water and get moving. In times of stress, clean – isn't that the only tonic?

A few minutes later, Aria appears. 'Can't that wait?' she asks impatiently, checking her watch. We're some of the last to leave, the field almost deserted and eerily quiet without the merry band of nomads and book lovers. In a strange way I miss the chaos, the noise. She's keen to get on the road and I can't understand why the sudden about face, when it's usually her holding us up.

'No,' I say. 'It can't, sorry. I can't let this dirt build up.'

'But we're about to drive out of here and Poppy's just going to get dirty again, probably more so if she's wet! Mud is going to flick up and drizzle down, there's seriously no point, Rosie. I don't know why you'd bother.'

I hold in a sigh. 'Well, I'll dry her too.' If I let things slide then who knows what might happen? Everything must be clean, stowed away, and orderly. 'I'll be quick.'

She rolls her eyes, and walks back to her van, shaking her head as she goes. Hurriedly, I scrub down Poppy, as the soapy water becomes dirtier with every dip of the sponge, I feel lighter, despite upsetting Aria who doesn't seem to understand.

It bothers me because I make allowances for her. Clearly she doesn't get how much it concerns me sitting amongst such chaos in her van and resisting the urge to clean. To right fallen disorderly books. To extinguish candles burning so close to paper without any worry from her. If you're not wired like me, you'd probably think *I'm* the one with the hang-ups, but I see it from the other side.

An hour later I knock on Aria's door. 'Ready to roll?'

'Finally.' I should explain so she understands, but I've protected that part of me for so long that admitting it feels like something to be ashamed of. Everyone has baggage, right? By the glower on her face now is not the time for deep and meaningfuls.

CHAPTER TWELVE

We drive soberly out of the field. I hear mud flick up the sides of Poppy and cringe. I'll have to wash her again as soon as we arrive at the next place. Nothing can be done, so I follow Aria as she bumbles along ahead.

At lunchtime she flicks on an indicator and pulls into a clearing. I park Poppy beside the little bookshop van and stand and stretch. Will I ever drive loose-limbed and carefree like Aria does? I feel like the tin man, body creaking and groaning as I get used to being an upright position again. As the blood flows, I make us a quick lunch: sandwiches with freshly baked sourdough, layers of fresh ham, a few slices of Swiss cheese and a mustard pickle relish Aria helped make the day before. Her cooking skills have improved under my tutelage, but she still gets distracted unless I'm there to prompt her.

She bursts into Poppy, carrying a thermos of tea and two mugs, and under her arm is a picnic blanket. 'Sorry, Rosie. I haven't been myself, but I shouldn't take it out on you. Will you forgive me?'

I'm grateful for the apology and it clears the tension. 'Sure, Aria. I'm here whenever you want to talk, you know.'

She gives me a watery smile. 'I know.'

We pack sandwiches into containers and I grab my jacket and leave. Apparently we have to soak up the scenery as we go, she says, and I plan to blindly follow along.

'Cake!' I say and dash back to grab a couple of slices of a dark chocolate mousse and hazelnut meringue layer cake that is so decadent we might be able to walk to our picnic spot but we'll have to roll back.

'So,' Aria says as I catch up to her. 'Your first proper festival went alright, yeah?'

I'm taking two steps to her one to keep up. 'Yes, I sold more than I predicted, so now it'll be working out that fine balance of what I make versus what I sell to minimise food wastage and make a tidy profit. And the tea blends – I can't keep up with demand!'

'I left an envelope of cash in your van to pay for what I've eaten.'

She grins and rubs her non-existent belly. 'Worth every damn penny!'

'You don't have to pay, Aria! You're my chief taste-tester. And you wrote about four million labels for the tea blends, I should be paying *you*.' In all honesty I couldn't have survived the festival without Aria's help, not just her opinion on each dish, but the multitude of things she did from helping serve when the queues snaked too far, to bagging and writing up teas and talking me down from the ledge when I had a mini freak out every now and then. Alone, I would have scarpered back to London without looking back once.

Again, I give a silent thanks to Ollie who recommend Bristol, and hooking up with a travel buddy. Sage advice that even an introvert like me understood.

Aria waves me away. 'Don't be silly, of course I have to pay. Anyway, I didn't mean all that business side of things, I meant it was a success in that you did well, you met some amazing people, enjoyed the experience on a whole. I can't pinpoint how but you seem changed.'

'Oh, right. I do feel different. Maybe not as on edge as when I started. Knowing I'm not the only one to have taken the plunge into this life with no real plan kind of helps. Being meticulous to a fault has its disadvantages in this world, and I'm learning to let go a bit.'

She gives my arm a squeeze. 'You're doing great, Rosie.'

We come to an embankment where the river rushes past, a gurgling russet-coloured mass. It's quite the loveliest little patch of paradise with lush green foliage acting as a canopy overhead, protection from the wind and light spring rain.

'What is this place?' We wind down a narrow path, coming to a stop under an alder tree. Aria sets up the picnic rug and takes the plastic containers from my hands.

'Magic tree forest. Isn't that the most incredible name?'

'Is it really called that?' The place *is* mystical, fantastical, as if we've stepped into a painting of a magical forest, lush and vibrant with various shades of green, the babbling brook the perfect accompaniment to the atmosphere.

'Yes,' she laughs, surveying my face which must reflect my wonder. This is what Aria always talks about, finding little patches of enchantment as we go.

'And this—' she moves to the magnificent tree nearby, kicking off her boots so her bare feet squelch in the soft, damp under-growth '—is *the* magic tree.' And she promptly gives it a hug. 'Come on,' she says. 'Give it a cuddle and let its magical powers restore you.'

'That might be going a step too far,' I say. 'It's an impressive specimen of a tree, I'll give you that but I don't think it has magical restorative powers somehow.'

Aria doesn't respond, she just inches her arms further around its massive trunk and lays a kiss on the bark. 'Ah, but you're wrong,' she says, her eyes twinkling. 'You can't see it, but right now this tree and this wondrous forest is healing me from my toes up. It's called earthing.'

Now I've heard it all. 'Rightio.' Aria has some kooky tendencies but I'm slowly getting used to her mumbo-jumbo. She's part bookworm, part sprite and it's impossible not to be swept away by her whimsy, even for someone as staid as me. But still, I pretend I'm going to ignore what she says.

'Rosie,' her voice rises. 'If you don't come over here right now and give this tree a hug I will wallop you with my umbrella.'

'You didn't bring an umbrella.'

She cocks her head.

'OK, OK,' I laugh.

Against my better judgement I take off my boots and cringe when my toes sink into the squishy mossy earth. Having a shower in Poppy is tricky at the best of times, if I have to bend and scrub mud from my toes that is a logistical nightmare on a whole other level!

Half-heartedly I throw my arms around the tree, thinking of my sandwich getting soggy, and how long this whole crazy process will take.

'At least *try*,' she says, her voice plaintive.

Laughing, I shake my head, and reach out a little further and hug the bloody tree. Honestly, what is this life? I'm glad we're alone in the forest.

'Now lean into it, pretend it's Max if you have to,' she giggles.

'It's about the size of Max,' I agree, thinking of the rough and rugged man mountain who helped me scale an actual mountain, stayed right beside me and made me feel safe, but I quickly cast the vision of him aside. He left without saying goodbye. Best not to dwell. Instead, I lean into the tree knowing if I follow Aria's orders this will be over quicker than if I protest. I rest my forehead against the bark, and wonder at how soft it is. Before long I'm so relaxed I'm almost floppy, and all thought is gone from my mind.

'See?' she says triumphantly. 'It's working! You feel different, don't you?'

Of course I can't admit to it. 'Nope.'

'Liar!' she says.

'Tree hugger!'

'Earthling!'

'What?' I release the trunk and double over laughing. She is the limit and I'm so glad I found a friend, as quirky as she is, to push me from my comfort zone.

'Now the magic tree *has* restored you, let's let your glorious food finish it off.'

We eat companionably at the edge of the river under the leafy canopy of the magic tree. I'm surprised when my phone beeps with a text message. It seems almost sacrilegious to use it in such a pristine natural environment, but it could be a supplier set to deliver at my next location, so I unearth it from the depths of my coat pocket and click on the message – and immediately wish I hadn't.

My sandwich falls to the ground and splits apart. I hastily pocket my phone and clean up my mess, stashing the sandwich back in the container to throw out later. I've lost my appetite anyway.

'What is it?' Aria asks. 'You've gone lily-white.'

I swallow back tears, mortified to drop my guard in front of Aria. I don't have messy outbursts. I don't cry in public. I don't like to show my hurt. But it threatens to bubble up and out. Why does this never end? It's a constant merry-go-round and I'm stuck on it. 'Oh, just some news from home. A… a work thing.'

She rubs my back, her eyes reflecting my grief. 'It doesn't look much like a work thing, Rosie.' Her voice is full of warmth, so gentle that it nearly undoes me all over again. 'Why don't you ever truly open up?' she says. 'Whatever you tell me won't go any further.'

I remember a girl in high school uttering the very same words, and I know how that turned out. My father was a laughing stock.

My shame became public knowledge. But I suppose this secret is different. It's not noteworthy; we've all been heartbroken once upon a time.

'Callum has announced in the *London Herald* that he and Khloe are expecting a baby.' I pull my knees to my chest, wanting to curl into a ball and disappear. 'Our divorce still isn't finalised and he's going to be a dad!'

'Oh, Rosie. I'm so sorry.'

'Just when I feel like I'm doing OK, something else crops up that reminds me of what I've lost.'

'How long ago did you split up?'

My throat burns as I will myself not to give into tears. 'He announced he was leaving me on my birthday, the 2nd February.'

'Oh god, on your *birthday*? Who does that?' She grimaces. 'So that's why you left London.'

I nod, not trusting myself to speak, as I picture Khloe holding a bouncy baby girl in her arms, with my husband beside her staring lovingly at them both. Mario must've been trying to spare my feelings saying Callum regretted leaving, because clearly they're marching on with their lives.

'Do you still love him?' Pity shines from her, and my bottom lip quivers in response.

'I love what we had, but I can't love a man who does that. That's why I don't understand why it has to hurt so badly, like I've been punched in the gut. And how unfair is it, when he's all doe-eyed over another woman. A woman who isn't me.'

Shuffling closer she wraps her arms around me and squeezes out what air is left in my lungs. 'It's not fair at all.'

I hang my head as the tears fall. Will these rivulets leave scars?

I take my phone from my pocket and read Sally's message once more:

My darling Rosie, I wanted you to hear it from me first, and there's no easy way to say this… in the London Herald *today Callum has announced Khloe is to have a baby. It says she's four months along. I'm so sorry, my dear girl. Sally xxx*

'This baby was conceived when I was still in London, still living with Callum.'

'He doesn't deserve you anyway, Rosie. But I believe in karma so I hope he eats undercooked chicken!' she bursts out vehemently. 'And I mean *really* undercooked!'

In spite of it all, I laugh. 'I hope so too.'

'Really though, Rosie, you're well shot of a man like that. While this feels absolutely heartbreaking right now, you can see you dodged a bullet?'

I nod. On paper I can rationalise it all but in my heart it's another story. 'Yep, I know. I just loved him so much, despite all our trials and tribulations. I loved him and never imagined he didn't love me just the same back. And to find out the whole thing was a lie? That he was seeing her and coming home to me? It makes me feel sick. And worse, it makes me feel like you can never really know anyone. It could all be an act, and how would you ever know?'

'Not everyone is like that,' she says. 'In fact the majority of men aren't. I bet he loved you just as much, Rosie, who wouldn't? But then he made a bad choice and he has to live with that now. But you don't! You can be free and clear of him. He's going to be saddled with a baby, with a woman who will probably find out, once a cheater always a cheater, and then there's you, skipping from one place to another, no ties, no ball and chain, just, I don't know… hot specimens like Max wandering around, waiting to be kissed.'

I smack her playfully on the arm. 'You just couldn't wait to drop him into conversation again, could you?'

'Don't shoot me.' She holds her hands up in surrender. 'I'm

sure it's been scientifically proven that the best way to mend a broken heart is by being in the arms of a delectable hottie like Max. I mean, *phwoar*.'

I fall back on the rug and laugh, at the situation, at our muddy bare feet, at the crazy idea we're beneath a magic tree, but soon the laughter dies in my chest as I picture Khloe and her burgeoning baby bump. Another woman is now sleeping in my bed with my husband while a new life grows inside of her. Khloe is living my life and here I am on the run.

What have I got to offer the world? Will anyone love me ever again – *did* he even love me?

'Sweetie,' Aria says, placing her hand in mine. 'I can actually hear the cogs ticking over in your brain, you're beating yourself up, I know you are. Listen, this is going to be the making of you. So you married a pig? It happens. It happens a bloody lot. But it's not like you're 80 years old, is it? The right person is out there, you just have to take the leap and find him. But first you need to figure out what makes *you* happy, and then have it in spades.'

I mull it over, knowing she's right. There's really no point dwelling on it so much, I can't change it. I can't rewind. 'Cake, cake makes me happy.'

'The eighth wonder of the world!'

'Do you wonder who you *ever* know completely?'

'Your best and most loyal travel buddy,' she says brightly, hand on chest. 'Your confidante, and fellow cake aficionado.'

But I don't know her really, do I? I seize my chance. 'Why do you wear a wedding ring?'

She gives me a sad half smile. 'I also had my heart broken,' she says. 'Life can be so cruel, sometimes, Rosie. But then I wake up to blue skies, and fluffy white clouds in some remote corner of the country and I think, we might have these trials, but we also have a lot of triumphs too. And we must put one foot in front of the other until the pain subsides, and the sun comes out on another day…'

'Where is he?'

'Gone.'

Is that why she wanted to quit this life when we first met? Had she lost the man of her dreams too? Maybe he's a nomad and she's worried about bumping into him again. I don't think I could handle hearing Aria's tale of woe, and believe in love ever again. If a man could love her and leave then I had no chance. Aria, with her coppery locks and ready smile, is an actual living breathing goddess. If a guy left her, then what hope did a mere mortal like me have?

Maybe they were opposites? I go to ask but she's already packing up the picnic things, her back towards me, as though the conversation is closed. For all her prodding with me, she's a bit of a closed book when it comes to talking about her own private life.

'What happened to him, Aria?'

CHAPTER THIRTEEN

Her lips remain pressed tight, but after my conversation with Nola, I realise it's up to me to show Aria I can be trusted with her secrets. 'You're the biggest cheerleader for love, yet you don't bother for yourself. Why is that?'

I can't always be the project, after all.

She sighs. 'I'm only trying to help you.'

'And I'm trying to help you too. What's the story with the guy in the gold frame?'

Her eyes widen ever so slightly. 'You went through my things?'

'No, of course not. But it's not hard to see it's special when I walk into the little bookshop and you're hugging it to your chest, and your eyes are swollen from crying.'

She deflates, and guilt rushes me. I've put my foot in again, asked the wrong way.

'Don't look so pained, Rosie. It's OK, you know, it's just still so raw.' She sniffs and takes a balled-up tissue from her pocket.

'What happened?'

After a beat she swallows hard and says, 'He's gone. It was the two-year anniversary that night you walked in.'

We sit back down on the rug.

'We need tea.' It's my go-to in times of need and this is no different. I take the flask and pour us a cup, handing one to Aria.

'It's not a happy story, Rosie.'

'But it's *your* story, Aria and that makes it special.'

She casts her gaze to the tea, curling her hands around the mug. 'About two-and-a-half years ago my husband TJ came home early one day and went straight to bed. Flu, I thought. I made him chicken soup, which I burned, and made sure he kept his fluids up, that kind of thing. A few days later he went back to teaching, but he still wasn't quite right.'

I nod, waiting for her to continue.

'He couldn't shake that fatigue. You know what guys are like though, have to lose a leg before they go to the doctor. I kept at him, but it was almost like he didn't want to face it, almost like he knew it was going to be bad news. He put it off for an entire *month*, until eventually I had the mother of all meltdowns and forced him to go to the doctor, who then sent him to a specialist and on it went.'

I sip my tea opposite Aria as various emotions flicker across her features, regret, remorse, sadness…

'The prognosis wasn't good. Cancer, stage four. It had spread already and they wanted to try chemo, but they didn't think it would do any good, it was too far gone.'

Tears well in her eyes, and mine follow suit. How could they say that? A man's life hanging in the balance? But I don't speak up, I don't interrupt her.

'He decided against treatment, knowing it would only make him worse, it would affect the quality of what life remained. He'd always wanted to see the Lake District, so we bought the van, and set off. Of course, it wasn't the little bookshop then, it was just a rusty old van, but it was our sanctuary, our haven. The place I cocooned him in my love and prayed for a miracle.

'He got his wish and explored the beauty of the Lake District.

Jeez Rosie, if you didn't believe in magic you would after seeing that place. A total nirvana, and a panacea for him for a little while. But not long enough. As the cancer marched on he became bedridden and we returned home, but he refused to leave the van. I parked it in our driveway and we stayed there for the duration so palliative care nurses could come and help.

'I did a lot of caring by myself, as best I could, always worrying I was administering the painkillers wrong, hurting him with my incompetence, but he never complained, he'd just rub my shaky hands, and tell me he loved me.'

I swallow a lump in my throat, knowing the story doesn't have a happy ending like Aria's romance novels do.

'Towards the end, those last few days he would talk to someone just over my shoulder, and say things like "I'm almost ready", or "Just one more day". I'd put it down to the morphine, the concoction of meds, but afterwards I knew, he was making a deal with whoever had come for him. And then… he lost the fight, which was more a devastating sort of surrender, than anything. His last words were…' Her voice breaks and tears run in rivulets down her cheeks. 'His last words were, "Only parted until we meet again".'

I move to hug her, feeling the quake in her tiny shoulders. 'He believed in reincarnation?'

'That we'd meet in the next life.' She gives me a wobbly smile. 'Crazy, right? But when you're faced with death, suddenly you become a believer. I hold on to that, it's all that gets me through some days.'

She swallows hard and dabs her eyes with tissue.

'It's such a beautiful notion, Aria, to have that knowledge that you'll be together again. One day, in another life, another location, maybe in another language.'

She nods, and bats at her eyes with a tissue. 'He's waiting for me. Just as I wait for him. There's no chance of me loving anyone besides him.'

I hold back the first words that threaten to spill out. Is it fair though for her to be alone the rest of her life? 'Are you sure he'd want that, Aria?'

She shrugs. 'No. He wanted me to fall in love again, get married, have babies, but there's just no way. There's no one who could possibly live up to him, not in a million years.'

Would time change that? Dull the memories and heal the heart, so she is ready to move on? But I understand her motivations. She's still in love with her husband, and always will be. And no man would live up to him for a while, maybe never completely. 'I'm sure he wouldn't want you to be lonely, Aria.'

She tuts. 'I have my romance novels and I have you, I have this epic journey, nomadic friends as far as the eye can see. That's enough.'

It's only been two years since she lost the love of her life, not long enough to do anything except cope as best she can.

'Did TJ want you to continue to travel?'

She refilled her tea, as ever the tonic to any deep and meaningful and a way for us Brits to cope with whatever life throws at us.

'Yes, our quick trip to the Lakes inspired us on every level. But after he left I didn't know what to do or where to go, and one day I ran into a group of festival nomads and we got to talking about where they'd been and where they were off to next. It dawned on me I could be just like them. I could go from place to place, never set any roots down, and I could be free. No one would speak in clichés about loss to me, no one had to know my past. So the little bookshop was born, and I think, out of the ways my life could have gone, this was the best course of action for me. A rolling stone, and all that…'

She pauses and I know her meandering hasn't been quite a carefree as that.

'But of course, you can't outrun grief, it's always there

117

hovering behind like a shadow. The day I met you, I had just asked for a sign, something fantastic, something big, so I'd know instantly I had to *stay* on the road, not go home with my tail between my legs. Before I'd even finished my plea you zoomed up, almost ran me down and then fell face first into the mud. I imagined TJ right at that moment, laughing saying, "Here's your sign, stay free woman!" And for some reason it made so much sense! Who else would send me you, but him? This strange beautiful creature appearing out of nowhere just when I needed her most.'

The fine hair on my arms stand on end. 'You think somehow he orchestrated my appearance in your life?'

A dead guy I didn't even know? But for some reason, I feel a curious sensation, almost like déjà vu, as though whatever I'm supposed to remember is just out of reach. Had I met TJ? Impossible. All this talk of death and reincarnation is sending me cuckoo, but for one lonely minute I want to believe I am the missing piece of the puzzle and essential in someone's life.

'Don't you?' she says incredulously.

'Well…' My life *had* inexplicably gone off tangent, but the idea seems preposterous. 'It's not out of the question, I suppose.' I stumble over the words, and yet somehow they ring true. As Alice would say, curiouser and curiouser.

'Rosie, don't you see? You weren't happy either, were you? You managed to fool yourself for years that you were living this fabulous life and yet you were empty – you told me in so many words. And there I was, about to give up, and our paths collide. It might have been fate, or written in the stars, *or* more realistically your appearance in my life is a gift from TJ, and one that I so desperately need.'

'You think I'm a gift?'

'The best kind.'

I flush with the compliment, stunned.

We lapse into silence for a while but I'm still curious about her reticence in speaking about her past, even just to me. 'Why do you keep it a secret, Aria?'

After a beat she says, 'Because then I can pretend he's stargazing on the roof again, and he'll be back as soon as I finish the next chapter…'

CHAPTER FOURTEEN

After a few leisurely days playing tourist on our travels, we arrive in Glastonbury and I'm amazed to see a field of teepees lined up in smart rows as far as the eye can see. It's like one big camp for adults! Thick crowds bring out a rash of eagerness. We have the potential to make a lot of money here, so I get moving. First I connect Poppy to the power and tape down the cords, before doing the same for Aria's van. Surreptitiously I search for Max, but he's nowhere to be seen and I try not to let it bother me. So the guy made me believe in romance again for one lonely minute, doesn't mean he felt the same.

The sun is shining and it's a glorious day, but lunchtime rain is forecast so I hunt out the big table umbrellas.

'Can you do the tables?' Aria hollers, her brow furrowed. 'I've got to run into town to the post office.'

'Sure,' I reply. 'Don't leave too much cash in your tin, will you?'

She rolls her eyes, used to me nagging at her about leaving bagged up pounds in her cash tin, burning unattended candles ready to turn her van into a cinder box, and the fact that she *loans* her books with no hope of them ever being returned.

She does have a storage problem. Our vans are so tiny and

Aria's is filled to bursting. I've tried to help her declutter but she wants no part in it – surely all those dust bunnies are a health hazard? But she just does that same frustrating laugh as if I'm crazy for worrying about such trivialities.

Aria props up her little bookshop sign, a rustic chalkboard that's seen better days but is appealing in that shabby chic way, and jogs over to give me a hug. As always she smells like musty books, vanilla, and kept promises. 'See you soon.'

As soon as she leaves, hitching a ride on the back of a stranger's motorbike I stealthily creep into her van and hide her money tin out of sight. I blow out all of the candles, right fallen cushions, fold the throw rugs, and quickly wash a smattering of tea cups left lying here and there. Not on my watch will the Little Bookshop of Happy Ever After be robbed or burn down! I have time to run a duster over the books, but figure then I'd need to sweep the floor and that might just be overstepping the mark.

Back outside, more caravans and campervans belch their way into the field. I ready our outdoor area, and try and light the fire in the iron grate, hoping that it'll draw people over if we do get a sprinkling of summer rain. This flucker has beaten me in the past, so I'd watched some YouTube videos about the correct way to lay a fire and I will not give up until it's a crackling success.

'Need a hand?' a husky deep voice sounds over my shoulder.

As I turn to it, the world darkens. He's literally that big that he blocks out the light. Max.

'No, thank you,' I say, joy pulsing through me, but I make a show of hiding it. He didn't say goodbye in Wales, did he? I must play it cool.

'Shove over, I can do it.'

I bristle. 'Do you assume because I'm female I can't light a fire?'

He gives me that trademark rueful grin and holds up his hands as if in surrender. 'Nothing to do with you being female, just an offer made out of common courtesy.' He stares at me for so long my skin tingles, so I avert my gaze. I bet he's lit a lot of fires, being so manly, so… outdoorsy. Like the type of guy who'd wrap you in his arms and carry you to safety.

To safety?

I've clearly been overindulging in the wine lately, or having too many late nights. To safety! Like this is some kind of romance novel, and he's the swashbuckling hero!

'Well, I'm fine lighting it on my own.'

'Fine. I've got berry swirl cheesecake on the menu today,' he says.

I smirk. 'A cheesecake made without cream cheese? I don't think so. Soaking cashews in water and then blitzing them up does not make a cheesecake, Max! We been over this before!'

He tilts his head. 'Oh, yeah?'

'It's offensive! It's a crime against cake. It's…'

Folding his arms, he butts in, 'Have you ever tried it?'

Not this again. I remain mute. I will not bite.

'Well?'

The blasted fire won't catch, and he's blocking out the light of the world, and I can't quite think.

'Well, what?' Can't he see I'm otherwise occupied? I don't have time to school him on how he's sucking the joy from life by not using sugar and butter and everything that is good in this world. Yeah, sure his smoked quinoa and cacao bars were good but imagine how much better they'd have been laced with sugar, butter and dark chocolate!

'I think it's only fair for you try it. Why don't you bake a berry cheesecake and I'll bake one and we can put it to a vote?'

I give him a half-smile as it piques my curiosity. 'A vote?'

'The customers can vote for their favourite and we'll see who sells more.'

My smile disappears. Half the population walk by Max's van just to catch a glimpse of him. I've seen them go back and forth, eyes wide, mouths slightly parted, dillydallying when they see his silhouette in the half-sunk sun. It's really quite distracting to see so many women cavorting around like that. Haven't they got work to do or a festival to enjoy? But I have a few secret weapons... sugar, butter, and cream cheese. There is absolutely no way to replicate the original and have it taste as good, is there?

'Fine,' I say at last. 'I'll make a berry cheesecake and you make an imitation version and let's see who wins?'

'What does the winner get?'

I grin. 'The winner gets to make dinner for the loser and that includes using *real* sugar!'

'Hello diabetes,' he mumbles.

I wrinkle my brow. 'Are you admitting you're going to lose?'

He lets out a scoff. 'Hardly. Say goodbye animal fats and hello coconut oil.'

'You ever think coconuts might have feelings too?'

His lips part. 'No, I don't think so. If they did they wouldn't fall from trees when they're ripe, would they?'

'Plants scream when they die, did you know that? It's true, I read an article about it, more reason to eat cake rather than salad.'

He squints, amused. 'Are you purposely wasting my time?'

'Need longer than me, do you?'

The fire returns to his gaze. 'Nope. Let's say cakes on the table by—' he checks his watch '—12 p.m.? That gives us four hours for them to set if we get cracking now.'

'And the challenge finishes at 1 p.m.?'

'Done,' he agrees, and we shake on it. My hand disappears into his bear-like paws, and I get the strangest zap from it. No time to rue, I forget about the bloody fire, give the grate a kick sideways for good measure and rush into Poppy to start preparing.

A few minutes later, a crackling sound catches my attention and I crane my neck out the window to see the grate standing upright, a roaring fire burning away.

That man!

CHAPTER FIFTEEN

A few hours later, Aria returns, and bustles into Poppy, unwinding her summery scarf. She pretends she's coming to check in on me, when really she's sniffing around for lunch. I'm just glad she's alive after hitching a ride with a stranger into the never-never.

'There's a Cornish pasty in the warmer for you, help yourself and there's a jar of tomato relish to go with it.'

'Ooh.' She rubs her hands together. 'I wasn't even thinking of lunch, but since you offered.'

I grin. 'Is that so?'

She turns her doe eyes up to me. 'Why, yes.'

'Liar.'

Laughter bursts from her, that same machine-gun cackle. 'Totally.'

As I pour my third cheesecake mixture into the tin I fill Aria in on the competition and how it came about. 'Really?' she says. 'You're going to win, hands down!'

I blow out a breath as a jolt of nerves dazzles me. 'Jeez, I hope so! You can't beat a classic cheesecake, and any imitation is just bluster. Especially one made with cashew "cheese". Can I put this cheesecake in your fridge? Mine is full up.'

'Sure,' she says. 'And let's hope you forget it's there and I have a mighty midnight snack…' Her laughter trails behind me as I go to her van and pop the cake in the fridge.

Dashing back to Poppy, I see a queue has formed already. Max must've got the word out somehow. I'm happy to note they haven't chosen a side yet, they amble in one group in the clearing between his van and mine.

Aria polishes off the Cornish pasty and helps herself to some vanilla bean ice cream.

'I'm nervous! There's a bunch of people outside already.'

She waves her spoon at me. 'Use your charm, Rosie. Dig deep and show the world the funny, sweet girl I know and love. Otherwise you won't win!'

When twelve o'clock gets close I do the unthinkable, and step from Poppy into the waiting crowd and spruik my wares, colour rising up my cheeks. I tell them about the competition and my history, namely that I'm a professionally trained Michelin-starred chef. When that produces confused looks, I change tact, and mention I'm new on the scene and trying to win a bet against a man whose principles I'm iffy on, to which they respond far better.

I glance at my watch. With only five minutes to go I race back to Poppy and pop on my apron. 'Are you ready, Max?' I holler over, only to see his smug face stare back with 'challenge accepted' written all over it.

He winks, which only galvanises me. 'Roll up, roll up for a slice of luscious, velvety smooth raspberry ripple cheesecake, the best you'll ever taste!'

Max raises a brow as if to say, 'Is that all you've got?' 'Attention festival-goers! Come and try a slice of my raspberry ripple cheese-cake *without* the artery-clogging ingredients! Guilt-free cake!'

'Everything in moderation!' I holler. 'Made with *organic* cream cheese from a local farm!'

'Ethically sourced ingredients!' Max bellows.

'Proceeds to be donated to the local children's charity!' I yell.

'All profits to PETA!'

Aria appears at the fold-down counter and munches away, her head going back and forth as though she's watching a tennis match. Finally, *finally* a customer approaches and I send Max my *take that* smile. The man reaches the window, and grins, revealing tobacco stained teeth. 'Max says your cheesecake is laced with so much sugar it's enough to produce a heart attack, and I thought to meself, what a brilliant way to die.'

Just as I wonder if the man is joking, or instead plotting death by sugar, he lets out a roar loud enough to scatter the birds.

I slice a generous portion of cheesecake, and hand it over, not before adding dollops of freshly whipped cream. 'Sugar is god's candy, and don't let him tell you otherwise,' I say with a smile. 'Don't forget to pop your vote in the box.'

Max has set up a little ticketing system on one of our tables. Blue slips for him, pink for me. As word spreads, I get more customers. Aria helps serve, winning everyone over with her sense of humour and bawdy laugh. Before long we've sold out and Max still has a line of customers snaking down the path.

'Time's up!' I announce, glancing at my watch. Have I done enough to win? It's hard to tell.

'Time to count the votes!' I motion to Aria who nods and goes out front. Max strides over and I ball up my apron and dash outside to watch the tally.

'You think you've won,' he says.

'Maybe.' I grin. I've never been on such public display before. I've never stood outside and tried to hustle customers, I've never screamed or shouted to woo patrons. This scenario is so removed from my old life in London it's enough to make my head spin in a flurry of anticipation.

'We have a winner, folks!' Aria stands and waves everyone over. I can't see her face; her back is toward me. 'Rosie has thirty-seven votes for her raspberry ripple cheesecake made with *real* cheese,' she ribs Max. 'And Max has thirty-six! So that means

127

Rosie is the new cheesecake champion! Let's all give Rosie our congratulations!'

There's thunderous applause, and I feel my cheeks flush. Max grins goodnaturedly and holds out his hand to shake. 'All's fair in love and war,' he says in that husky voice of his.

'Are we at war, Max?'

He lifts a shoulder. 'Well, we're not in love, are we?'

'Definitely not!' I sputter.

He smiles.

I shake his hand, and he pulls me in for a hug, quite knocking the breath from my lungs. He smells exactly like I thought he would, peppery, earthy, elemental. I shake myself back to the moment, to reality.

'So what's on the menu?'

'Never you mind,' I say, mind scuttling with ideas, and realising just how hard it's going to be to cook for him, if I can't use meat, flour, eggs, butter, or cream. How did I *think* this was a good idea?

'Let's do dinner Monday night, once we've wrapped up the festival and packed up?'

It makes sense, we don't want to shut down and lose the customers that keep on into the evening.

'Yeah, good plan.'

I kick at the ground, while he slings his hands in his pockets. The air feels charged somehow, maybe it's my victory, or Max's good sportsmanship. Either way, it's difficult to form words so I scramble about for an excuse to put some distance between us.

'Oh, golly, I've left my mixer... mixing. I'd better go.'

'Goodbye, Rosie.'

Sheesh, what power does that man have over people? My heart thumps double time and it's all I can do to remain upright.

Aria holds the fort while I try to shake the sudden fog from my head. Thank goodness one of us has a modicum of sense!

128

The queue has grown as people have wandered over to see what all the kerfuffle is about. Aria is red-faced serving them.

I smile and help serve, whipping up knickerbocker glories as fast as I can make them, dolloping jam and cream on scones, and scooping generous serves of vanilla bean ice cream into waffle cones.

Once we've caught up, we take a breather, and put up a *back in five* sign. I need a pot of *Sense and Sensibility* tea to calm my nerves and settle my pulse.

'You totally dominated the crowd for the competition!' she says. 'You're going to have so much fun on your date!' She pulls down a teapot and boils the kettle.

'It's not a date.'

'Of course it is!'

'No, it's not!'

'Well, why did you choose such a prize?'

Why did I? Oh! 'I guess because, well, he acts so superior drinking kale juice and what not...'

'I think subconsciously you wanted a date.'

'Oh, Aria are you that desperate to marry me off?'

She laughs. 'No, but I'm calling it as I see it.'

I roll my eyes dramatically, taking lessons from Aria herself.

'You, my friend, need to entertain the idea of romance, just to prove to yourself that Callum is in the past, and life goes on.'

I sigh. 'I know, I know. That was my original plan. Callum predicted I'd be alone my whole life because I am a stickler for details. But look, here I am, completely *un*scheduled.' I dart a guilty glance at my pin-up poster board with my travel routes marked out, petrol stations highlighted with yellow pins, hospitals with red pins, expected travel times, and distances, tyre air pressures. Then there's the daily list of chores and at what point in the day they need to be done. 'Anyway,' I hastily continue, 'being so busy as we are, there's no time to even consider love, and I've sort of got cold feet about the whole idea. I mean being single isn't the worst thing that can happen to a person, is it?'

She cocks her head and I wish I could snatch back the words, since Aria is self-exiled to the land of singledom. But then surely she understands? And really, how can one sustain love when you live the way we do? People flit in and out of our daily lives, there's always new faces, and so many goodbyes.

Clucking her tongue, she says, 'You're nervous about the date with Max and that leads me to believe that as much as you try to hide it, there's a sizzle of attraction there.'

I scoff. 'The only sizzle will be the nice big juicy steak I cook for myself while I make him a bowl of...' What? 'Quinoa.'

With a world-weary sigh she says, 'You two are like Bridget and Mark, or...'

'Who?'

'Bridget Jones and Mark Darcy, darling. OK so you're not quite the disorderly hot mess that is Bridget, but you're the same in that you and Max are totally opposites, and yet perfect for one another, just like Bridget and Mark.'

'Book couples, Aria, are fictional!'

'Well, clearly, but the ideas have to come from somewhere!'

'Not everything relates to romantic comedies you know.'

She holds up a finger. '*Ah*, yes it does. You'll see. When Cupid strikes there's little you can do about it. Take Scarlett and Rhett, two complete opposites, but they were the making of each other.'

'*Gone with the Wind*, now? Really?'

'You don't need to marry the man, just get back on the bike, sort of thing.'

'Are you implying casual sex?' I pretend to be scandalised. OK, I am a little scandalised.

'Yes, and lots of it!'

'You romance reader, you.'

'Guilty as charged.'

Squirming, I finally tell her the story of the near-kiss interrupted by the world's cutest pony with the worst timing.

'You nearly kissed and you're just telling me this now?'

'Well, *I* nearly kissed him, not the other way around, and then he didn't really say anything after that. In fact, he disappeared and has only *re*appeared now as if nothing happened. And if I'm honest, I'm not sure he's the right sort for me. We are far too different.'

'I don't think there's such a thing as too different.'

'He's not my type.'

She waits me out.

'He's not.'

Her brows pull together and still she stays schtum.

'I'd say if he was,' I lie.

Eventually she relents. 'OK, so if not Max then who? Surely there's someone who has caught your eye?'

'Well, there is Ollie,' I say, scratching for someone safe. Someone who isn't here so she can't latch on to the idea. 'But he's just a name on an email. However if I *had* to choose, he seemed more the dependable, boy-next-door type who definitely wouldn't cheat.'

'The online forum guy?'

'Well, yes, but before you go planning my engagement, I'm not certain at all, it's just he has this sort of poetic, charming way about him. He's caring and compassionate. He seems lovely.'

'He sounds like The One.'

I wave her away, laughing. 'Didn't you warn me about the problems with insta-love?' Aria and her romance-novel advice for real life never fails to amuse me.

'Insta-love is OK, but I doubt the longevity, you know?'

I can only shake my head. 'I don't know the guy really, there's just this little inkling at times that I'd like to *get* to know him, that's all. He's shared a lot of personal things with me, been very open and honest about his life on the road, truthful, you know, not sugar coating it, and I just feel sort of a connection with him, but he might just be that polite with everyone.'

'I doubt it, Aria. Have you swapped pictures of yourselves at all?'

'We're on Facebook.' I'd broken my own cardinal rule and accepted him as a friend on social media. I kept my pages private for a number of reasons. Firstly, celebrity reporters had hounded me for the inside scoop on chef Jacques, and secondly, I didn't like my privacy invaded by people I hardly knew. But what was the worst that could happen by accepting Oliver? So he might see some pictures of me and Callum in Cornwall? A million pictures of plated up degustation dishes? I wasn't that exceptional that it mattered, surely? And I'd scoured Oliver's profile and aside from a few close-ups of his face, his page was filled with his captivating photography.

'Then he's keen.'

'Why?'

'You're stunning, Rosie, even though you have no idea that you are. I bet he's counting down the minutes until he runs into you.'

I guffaw. 'Oh please.' Next to Aria I'm so plain I'm invisible.

'It's true.' She shakes her head. 'Do you *want* to get to know him?'

'Well, yes, I suppose. He's gorgeous, in that really down-to-earth, stable sort of way. But the whole thing is ridiculous, isn't it? You can't develop feelings for a name on a screen! From a picture—' I make a tiny square with my fingers '—this big.'

Her scoff echoes. 'Darling, it's the way of the world these days! No one falls in love at first sight anymore, they fall in love at first Snapchat! Especially travellers – while we might be surrounded by people, we spend an inordinate amount of time alone, usually on the way to a new place, the people you met earlier off on a different route. This lifestyle is really all about connecting, and what better way to do that than via the internet?'

I shake my head. 'It seems a bit… desperate.'

'You're not marrying the man, you're simply opening yourself up to friendship with the possibility of more.'

'He did mention his journey started after a break-up too.'

'See,' she says, as if that's a sure-fire sign. 'Email him now and just be yourself, without filtering everything you think.'

'Mm,' I say, not convinced. I tidy the bench in Poppy, wiping down crumbs and filling the sink full of soapy water. 'I'll write him a quick email without second guessing every word, but that's it.' And maybe I won't send it. Or maybe I will. What if he thinks I'm a stalker? Or what if…

'Don't start with those end-of-the-world scenarios,' she warns, and knocks me out of the way before she plunges her hands into the sink and washes the cake tins, stacking them on the draining board. 'Just be free, say what you feel. It's so much easier by email! Off you go before you change your mind.'

I give her a quick hug, head down the back of Poppy, grab my laptop and fire it up.

Hi Ollie,

Too informal? I delete it and type *Oliver*, the delete and type *Ollie*, before it occurs to me I'm already second guessing myself!

Thanks for your email and sorry about the delay responding. It's been a tumultuous time in certain ways. A former work colleague sent me a text to tell me my ex-husband is expecting a baby with my replacement. Normally, I wouldn't bother telling anyone about my private life, especially something as hurtful and mortifying as this, but Aria has convinced me opening up is the way forward and how can I argue with the most popular girl on the circuit?

If I'm being pragmatic, I know in time this betrayal won't keep me from sleep, it won't plague my thoughts, but right now it does. But I suppose that's because I loved the guy, heart and soul. I'm sorry that your journey also started because of the same reasons. I guess it's one way to spur on a person, by breaking their heart...

Whoops. If Aria read the opening she'd make me delete it. No one wants to hear about previous relationships, not the nitty gritty details. She probably expects me to be fun and flirty with him... But if I'm going to open up my heart to possibility, it has to start with the truth. I'm sure Ollie will understand, and might empathise having gone through the same thing.

Where are you now? How is your photography work going? We're in Glastonbury and there's a really cool vibe here. It's absolutely jam-packed with people! Aria has been a godsend and helps out whenever she notices a queue forming. Without her I doubt I'd cope, so I thank my lucky stars I have a friend who expects nothing in return, except maybe a slice of treacle tart!

In my old life I hid behind the kitchen walls, hid behind my cooking, hid from the world, and here I can't do that. I am exposed and it's been a steep learning curve, but I feel like I'm halfway up the hill, if that makes any sense at all?

So Ollie, if we were to cross paths I'd love to meet for a coffee and a chat, and hope to count you as another friend on the road...
Rosie

I hesitate and then remind myself to stop overthinking things. Send. Off it goes to Ollie. Ten minutes later my inbox flashes with an email.

Rosie,

> *I'm in and out of range, so wanted to say hi while I've got the chance. Full reply soon, but crossing paths sounds magical to me.*
>
> *Ollie x*

Magical? Maybe that's what I'm after, a little magic in my life and Ollie is fast becoming another reason to smile.

***

I sense him this time before he knocks. It's only ever Max and I who wake before the birds these sunny bright mornings. He raps quietly and this time I'm already dressed.

'What's the plan today, Max? Jumping out of a plane, white-water rafting?'

'How did you know?'

'Oh no way, Max, I'm joking!'

He laughs. 'Me too. Let's go visit Glastonbury Abbey before the crowds descend.'

'Why?'

'Why not?'

'Don't you have friends?'

'We're neighbours, that's why.'

Sure, Max makes my heart beat double time but how could I ever relax around him? He's constantly surrounded by a bevy of beautiful women vying for his attention, and that would turn anyone's head. My confidence is at an all-time low after Callum and I won't risk my heart to a man like Max, who for all his sins, is just too popular amongst the ladies. I feel like such a plain Jane compared to all the ethereal goddesses who practically throw themselves at him. Too much angst, too much risk.

What am I even thinking? Max likes me as a friend, as a

neighbour, and because I'm the only one awake at this damn time of the morning.

Twenty minutes later we pull up at the abbey where a weathered-faced man in a grey cap is there to let us in. He seems to know Max well and tells him to take his time, asks about Nola and Spencer and some of the other nomads. Maybe this man was one of them before settling down as caretaker of Glastonbury Abbey?

Max thanks him and we make our way in the dewy morning. The ruins are heavy with low hanging fog like something out of a Grimms' fairy tale. We trudge through the mist to find half of the façade gone, which is confronting somehow; almost as though it's missing a portion of its face. Inside the ruin ivy creeps through stone. There's a hush; no birdsong, no bees, just this sense of desolation in the most romantic way as if previous inhabitants had abandoned the abbey and nature claimed it. The grass however is mowed with military precision. Strangely I'd prefer it growing wild and free and protecting the remains, hiding them partly from view. But either way, it's beautiful, especially in the diaphanous light.

'It's incredible,' I say.

'Have you heard of the legend of King Arthur?' Max asks, raising a brow.

'Yes, of course, but it's all folklore, right?'

Max scoffs. 'Folklore!' He looks offended as if he's a personal friend of King Arthur. 'He was a medieval legend, a force to be reckoned with and it's believed he's buried right here with his wife, Queen Guinevere.' Max points to a rectangle of grass, unremarkable, except for a small plaque engraved with historic details.

'Imagine being buried here,' I say, goose bumps prickling my skin. Do ghosts have the run of the old abbey, sitting ever watchful of visitors? Do they hover unseen in the fog? The thought sends a shiver through me. As I get older history becomes so much more alive and interesting, as my horizons broaden and times gone by take shape in my mind.

'Not a bad place to spend eternity, eh?'

'Pretty spectacular.' While the abbey is a shadow of its former self, it's breathtaking in its ruinous state. 'Let's keep going before we have to share this with the public!' I take out my phone and snap pictures, wondering if I'll catch Queen Guinevere just out of focus…

A few hours later we wave goodbye to the caretaker and hop back in Max's van.

'Hungry?'

'Famished.'

'Did you know Glastonbury is absolutely *full* of vegan cafes?'

I laugh. 'Of course it is.'

'Can't beat a new-age, funky, ancient market town who cater to the more holistic of us, now can you?'

'What are you suggesting, Max? Gluten-free bread with tofu?'

'A café that caters for the herbivore *and* the carnivore, I suppose.'

I make a show of munching on his arm, and then snatch my hand away as colour races us my cheeks. What on earth am I doing! Damn the man, even his skin tastes good!

'Sorry, I'm starving after that long walk.'

At the café I order a quinoa salad just the same as Max. Once again I'm surprised by how tasty it is considering it's so healthy, so free of butter, salt and meat! It's packed with nuts and vegetables that have been slow roasted in coconut oil, and I begin to see the merits of his way of life.

'Have you travelled abroad in your van, Max?'

'I have. I've been up and down France, and into Spain, over to Italy. I'd love to go to Croatia, and Germany, and so many other places, but there's still time, right? It's not as easy to make money there, though.'

'So you'd have to save here and just travel in the van there?'

'Ideally. And there's so much to see and do, why would you want to work?'

'True,' I laugh. 'I can't imagine having enough surplus to fund that amount of travel.'

'It'll happen, Rosie. Each day is a blessing whether you're under British skies or Italian sunsets.'

'I guess.' Will I ever be as relaxed as Max is? Patiently waiting for the universe to provide what I need to move on? It goes against the grain of the planner in me.

'What about you, Rosie. Do you want to venture elsewhere?' He stares so intently at me it untethers me for a moment.

'I'm not sure. I'd love to be that free-spirited wanderer, but I'm the type of person who needs to feel secure, to have even a rough plan in place, so I know if I get stuck I have a way out.'

'We're so different,' he says and I can't tell if he means it's a good thing or bad.

'I'm usually the anomaly in every group.' I try and laugh it off as a joke.

'Anomaly is just another word for extraordinary, and who wants to be ordinary, anyway? To me you're a shining light in a crowd of beige.'

I blink, taken aback. Is he just being polite or is it something more? I half choke trying to reply. 'Er, um, thank you, Max. That's quite the loveliest thing anyone has ever said to me.'

He shrugs as if it's nothing. 'It's true.'

No matter how he means the sentiment, it makes me feel warm and fuzzy and bolsters me. Max really is an enigma and I hope I get to know him better.

CHAPTER SIXTEEN

By the time Monday arrives, half of the Van Lifers are packed up and ready to leave. The other half use the time to sleep in. Awnings are down, windows covered and it's quiet. I make a pot of rose infused tea (promotes healthy, radiating skin) head out to Poppy's tiny deck and scroll mindlessly through social media willing the sun to shine more brightly.

I'm flicking through Facebook when I spot Callum and Khloe mentioned in a foodie page I follow. Of course, there's a picture of the happy couple smiling benignly at the camera.

She rests a hand on her teeny tiny baby bump and Callum has his palm over hers. I put the phone down, not wanting the picture burned into my retinas any more than it already is. But it's too late, I can still see their wide smiles, the love in their eyes.

I touch the slight swell of my own belly (AKA a cake baby) and wonder if I will ever be a mother. A stray tear rolls down my cheek and I'm glad no one is around to witness it.

How could they have made a child when our divorce is still pending? Was I just a stepping stone for him, until he moved on to brighter, better things? Khloe is eye-catchingly beautiful, and whisper thin.

But Jacques told me you should never trust a skinny chef. *Especially* a skinny chef de partie. If they're not at least a little curvaceous, it implies they don't want to eat what they cook, and what's that saying?

Khloe will probably be one of those mums who shares her post-baby body pics flaunting her flat tummy, nary a stretch mark in sight. As though the baby just showed up one day, out of thin air. My jealousy is talking, and I try not to think that way.

Across from me, Max's van door wobbles before he bursts out of it larger than life. I hastily swat at my face, hoping he won't notice.

'Hey, Rosie,' he says. 'Dinner still on for tonight?'

Oh god, the dinner from the bet. I'd completely forgotten. 'Erm, yes, sure is.'

Go back into your van.

He wanders closer, and peers at me. I drop my gaze, and fuss about with my phone.

'You OK?'

'Blooming marvellous.'

'What's wrong?'

'Sun in my eyes, just a little bleary, that's all.'

'There is no sun.'

'Are you some kind of detective?'

I expect he'll crack and smile and we'll make light of it, but he doesn't. He drops to his knees in front of me, placing his hands on either side of my legs.

'Has someone upset you?'

'Why?' I ask. 'Are you going to pummel them?'

'I'm a pacifist.' He smiles disarmingly. 'But if you want me to I will.'

I can't help but laugh. 'That's very kind of you. I'll keep it in mind.'

Aria jogs over from the clearing. Has she been exercising or something? Her face is ruddy from the morning chill. She's as adventurous as the rest of them, but isn't usually up as early as this. She's more night owl than early bird. 'Morning,' I say.

'Morning, sunshine. Have you heard from Ollie?' she says out of breath.

'Who's Ollie?' says Max.

'Oh, he's this *very* handsome guy from the Van Lifers forum. He's a little smitten with our Rosie.' I want the ground to swallow me whole. What is she doing?

Max's eyes flash.

'Be careful,' Max warns, his voice almost a growl.

'Of what?' Aria asks.

'Of people you meet on the internet.'

She makes a show of rolling her eyes and snorting as if that's the stupidest thing she's ever heard. 'Do you know what year it is? *Be careful of people on the internet!* Half of us wouldn't be here if not for the internet. What are you... jealous or something?'

He clenches his jaw and stands to face her. 'Jealous of what?'

'Jealous of Ollie.'

'I'm not jealous, I'm protective. What happened to meeting people face to face?'

'No one's done that since the Nineties,' Aria says, scoffing.

I watch them bicker and don't know what to say or who to stick up for. They're acting like they're my parents or something, which is just plain weird. Eventually their rebuttals die down and Max turns to face me. 'Apparently I'm living in the past,' he shrugs. 'But just be careful, OK?'

'OK,' I manage.

He storms away, taking a cloud of dust with him. It's all very theatrical, very Hollywood blockbuster-y.

Once I'm sure he's out of hearing range, I hiss, 'What the hell was that all about?'

Aria giggles and muffles the sound with her palm. 'Wasn't it *genius*? Nothing like a bit of competition to get the romance revved up.'

'Romance? Are you crazy? You are crazy, aren't you?'

She laughs. 'A little. But only in the nicest possible way.'

'You made it sound like Ollie and I were in some kind of relationship!' Her antics beggar belief.

'I know! It just came to me. Look,' she says more seriously. 'Max was all up in your face and trying to dazzle you with those broody eyes of his, so I just thought I'd up the ante. If he's interested, he'd better know that he's got some stiff competition, yeah? I got the idea from this book I'm reading where the best friend nudges the two completely befuddled characters together. Plus I did it to *save* you…'

Aria and her romance books! 'From his evil clutches?'

'I wouldn't exactly call him evil, I'd call him – *hot damn*, here he comes, change the subject.'

'But I told you I wasn't interested in Max, anyway,' I whisper, willing her to believe the lie.

As he snakes his way behind our vans to head to the field he glowers at Aria who tries hard to stifle another bout of giggles.

'Why, though, did the thought of another man affect him so?' Wonder colours her voice. 'You've got to ask yourself that.'

CHAPTER SEVENTEEN

Cooking for Max turns out to be a lot more panic-inducing than I'd imagined. Why did I think this was a good prize for the winner? What if he hates my food? I'll have to sit by and wait for him to painfully fork every bite into his mouth and try not to be distracted by his larger than life presence. There's something so primal and real about Max and it tends to send me a little batty.

As I survey the contents of my fridge, I find nothing suitable. The pantry is much the same. There's a big part of me that wants to impress him with my cooking style – it's the one thing I feel like I excel at, and what better challenge than a vegan who doesn't eat processed carbs or sugar? Even though I joked I'd lace everything with sugar, I can't do that to the guy who takes his lifestyle so seriously for his health, the planet, and animals.

I spend an hour on the internet, and finally make a plan, which includes walking into town to the health food shop to source ingredients I don't normally use.

When I arrive, the woman in the shop is bubbly and friendly. She smiles and introduces herself as Darla. I explain this method of cooking is alien to me and Darla helps me find everything on my list.

'You'll lose yourself in this new lifestyle, and won't look back, trust me. I've been vegan for a decade now and I only wish I'd started sooner.'

'Oh, no no, it's not about me. I'm only *cooking* a meal for a vegan.'

Darla raises a brow. 'You say that now, and so did I, and before long I realised how much better I felt following a vegan, gluten-free, sugar-free, wheat-free diet.'

I cock my head, already considering all the delicious food she'd have to give up with so many restrictions. 'But don't you miss real bread – there's nothing better than a still warm sourdough straight from the oven.'

She smiles, two tiny dimples appear. I'm guessing Darla's around fifty, her complexion is clear. She *does* look the picture of health – I suppose a prerequisite when you work in such a store.

'Don't miss it at all. There's plenty of substitutes if you're a bread-lover, and after a while you don't even think of all the things you've given up, because there's plenty of delicious food on offer. You just have to learn more about what you're eating, and how to jazz up say a simple salad into a meal that's filling and nutritious.'

'I'm a chef, so I can't ever imagine using a cheese substitute or foregoing sugar for the rest of forever.'

'Yet here you are,' she laughs.

With a grin I say, 'Yes. Here I am.'

'Do me a favour, once you've cooked this amazing three course meal up—' she indicates to the sheet of paper with my recipes and ingredient list '—send me a message and tell me you're not tempted to try this lifestyle out?'

I nod. 'Sure, I'll text you.' I take her proffered card. 'But as I said, I'm a chef by trade, my middle name is dairy hyphen sugar hyphen sourdough.'

This time she throws her head back and laughs. Even her teeth sparkle; she really does look amazing. 'I'm sure the man you're cooking for will be very impressed with the amount of effort you're putting in.'

'Oh.' I wave her away. 'It's not that I'm trying to impress him, it's more that I want to show him that…' That what? That I show my love through food? 'That I'm a good cook,' I finish lamely and blush to the roots of my hair. The point is I want Max to enjoy the meal, which will reflect well on me – I can't harp on about being a Michelin-starred chef and not be able to dish up a delicious vegan meal now, can I?

Cooking is my daily meditation, my happy place. Everything makes sense in the kitchen so why is my stomach in knots? Maybe it's because at Époque I was faceless, a real behind-the-scenes chef, and that gave me the confidence to plate up time and again. Here I'll be on show in front of Max of all people.

I thank Darla and head back to Poppy, mentally assessing the order of everything I need to do. I unpack the shopping, and get to work, looking up hours later to find the sun slowly sinking into an amber sky.

Flinging my apron on a hook on the pantry door, I throw myself in the shower and wash my hair, before dressing entirely for comfort in an old pair of frayed jeans and a loose tee. I swipe on some mascara and a quick coat of lip balm. If this *was* a date, I'd wear a full face of make-up and curl my dead straight hair, so this proves once again, it's just a casual dinner between two Van Lifers, right?

My email pings as I'm clipping a pair of earrings on, which scream *trying too hard* so I rip them off.

Dear Rosie,

Finally, I have Wi-Fi again. I manage to use up whatever data I buy way too fast and then have to rely on finding it elsewhere.

About your email – you could be my twin, in spirit at

any rate. I felt exactly the same as you on so many levels when I first started out. Leaving an ex who'd broken my heart, my trust, and put a dent in my bank balance too, I felt so alone in the world like I could have just kept walking away and no one would have noticed I'd gone. But eventually I realised that was a freedom in itself, and how liberating it was not to have to get permission for anything ever again. To sleep all day, or stay away all night, to work when I chose, to drive until the sky changed or the moon rose. To sleep under the stars with only a dog-eared paperback for company.

My first friends on this journey were fictional, and they stay with me still. When I'm having one of those doubtful *why am I doing this* kind of days, I go to them. Pick up that same book whose pages are bent and skewed, swollen with wind and rain and I'm whole again. Does this make me sound crazy? Probably! But what I mean to say is, that man never deserved you, and while it's tough now, in six months' time you'll catch yourself remembering, but it won't hurt anymore. You'll be too swept up in this.

You already have your friend Aria, and I'm sure you've met a bunch of other people who want to be in your spotlight. That says a lot about you, Rosie. Aria sounds like a tonic, and I know how it adds to the trip to have someone you can count on even just to share a pot of tea and a chat.

I'd love to catch up with you if we're ever close enough to do that. I'm heading for Edinburgh next, to shoot the opening ceremony of the local library. Are you going to the Fringe Festival? If so let me know and we can tee up a time. And if not, I'm sure we'll eventually run into each other. It's the way it goes in this life.

I've included my phone number in case you ever want to chat. Or we could video call, but reception is always dodgy

when you're using some bloke up the road's Wi-Fi. Admit it,
we all do it!
  Until then,
  Ollie x

I read the email again. We are so likeminded, so similar, and I sense a cautiousness in Ollie too. Which I like. He doesn't seem pushy, or probe too much, he just genuinely seems to care and offer support and compassion because he's trodden the same path. And he's happy now, at peace with his life which gives me so much hope.

I decide to shoot off a reply before Max arrives, breaking my usual rule of processing every last detail and weighing up the pros and cons of every kind of response. Instead I write from the heart, my fingers fly over the keyboard.

Hi Ollie,

  I'm sorry to hear your journey started after a break-up too. Perhaps it's the catalyst for many of us? That desire to flee, to change, and grow. In my case it felt more like running away but that mindset is slowly changing. I didn't want to be the fodder for gossip, the one left behind, whispered about. Callum made some dire predictions about my future, and deep down I think he might have been right. So of course I must prove him wrong!

  The week was a little quieter, the festival on a much smaller scale and my profit was slightly eaten away by baking too much and not selling all of it. I have to get the balance right, but really how can you with so many unknowns?

  We have the Festival of Speed in West Sussex up next (car racing, of all things!) and after that we are heading to Edinburgh for Fringe...

  Shoot me a message when you've wrapped up your photography work and maybe we can share a pot of tea in Edinburgh,

since you'll be close by? I'd better run, I'm cooking for Max
tonight after he lost the cheesecake bake-off!

P.S what are the favourite books you spoke about in your
earlier email? I'll see if Aria has them.

Talk soon,

Rosie

I always feel a little more upbeat after emailing Ollie. While
I'm setting the table my email pings.

Dearest Rosie,

My old friends, my cherished travelling companions are
On the Road *by Jack Kerouac, a classic, but still so relevant.*
I get a real thrill imagining their journey, and I do love the
beat generation.

Also The Beach *by Alex Garland, the premise being that*
what we seek is all an illusion… If so that would mean we're
out here now searching for that which is unattainable, but
then I remind myself it's fiction, not fact, and just enjoy being
lost in the story.

I'm replying so hastily while I have Wi-Fi. I'll message you
once I've wrapped up the shoot. Edinburgh sounds like a plan
then! I understand you'll be run off your feet so I promise I
won't take up much of your time. Until then, enjoy the Festival
of Speed!

All the best,

Ollie

P.S Please don't feel pressured or anything! It would simply
be a pot of tea between email pals!

P.P.S Who is Max?

Email pals? I smile at his hastily written, and what reads as
a somewhat nervous email. I jot down his book suggestions
so I can ask Aria to order them in. But his question about

Max... Do I go into it? But what exactly? Max is just a guy who happens to park next to us. Really, nothing has happened so why muddy the waters trying to explain what is unfathomable even to me.

I shut the laptop and ponder it all. What if Ollie sees me and flees? The only pics he's seen of me on Facebook are years old. I'm not a fan of the selfie, and I just don't get the point of pouting and uploading myriad pictures of myself with a trout pout. It's probably a lack of confidence thing on my part. What if *his* photo is years old? He could be old and grey, I've never actually asked his age. Before I can get carried away mulling over worst case scenarios, Max bangs on the door.

He doesn't wait to be invited, just strides right on in wearing that same disarming smile of his that I'm sure has weakened the legs of many a girl.

'Make yourself at home,' I say, but the sarcasm is lost on him, as he goes to the fridge and deposits a six pack of beer, ripping two from packaging.

'Allow me,' he says and pops the caps off, using brute strength and not the bottle opener.

'Nice party trick.'

'I try.' He grins and sits down at Poppy's tiny dining table.

I smother laughter. It's like someone sat a giant in a dollhouse.

'So you don't eat sugar or butter but beer is OK?'

'It's wheat-free, and a man's gotta have a vice.'

'Don't we all?'

'So what's on the menu?' he asks, taking a swig of beer and emptying most of the bottle in one fell swoop.

'You sure don't do anything by halves, do you?' I laugh.

'Nope.'

I feel pressed for space with him in the van. I'm not used to anyone besides Aria visiting. 'We have pistachio crusted maple and Dijon tofu for entrée, followed by seared king brown mushroom with cauliflower puree and mushroom compote, and for dessert, hold your hat, because I've made a delicious "raw" walnut coffee cake with a vegan brownie base.'

His mouth falls open. 'Wow.'

'Wow, indeed,' I say slightly tickled that he's so shocked. 'What were you expecting?'

'Not that much effort for starters, and maybe spun sugar with a side of sugar, just because you could. I agreed to the bet after all.'

I tut. 'Well, you're a lucky man. I do respect your—' I pause '—sugar-free veganism, and I actually found myself excited to try this method of cooking. You just have to wrap your head around all the alternatives.'

His eyes twinkle. They actually twinkle. 'So you do have a heart?'

'A tiny one.'

'Thank you,' he says more seriously. 'The thought of eating sugar after all this time was a worrying one. I'd probably be climbing the walls…'

'I can picture you doing that somehow.'

He lets out a deep laugh. 'Maybe you'll become vegan too?'

'Never,' I say.

'Never say never.'

'Never.'

'Do you always have to have the last word?'

'Yes.'

We share a smile.

My hands quake a little as I pour us a glass of red wine and serve up the entrée.

'Your mum told me you were formerly in the US Army. I find it hard to picture you as a solider, Max, what with your, with your…' Golly I'm doing it already, stumbling over words. I clear my throat. 'With your peaceful nature. What made you decide to join?'

The fork looks downright minuscule in his hands as he stabs at the pistachio encrusted tofu. 'You spoke to my mum?'

'Yeah. She's glad you're back to living a nomadic life.'

He weighs up how to answer, probably how much to say. 'I sort of fell into it, as crazy as that sounds, and once I started the training I had this real sense of belonging, this comradery with the team. It was us against the enemy, and I enjoyed the physical endurance side of things, pushing myself to my limits to see how far I could go. And I wanted to help those who couldn't help themselves.'

'A real-life GI Joe?'

His lips twitch with a smile. 'Something like that.' He considers it more. 'There was order, and routine, and as you can imagine growing up with my wandering parents, I didn't have a lot of that. I liked knowing what each day entailed; even when it was more nebulous in the field, we still had a game plan.'

That I can understand! Maybe Max is more like me than I realised.

'So why'd you leave?'

His face darkens. 'There was an incident in Afghanistan, a small child walked into the fray...' His voice trails off and I know instinctively that moment changed Max's life forever.

'You don't have to explain,' I say, patting his hand. With his twisted features, and grief-filled eyes, I sense the ending.

'For the next few months every time I closed my eyes, I saw her innocent little face, and I couldn't do it anymore. I couldn't get to her on time, and I relive that moment every day.'

There's so much more to him than I imagined, part of me feels guilty for judging him on shallow things without really getting to know the man within. 'I'm sure you did as much as you could,' I say softly.

He nods sombrely. 'I've set up a foundation,' he says. 'For children like her, ones stuck in the middle of a war zone, my way to atone for what happened. It will never bring her back, but maybe it will save another child, a child who should be in school, not stumbling through war-torn streets.'

What he must have seen! It makes my journey seem frivolous, and it strikes me how strong these people I live amongst are, suffering with grief and tragedy yet still there for everyone else.

'What can I do to help with the foundation?' I say.

He turns to face me. 'You really want to help?'

'Of course,' I say.

'You could help me fundraise.'

'Why don't I donate a portion of profit of every tea blend I sell? I'm sure we can ask a few of the others too?'

'That would be amazing,' he says.

We draw up a plan and brainstorm ideas before shelving it for the night and moving on to cheerier topics such as the fact that Nola is quite the prankster, and his father Spencer is a closet writer. Max tells me about his siblings who are living all over the world, some staying because they'd fallen in love, others because they liked the country or found long-term jobs there.

'So how many siblings have you got?' I ask.

'Ten,' he says and shakes his head. 'Not all of them are biological,' he laughs. 'Nola sort of collects people as you might imagine, so even while they might not be blood-related, they are in spirit.'

'You're so lucky having such a big family.'

'You don't?' he asks.

I shake my head. 'Just me.'

'What about your parents?'

This is when I'd usually change the subject, put my foot in my mouth, act frozen, but that's the Rosie of the past. 'My mum left us when I was young, and my dad died a few years ago.'

'I'm sorry, Rosie.'

I shrug.

'My dad had lots of emotional issues and he became a recluse, lived in squalor type of thing. He started collecting newspapers, then magazines, and next minute the house was full to bursting as he hoarded garbage as if it were precious. I couldn't throw away anything, not even empty milk cartons. Before long we were the laughing stock, our front yard full of rusted bikes, car parts... It was as though he tried to fill her absence with tangible things – junk, but in the deep recesses of his mind it mattered to him, all those piles of rubbish, those senseless mementos.'

'That must've been tough on you, Rosie. But it's obviously shaped you into who you are today, in a good way?'

I consider it. 'Maybe, but it comes with compulsions of its own. I'm so scared of waking up one day with my life full to bursting of things, that I'm the extreme opposite. Everything has a function and a place and must be cleaned by a strict schedule I keep.' I laugh to soften the weight of the words. 'I'm a little OCD about it all.'

'Is that so bad though?' he asks gently. 'So you like things neat and orderly? It makes sense to me. I yearned for structure, for routine, because I had none growing up. It doesn't mean we're not right in searching for our own truth.'

'How did you get so wise?' I smile and it lights me up from the inside.

'Sometimes I feel like I've lived a thousand lives already,' he laughs. 'And one thing I've learned is there is no right way to walk this earth, and we can only learn from those in our lives, take whatever lesson we can from it and keep going.'

I'm surprised to find tears stinging the back of my eyes. Max speaks of these things I've hidden as if it's a learning curve and nothing to be ashamed of.

'You make me feel good, Max.'

'Did you ever think that's the vegan food working its magic?' His eyes glimmer with mirth.

'And then you say a Max-ism and we're back to reality.'

'A Max-ism, I like it.'

'I bet you do.'

'You make me feel good too, Rosie.'

'Get in line, Max, that's my mad chef skills wooing you.'

'Do you miss it? London, that life?'

I think it over. 'Less and less.'

'Will you stay on the road?'

'If I can survive financially, I can't see why not. It's not like I have anything to go back to, and as each day passes, I fall in love with it a little more. Not just the lifestyle but the way it's changing me as a person.'

'Some people will never get to experience the true freedom that comes with being nomadic. Truth be told, while I enjoyed the structure of the army I did miss being on the road. Waking up in some foreign locale wondering what the day would bring, who I'd meet...'

'What about love though, Max? It's not conducive to long-term relationships, is it?' My toes curl, I can't believe I've just blurted that out, but Max doesn't seem to notice my sudden discomfort.

'Depends what you're looking for. People come into your life when you need them or they need you, and then they flit off again. There doesn't need to be a time limit attached to it.'

Does he mean he's not the settling down sort? I don't dare ask in case I don't like the answer.

The evening continues on and it's only later once he's left and all that remains is his peppery, earthy scent, that I realise I haven't laughed like that in aeons. Proper belly clutching, eyes streaming kind of laughter. Max is nothing like I pegged him for...

The next day I send Darla from the health food shop a quick text message:

OK, so maybe your lifestyle isn't all so bad. Thanks for the tips, I might just have to consider adding some vegan dishes to my repertoire... Rosie x

***

When I wake the next day there's another email from Ollie, and attached is a picture of his jean-clad legs, an open book in his lap and what must be the view out of his van: some undulating lush green hills and a sky that spans for miles. It simply says: *A busy day ahead doing this.*

I grin, imagining him in some rural hamlet, a pot of steaming hot tea at the ready, a new novel to sink into and nothing else to do all day besides enjoy the solitude.

I hit reply:

So you must have wrapped up the shoot then? It looks like you've found the perfect spot to stay idle and recharge the batteries. Life has been busy here but after your pep talk I'm definitely feeling more at peace.
   Talk soon,
   Rosie

CHAPTER EIGHTEEN

July rolls around bringing a thick humidity that manages to frizz my ultra-straight hair. We arrive at West Sussex for the Goodwood Festival of Speed which Aria assures me I'll enjoy. Max seems to think I'll enjoy the spectacle and the atmosphere, he reckons it's one of the best festivals in terms of vibe.

A huge weekend is expected with crowds forecast in excess of a hundred and fifty thousand, and hopefully that means we can bank some much-needed funds. Not sure rev-heads will delight in literary tea, but as I've come to learn, you never really know people and what makes them tick, and that first impressions are a judgement best not relying on.

As the racing starts, the zooming of engines becomes half normal and I serve the punters scotch eggs, and pork pies, which they buy fresh from the oven. I can barely keep up with demand.

The first day draws to a close and I swear the smell of burning rubber envelopes me. I'll have to wash Poppy, and also myself. Before I close the awning Max appears, his feline eyes shining with a look I now recognise: challenge.

'Whatever you're about to say, stop.'

'You know you want to!' he laughs.

I gaze around me, knowing it's going to be something far

outside of my comfort zone. I don't know how to race a car – I can barely drive Poppy in a straight line – so it can't be that.

'What is it?' I ask as curiosity gets the better of me.

'A friend of mine is doing the forest rally at the top of the hill, they're allowing a few spectators a thrill ride, and I put your name down, and as luck would have it, you got chosen.'

'Why did you put my name down? Why not yours?'

'Because last night you said you wanted to stop letting fear drive you and say yes to new experiences even when they scare the hell out of you, did you not?'

Red wine, how you constantly let me down! Max had stopped by for a glass of wine, one thing had led to another and before long there'd been a bunch of us on Poppy's deck toasting to new horizons. 'I didn't mean a thrill ride down a mountain! It was a figure of speech.'

'You should have been clearer.' He smiles.

My heart threatens to burst out of my chest. Pure fear grips me. 'No way, Max! No way am I going in a car that spends its life going sideways downwards through a *forest* at extreme speeds!'

He shoots me a disappointed look. 'There's about a hundred and forty thousand people here who would kill to be you right now.'

'Unless I get *killed*, which is very likely!'

He waves me away just as I hear my name called over the loudspeaker. 'Rosie Lewis report to the top of the hill for your thrill ride!'

'Quick,' he says. 'You don't want to miss the safety briefing. All those rules you can memorise.' He sends me a *take-that* look.

I throw him daggers. He knows I won't be able to resist if they're expecting me. I don't want to hold anybody up, or disrespect them.

'You are *evil*, Max.'

'You can thank me later.' He grins, monster that he is.

I make my way up the hill, muttering belligerently to myself.

157

I meet the smiley team who act as if I truly am the luckiest person in the world and not someone walking to their death. After a briefing about safety, they give me a fire-retardant race suit to wear and a helmet.

I feel dizzy with fear, and my legs wobble as I pull the suit on. What am I doing!

Eventually I'm harnessed into the seat, and I give the driver what I hope is an encouraging thumbs up. 'You can go slow,' I say, 'I don't mind checking out the scenery.'

He chortles and revs the engine and takes off down the mountain *sideways*, flinging the car into angles I didn't know were possible. The trees are a blur as we fly by at full speed. A scream gets the better of me as the driver hangs heavily on the steering wheel and we go sideways in the opposite direction, but it's a screech of pure adrenaline and before too long I realise this is the most fun I've had in ages.

How he maintains control is beyond me but he commands the vehicle to go this way and that on the dirt track, as rocks and debris fly up and coat the passenger window. I feel my body start to relax into the turns as my trust in him gains momentum. The sound of the thrumming motor and the screech of brakes is heavy in the air along with my manic laughter which thankfully has replaced my spate of screaming.

I want to pepper the driver with questions. How does he know which way to go without hitting a tree? How long did it take him to learn to drive like this? But I doubt he'd hear me over the noise with our helmets on and I don't want him to lose his laser-like focus.

As the forest rushes by as fast as lightening, I think of Max and how he just *knew* I'd love this, even when I didn't.

When we reach the end of the course, I face him. 'Let's do it again!'

The driver laughs as Max pulls open my door. 'Say it?'

I grin. 'WOW!'

Max helps me unbuckle and exit the car but when I go to stand my legs won't hold me.

'The adrenaline,' he says, and props me up in his arms. I fall against him, waiting for my body to catch up on the fact I'm safe, I'm good, I'm OK to walk. While I lean on him, my cheek pressed against his chest, I feel his heartbeat, and strangely enough it's knocking just as hard as mine.

***

The festival whizzes past as fast as cars race down the straight and before I know it, it's time to pack up and prepare to head to Scotland. Aria and I have planned a week off, so we can veer off course and see what we find. It's midday and I'm consulting a guidebook when Max appears, making no bones about peering over my shoulder.

'Stonehenge, huh?'

I pretend to be annoyed at his intrusion. 'Do you always sneak up on people?'

'I'm part ninja.'

'And part nosey parker.'

'Touché.'

Aria joins us, carrying a pot of tea and the biscuit tin. 'Max can you grab some mugs?'

He nods and dashes into the little bookshop returning with three mugs clasped in one giant bear paw. Golly.

Aria squats down on the deck and makes tea, handing us all a cup. 'So what's the plan, Max? Where are you off to next?'

He rubs his chin. 'I've been considering a visit to Stonehenge, and you?'

I hide a smile. No he wasn't!

'Rosie wants to go there too!' She shoots me a cheeky grin. 'Why don't you go together? I might go to do that local course on astral travel, and it's not really Rosie's thing.'

'Astral travel? What's that?' I'm sure she hasn't mentioned any course on such a thing.

'Oh.' She waves me away. 'It's just consciously having an out-of-body experience where my astral body leaves my physical body and travels around the universe. It's sublime, and a must do when you are sort of... telepathically ready.'

'What?' I'm completely bamboozled and can't tell if she's having a lend of me or if it's actually real. You can never really be sure with Aria who spends a percentage of her life in fictional lands.

'I'll explain once I've done the course. Why don't you and Max head to Stonehenge and I'll meet you both in Bath and we can park up there for the next few days?'

I can't help but feel as though Aria's set me up again. Astral travelling sounds a little too mystical even for her.

'Great,' Max says. 'You can follow my van, Rosie.'

And just like that she floats away, little minx that she is. On one hand I'm excited to spend more time with Max, but on another it concerns me that we're getting close. What if he sees me as one of those flit in, flit out people in his life? I don't want to be a stopgap for anyone.

When we arrive at Stonehenge, I can barely see the stones for the crowds and I deflate a little. What did I expect? This magnificent UNESCO world heritage site empty except for Max and I?

'Just wait,' he says. 'Once the tours are over for the day, and all the buses leave, we will have the place to ourselves and have our own private tour.' Again, he's read my mind, or the disappointment on my face.

'And how is that so?' I tease.

'I know a guy.'

'Of course you do.' I wonder if I too will know a friendly face in every town once my journey is over. Like some kind of special group, we'll recognise each other in our regular lives, doing regular jobs, and without a word look after one another, remembering times gone by, a life well lived on the road. The thought makes my heart clench, thinking that one day this adventure will be over, and I'll be back to a mundane life, with mortgage payments, and real responsibilities once more.

Because if I'm honest, I want to be married, I want to raise a family and I can't see myself doing that in a little bright pink van somehow. Am I counting my chickens a decade too early though? Don't you have to be in love to plan such a thing?

I glance at Max's distinctive chiselled profile, the epitome of a hero in romance books, and wonder what he yearns for. He harks about freedom all the time so maybe a married life with babies isn't for him. A house with a steep mortgage and bills to pay just doesn't seem like something he'd go for.

He catches me ogling and I quickly look away, coughing unbecomingly. 'Allergies.'

He lifts a brow. Even his brows are distinct, thick and wild which adds to his ruggedness.

We wander into the visitors' centre, and partake of all the interactive displays. I learn a lot about Stonehenge and its heritage. It's thought to be a burial ground; which archaeologists believe was constructed somewhere between 3000BC to 2000BC. It's another marvel and I wonder how I spent my whole life up until now missing out on such eye-opening, breath-stealing experiences that I feel are somehow shaping me into a different person, opening up my imagination, my heart and mind.

'Let's go have an early dinner and we'll come back later.'

It feels natural when Max takes my hand and leads me out.

We arrive at a cosy little gastropub; ivy climbs a weathered brick wall like a closed curtain of green. Inside, a fire crackles in the grate despite the warm day. It adds to the ambience and adds a certain old-world charm to the place.

We order drinks and a ploughman's, and I mentally scan what vegan morsels are included and think Max might leave a little hungry. He doesn't seem to mind, and laughs and jokes with the bartender about fad diets, taking it in his stride when the man guffaws with surprise when he finds out it's Max who's the vegan and not me which I find oddly discriminatory.

I suppose I'd thought the same when I first clapped eyes on Max. How a man of his sheer size can subsist on mainly vegetables *is* incongruous.

Nursing our drinks, we sit in the corner near a window. 'I thought he was a little rude,' I say, wondering why I'm now wanting to leap to his defence when I had practically acted the same way.

He nods, his top lip frothy with beer until he licks it away, for some reason the gesture is slightly erotic and I drop my gaze to the table. 'It doesn't bother me. I get that people think it's almost like a punishment, like I'm missing out on life by not eating meat. It's not their fault, not really. Most of us have been conditioned to eat a certain way, whether we realise it or not.'

'Yeah, I understand, but still it must get annoying to constantly have to defend yourself.'

'I stick to vegan cafes usually, places like this don't cater all that well to my lifestyle.'

'So why are we here?'

'Sometimes you gotta look after the carnivore too.'

I smile. 'Why, thank you.' Max seems to look after me each and every time, and I vow to return the favour.

We lapse into silence so I wrack my brain for something to say. Max seems unruffled by the lack of conversation and stares intently at me as if he's looking deep into my soul. Of course, that makes me feel decidedly nervous so I grasp at straws. 'So, where do you see yourself in five years?' The words come out stiffly, formal somehow, like I'm interviewing him for a job. I resist the urge to smack myself upside the head as he lets out enough laughter to draw the eye of *every patron* of the pub.

'You're so lovely, Rosie,' he says when he manages to compose himself. Knitting his fingers, he contemplates and then says, 'I'm trying to go with the flow. But I'd be lying if I said I didn't have a rough idea of what I want and when I want it.'

'Oh...?' This sounds different from our earlier conversations about this lifestyle.

My mind spins with scenarios. He wants to live off grid. Become a survivalist and build a bunker. Climb Everest. Save Rhinos. Cruise Antarctica.

'I want...' He pauses for an eternity. 'To get married and have a brood of children who run wild and free, and spend cold nights with my wife wrapped in my arms, warm nights stargazing with my babies, and to roam the earth and teach my kids along the way.'

'I see,' I say, startled by his confession. Never in a million years would I have guessed he'd say that.

Then I imagine Max's children, beautiful bronzed healthy cherubs, with long curly hair, the same exotic eyes, running wild with abandon. Curiously I pop into the little montage, hand in hand with the little blonde girl, a mirror of the best parts of us, who stares up at me with a fierce love in her eyes. It shocks me so much I choke on my drink and sputter it all over Max. 'Sounds lovely,' I say, and dab at my mouth with a napkin.

It dawns on me I'm jealous of who his wife, the mother of his children will be.

***

Dear Rosie,

I'm suddenly inundated with work, a blessing and a curse. But I suppose I should be grateful to take up as much work as I can before summer scuttles away and the weddings slow down. I love my job, I do, it's just I also love the solitude.

What about you? Do you crave alone time?

I'll try my best to get to Edinburgh for the Fringe Festival but probably won't be able to stay as long as I planned, but we'll still get to say hello at least! Let me know when you arrive in Scotland and I'll see where I'm at work-wise.

Solitude is only good for so long before I also need the company of real people, and not just the ones who hire me to take pictures.

All the best,
Ollie

CHAPTER NINETEEN

Scotland is everything I expected and more. Aria and I are parked a short distance from the historic fortress that is Edinburgh Castle which sits regally atop a castle rock as if watching its loyal subjects from its perch high in the skyline. It's a sight to behold with its rocky cliffs above the sea. Crowds mill in the gardens, and by the fountain, waiting for their turn to tour the iconic palace and hunt out its treasure trove of wonders, including the crown jewels, the royal palace, and the Stone of Destiny used for the coronation ceremonies for the monarchs of Great Britain and England.

Aria and I are snuggled inside the little bookshop. While it's summer, the Scottish days are mild, and there's a chill in the air mid-morning. We stab at our cake while we ruminate about the upcoming Fringe Festival and how we hope to bank some much-needed money to add to the coffers. Lots of people we've met have moved on, chasing sunshine in other climes. Max has high-tailed it elsewhere, and I miss seeing him. Miss the way he makes me feel.

There's this strange sense of desolation when we leave a place now. Perhaps it's that I find goodbyes hard, even if I'm just saying goodbye to a feeling, a festival, a group of nomads off on another route. A place where I acted a little bolder, a little braver.

Summer rain beats down and I snuggle deeper into my coat. I peek through the window noting the leaves are already turning orange; autumn is not far away.

We're lounging in the warmth, wrapped in throw rugs, as nature plays a symphony for us, wind whipping through trees, rain drumming the roof. I'm getting used to these moments of stillness, where I don't clean, I don't make lists, I just exist. It's so strange, this almost meditative effect that only comes when the crowds go and we rest before readying ourselves for the next place.

'So,' Aria says, rolling to face me, placing her plate on the floor, crumbs raining down. 'What's the latest with Ollie? Did you email him back about confirming to meet?'

I make a show of forking every crumb from plate to mouth but Aria knows I'm stalling and snatches the plate from my hands. 'Hey!'

'Hey, nothing! Did you reply to the poor guy or not?'

'Well, he was going to meet us here, but I was supposed to call him once we arrived.'

'Oh for god's sake, Rosie, you didn't do that to him, did you? It's just a macchiato, not matrimony for crying out loud!'

'Excuse me,' I say, 'I've been a little busy if you haven't noticed. These vans don't wash themselves, you know.' I've taken to washing Aria's van too, I can't handle seeing it caked in mud, windows dusty. I don't know how she stands it.

She rolls her eyes and lets out one of her *you're impossible* sighs. 'If you don't want to call, then email the guy right now, and only then will I resume our conversation.'

'You're threatening me?'

She mimes zipping her lips.

I lob a cushion at her and still she stays mute. 'Fine, fine, I'll email him. He's probably still busy with the tail end of wedding season.' I'm happy she's forgotten about Max for the time being. She reads into every little nuance, even ones that aren't there. 'I hardly think Ollie's sitting waiting for a reply.' And I feel almost guilty replying to Ollie when Max keeps popping into my mind with alarming regularity.

Her lips turn white as she presses them harder.

'You should have got into acting, Aria. What with all your *dramatic* abilities.'

With a sigh, I find my phone and bring up Ollie's email address. What's the very worst that can happen sharing a pot of tea? Is it because I harbour something for Max and this feels all wrong? I can't quite tell, and I haven't seen Max for a while. He disappeared again without a word, even though he said he was following the same route as us.

Hi Ollie,

Sorry I didn't phone earlier! We're in Edinburgh now and just waiting for the Fringe Festival to commence if you still want to meet? You'll spot Poppy a mile away, look for the fuchsia pink van in a sea of white and that's where I'll be. Cake is on me.

Witty, Rosie…

'There, done, you can unclamp your mouth now.'

She sucks in air like she's been deprived and says, 'Yay! Finally, the ice queen melts!'

'Ice queen?'

'You do come across a little frosty, don't you think? If this were a book, you'd see you're sabotaging your own love life out of some misplaced of fear of rejection.'

'*My Life*, the romance novel, according to Aria Summers.'

'Doesn't that just sound perfect?' She laughs. 'Now all you have to do is meet the damn guy and see if there's any chemistry, any spark, and go from there, since you've had a million chances with Max and haven't acted.'

I sigh. 'Jeez, Aria. And thanks for the lesson, I get how it all works.'

'No you don't. I bet you've made a list of all the worst-case scenarios already, haven't you?'

I feel the outline of the pad in my pocket and blush. 'No.'

Too late, Aria notices and lunges for my jacket pocket and with one sleight of hand brandishes my trusty notepad with a flourish. 'I didn't know you'd trained as a pickpocket.'

'I have many hidden talents. Now…' she flicks through the pad. It strikes me I'm not all that embarrassed. A month ago if anyone read my jottings I'd have been mortified, but I trust Aria in way I haven't trusted anyone before. She's aware of my foibles and while she might tease me it's all in good fun. 'Pros: cute, sweet, has a touch of the poetic about him, creative, excellent photographer, quiet, studious, loves reading, and a great listener.'

'Well, I *imagine* he would be,' I say. 'I can't be sure.'

She lifts a brow. 'Cons.'

I cover my face. Why do I feel compelled to commit every thought that flitters through my mind to paper? Really, I'm too old for this.

'Could be a serial killer, be a fan of rap music, live a cluttered life, use salty language…' She pauses and stares me, before continuing. '*Salty* language? Be messy, hate mornings. Snore. He's not Max.'

She looks down her nose at me. 'He's not Max?'

I squirm. 'Well, I mean he's just different to Max.'

'So who do you prefer?'

'Neither. I prefer my tarragon plant to be honest.'

'You are such a bad liar. Why don't you meet up with Ollie at least, and then you can cross him off the list if your heart lies with Max.' She grins. 'And if you feel *anything* at all, you have to promise me you'll be brave and ask him out for dinner. And don't sit there making a list of all the disasters that might befall you.'

I heave a dramatic sigh, much like Aria does when she wants me to give in to her. 'Fine. I'll stop focusing on what might go wrong and instead focus on what might go right.' Max pops into my mind, and confused, I try and push the vision of him away.

'That's my girl!' She toys with her wedding ring, and it's then I notice the gold photo frame is gone.

'Where's the picture of TJ?' I ask.

'Oh.' She pretends to be blasé. 'In a drawer. I decided brooding over him every minute wasn't helping. Instead of cuddling the picture a hundred times a day, I'm down to once at bedtime.'

'Progress.'

She lifts her shoulder. 'Self-preservation.'

I know in my heart that Aria's long journey of healing has begun. She's pulling herself out of that interminable darkness slowly but surely. Maybe there's hope for us both, yet.

CHAPTER TWENTY

We're close to our allocated site for the Fringe Festival when Aria beeps frantically from her van behind me. The next minute my phone buzzes.

'Pull over!' Aria says wildly. 'You've got smoke billowing out from Poppy.'

'Fluck, OK.' I'd been in La-La land dreaming of my next menu, so I hadn't noticed. Now I see thick black smoke, accompanied by the scent of burnt oil.

I pull over to the embankment, and hastily exit. My heart lurches as I see Poppy belch and hiss, as if she's in real pain. Aria races over, and assesses the van. 'I have no idea what to do!' she says helpfully.

'I don't either!' I cry. My YouTube sessions never covered this! I can't even pinpoint exactly where the smoke is coming from, it clouds out from underneath Poppy in all directions. 'Poor Poppy! She's not going to… explode or anything, is she?'

Aria bites her lip as I struggle to make sense of what I can do. Smoke means fire, right? Something must be burning, but what? The engine? The radiator? What else is there? What if she does catch alight?

Just then a loud rumble sounds, and Max pulls over. I've never been so happy to see anyone in my life.

'Max!' I wave to him as if I'm drowning. 'Over here!'

'I'm sure he can see you, since he's pulled over and all,' Aria says.

I ignore her and run to him. This is an emergency, and Poppy might be just a piece of machinery to some, but to me she is my lifeline, my friend, the one I chat to on those long lonely drives, a confidante who keeps all my secrets.

'Poppy needs help!'

'OK,' he says. 'Don't panic. Let her cool down and I'll check the engine.'

I mentally calculate my funds and wonder just how much it might cost to fix such a thing. Poppy isn't exactly of the modern era, she's more of a grand dame, so I imagine any engine parts will be costly, and hard to come by. 'Sounds expensive.'

'It's OK,' he says, giving my shoulder a squeeze. 'Everything is fixable.'

Typical nomad talk! They're all so laidback and carefree. They don't get flummoxed, they take the good with the bad, and enjoy the ride. I'm not quite at that stage. I picture myself stuck on this roadside at the witching hour, shadows cast from the trees, shimmering on the road like ghosts, scaring the bejesus out of me. No, I have to panic, otherwise how will I get this fixed!

'I can't stay here! I'll die!'

Aria and Max exchange a look, and it's too quick for me to translate it, but I'm guessing they think I'm overreacting. Which I clearly am not. What if a wild animal finds its way into Poppy when I'm sleeping, or a pack of wolves wander by while I have the door open, or what if vampires are real...!

Max puts both hands on my shoulders and faces me. 'Take a few deep breaths, Rosie, everything is going to be fine. Once Poppy has cooled down, I'll take a quick look. If I can't fix it, we'll call a tow truck and get you towed to the festival so you

171

can at least take part, and we'll call a mobile mechanic to come take a look.'

'I won't have to sleep out here alone?'

'I'd never leave you alone.'

I want to demand to know where he's been then but I'm so relieved he's here that I fall into his arms, and press my head against the warmth of his chest. He's so comfy, like a big burly electric blanket, and I relax against him as my own heartbeat steadies.

Aria coughs.

'Yes?' I say.

'Shall I give you two some privacy?'

What am I doing! I blush to the roots of my hair and somewhat reluctantly pull myself from Max, feeling the cold once again and for a moment I want to throttle Aria. 'That won't be necessary.'

'If you're sure.'

Max grins, goes to Poppy, lifting the seat to expose her engine, and begins tinkering away, whistling as if this is not an emergency but just any other fork in the road.

Aria grabs me by the elbow and leads me away, presumably so Max can't hear what she's about to say.

'What was *that*!'

'What was what?'

'You were one step away from straddling him!'

My mouth falls open. 'I was not! In the heat of the moment I was grateful he was there, that's all! It was a hug of gratitude. I was cold, he was warm. You make it sound so sleazy.'

She pulls a disbelieving face. 'You can't see it, can you?'

'See what?'

'You adore Max! You had the whole puppy dog eyes going on, you bounded, *bounded* into his arms.'

'You don't need to emphasise every damn word! And you're wrong, I only walked in slow, measured steps into his arms because he'd made it very clear I wasn't going to be left alone on some desolate road. There's been some interesting studies done on ghosts and if they're...'

Max wanders over to join us. 'It's the engine,' he says, and pulls his mobile phone from a pocket. 'I'll call Lars, the tow truck driver, and then we'll see about finding a mechanic, yeah?'

'Yes, please.' Just how many buttercream cupcakes will I have to sell in order to pay for this? Really, I should have set up a better safety net. My savings had been slowly depleted as my journey started in earnest, and what I'd made I'd sunk back into buying more produce, more equipment. And living expenses between festivals. I'd expected to build my nest egg as I went. Stupid, stupid, stupid.

Aria rubs my back. 'Don't stress, Rosie. It happens to everyone.'

I nod, wishing I shared their Zen when disaster strikes. But all I can do is silently recriminate myself for not having a strict plan in place, like I've done *my entire life* for very good reason.

'Thanks, both of you.' To my surprise my voice breaks, so I turn away and pretend to root around in Poppy for my handbag. *Do not crumble, do not lose it.* This is what money is for, right? I'd so wanted to contribute to Max's foundation, setting aside some of my savings to surprise him with, and now I'd have to forgo that for the time being.

A few hours later, Lars the tow truck driver and I enter the site for the Fringe Festival with Poppy hitched on behind. Max refused to leave me – instead he brings up the rear in his van. Already I see a couple of vans I recognise, and Aria, who went ahead of us, is all set up in the distance, our tables and chairs out front.

Lars unhitches Poppy.

'You OK?' Aria says, coming over, wearing an apron dusted white.

'I'm great,' I give her a smile. 'Are you... baking?' Aria has taken our cooking lessons very seriously indeed but progress is slow only because she usually falls into the pages of a book and forgets whatever is bubbling on the stove or baking in the oven.

She blushes. 'Well, I'm trying to,' she says. 'I knew you'd be under pressure getting here late, so I made a batch of buttermilk scones and some chocolate chip biscuits. I thought that might appeal to the masses while you get everything else sorted.'

I swallow a lump in my throat. I'm lost for words.

'OK, so they're not *exactly* the same as your buttermilk scones, but I think with enough jam and cream no one will be any the wiser.'

Laughter burbles out of me which soon turns to tears.

'Aww!' Aria envelops me in a hug and doesn't say anything when my shoulders shake.

When we part, I swipe at my eyes. I know it's still evident I've had a bit of a blub, but that's OK. I'm with friends, and they're tears of gratitude.

Poor Lars is shuffling from foot to foot and doesn't know where to look. He says nervously, 'Ah, I've got the erm… bill here, but if it's not a good time?'

'I'll sort it,' Max says.

'No, no.' I stand in front of Max, blocking him from Lars. 'It's all good, sorry, I just had a moment, that doesn't happen to me often, I can assure you of that.' Oh stop! 'Thanks so much Lars for towing me. I'll settle the bill now, thanks.'

Almost sheepishly he hands me the invoice and I go inside Poppy to pilfer my secret stash of money, and hope the upcoming mechanical costs aren't too frightening.

Back outside Lars takes the money and shoves it in his pocket. 'Any other troubles, give me a call.'

We wave him goodbye.

'Oh, I forgot about the cookies in the oven!' Aria says and dashes back to the little bookshop.

We watch her race off before I say, 'Thanks, Max that was kind of you, but you don't need to keep rescuing me.'

He waves me away. 'It's not rescuing you, Rosie. Just being decent, and I know you'd do the same.'

I feel tears sting the back of my eyes again. How to show my appreciation? 'Can I buy you a drink at the Vintage Cocktail Bar later to say thanks? Say 9 p.m.?'

'Sure,' he says. 'It's a date.'

Before I can correct him he's done an about turn and is gone.

There's no time to fill Aria in and I set to work. There's a lot to be done, so I put on an apron and get into the zone.

**

Time flies by as Van Lifers stock up on sustenance for what is expected to be a busy week. I've kept my menu simple because I'm time poor, but no one seems to notice I don't have as many choices on offer and happily buy what I have – including Aria's rock-hard scones, which I give away for free when she's not looking, quickly explaining how they came about, which makes everyone coo with how sweet she is. And she is.

I've made piles of cupcakes which I'll frost fresh in the morning. I figure they'll sell easily, especially discounted in packs of four. Turkish delight, salted caramel, Kahlua buttercream flavours are made and cooling in the fridge. I've also made some fruity boozy trifles in single serves which I hope are popular, because they're such a delight to make.

When the kitchen is clean and tidy, I pull down the serving shutter and check my emails.

Dear Rosie,
    I'm almost done here. How about I head to you Sunday?
I'll look out for your van, it sounds eye catching!
    Can't wait to meet you.
    Ollie x

Flip! It's so soon, so sudden! I head to the little bookshop to tell Aria.

'Oliver is coming on Sunday, but now I'm not so sure…'

'Why?'

'Maybe I like Max? Maybe I don't?'

'Remember you're just meeting Oliver for tea, no big deal, right? Keep your options open! Is anything happening with Max?'

'We're going for a thank you drink tonight.'

She waggles her eyebrows suggestively.

'Tea with one, cocktails with the other. If I didn't know better I'd say our shy little Rosie is coming out of her shell…'

I give her my trademark *as-if* look. 'Do you want to join us for a drink?'

'And be the third wheel? Never. I've got a date with this bad boy, right here.' She taps the cover of a book adorned with a bare-chested bronzed man.

With a laugh, I say, 'Don't do anything I wouldn't do.'

'I won't. You look happy, Rosie. Even after the drama that was today.'

And I guess I am. My friends were there for me today, and they probably don't understand how much that means to me. 'Next I have to freak out about what to wear.'

'The red dress!'

'Not the red dress, that screams trying too hard!'

She scoffs. 'It screams sex appeal.'

I cock my head. 'It's too dressy.'

'It's a form-fitting bodycon dress that can be dressed up or down and shows off your curves! You'd be mad not to wear it.'

I give her a dubious smile. 'I'll think about it.'

Back in Poppy I try on the tight red dress and discard it for a simple black sheath, and then discard that for the bodycon dress again, before I sit on the bed and scrutinise my wardrobe, which doesn't take long, since I have the world's smallest cupboard and travel light.

The red dress is just too much for a simple catch up, so I compromise and wear a short black skirt and blue halter top, more casual but still form fitting enough that I feel confident and very different to the apron-wearing Rosie Max always sees. I slick on mascara, blusher, and some lip gloss. I give my hair one last ruffle, and survey myself in the mirror, surprised to find my eyes shining with... what? Anticipation? Happiness? Max does constantly surprise me, and my feelings for him, as hazy as they are, are growing every day.

Heading out into the night, I wave to familiar faces here and there, feeling a little burst of happiness that I'm becoming one of them, slowly but surely.

The noise level increases as I get closer to the Vintage Cocktail Bar. A jazz band plays jaunty music while patrons hover around tables. A fire burns in a grate in the centre of it all, sparks shooting out like mini fireworks.

Max is there, craft beer bottle in hand, surrounded by a posse of people, men and women alike, who gaze up at him adorningly. Now I have peeled back some of the layers with Max, I appreciate better why people have the tendency to flock to him.

He sees me and edges from the group, waving them goodbye. *Phwoar.* With the firelight dancing shadows across his body, illuminating the planes of his physique he is quite the spectacle and does bring to mind being ravaged... I make a mental note to stop reading Aria's romance books because this is the effect they're having on me.

'Let me get you a drink,' Max says.

'No, no, I'll get you another, beer or something else?'

'Beer is good.'

I make my way inside the Vintage Cocktail Bar, the most elegant van ever. There's a small plush deep blue velvet seating area, dark woodgrain walls, mood lighting, and the strange feeling you've been transported back to the jazz era. I sit at one of the small sofas which is barely big enough for one, let alone two.

Louisa the bartender comes over and I order an espresso martini and another beer for Max.

'Be careful,' she whispers. 'Don't let him break your heart.'

I only know Louisa in passing. 'Who... Max?'

'Haven't seen that boy quite so dazzled before, but he's got wanderer in his soul, you know?'

'Dazzled?'

She raises a brow. 'By you.'

It's suddenly hot inside the cocktail van so I take my little napkin and fan myself uselessly as Max joins us, giving Louisa a mighty hug that knocks her off her feet. *Got wanderer in his soul.* Is she warning me he'll never settle down, never grow roots, that it's in his blood to keep searching, keep seeking? He might have settled into military life, but even that couldn't keep him. Besides, he told me himself – even being married with children wouldn't stop his quest to travel the globe. But is that so bad?

When she brings the drinks back I do my best to avoid eye contact. She's trying to send me some message and I don't want to receive it.

But boy do those espresso martinis go down well. Too well.

Two hours later I'm pressed up against Max as we dance some sultry flamenco style dance under the moonlight to the Spanish strumming of a guitar. We fit together as if we were moulded for one another, and I can't remember ever feeling so intoxicated by a person – or the martinis. I push the thought away and focus on the now, the moment right here. As I gaze up at Max I see he's staring right back at me, a primal look in his eyes.

'If you weren't vegan,' I say, 'I expect you'd be the type to throw a pelt of fur on the floor of your van for your one-night stands, wouldn't you?' I can't imagine him taking the extra two steps to the bed. He doesn't look like the patient sort.

'One-night stands?' he queries. 'Is that so?'

'Yep. A wild night of passion and then you'd disappear, I bet. The poor girl would wake to too-bright sunlight and only the musky scent of the night before. You, you'd be long gone. Running in the hills with your pride of lions or something until she leaves. Right?' Or am I wrong, and he'd be there waiting with a cup of herbal tea, and the look of longing in his eyes? Why is love so complicated?

'Right.' He laughs and pulls me tighter.

In some deep recess of my brain I remind myself to behave but I get confused with him being so close, the wild scent of him, the rain in my hair, the heat from the fire. In a split second of *absolute knowing* I stretch up on tiptoes. If I don't kiss him *I will die.*

I press my lips against his and lose myself in the sensation. It is so unlike any kiss I've had before but there's no time to ruminate why as I savour the passion on his lips, and taste his desire. I fall down the rabbit hole as my body feels suddenly *electric* connected just so to his. Yearning makes my legs go to jelly and I wonder how I will ever live without him. Just as I'm hoping the kiss never ends he pulls away from me, and smiles, a sad sorry sort of smile.

'I think we'd better get you back to Poppy.'

To Poppy? But what about the pelt of fur? The ripping off of clothes? The wild night of passion? Have I misread the signals?

CHAPTER TWENTY-ONE

The next morning I wake with the most piercing of headaches, a silent scream, which only thunders louder when the previous night comes crashing back into my subconscious.

You'd be the type to throw a pelt of fur on the floor of your van...

Please tell me I did not say that to the man! More memories sledgehammer my brain. The kiss, oh god, the kiss! And then the inevitable let down, the rejection. Him walking (dragging) me back to Poppy! Mortification colours me scarlet and I am glad I'm alone so no one can witness—

'You're awake, sleepy head!'

I squint and make out Aria's shape at the end of the bed. I grab a pillow and stuff it over my face hoping to sink into oblivion. How will I ever face him again? Was Aria here last night? Does she know the level I stooped to?

'So-o-o, Max, eh?'

That would be a yes.

'Was it everything and more?'

Despite my better judgement, I'd succumbed – the fool, I am! Urgh. I hesitate with a response.

'Well?'

'Leave me alone. I want to wallow in peace.'

'No can do, I'm afraid. We've got work to do. The festival opens in an hour.'

'I'm calling in sick. In fact, I'm calling in dead. Pretend I never existed.'

She laughs and it's like a jackhammer to my brain.

'Come on.' She wrenches the pillow from my death grip. 'There's a glass of water and some aspirin next to you, take that and I'll fry you up the greasiest, fattiest breakfast and you'll be good to go, yeah?'

'I can't. I can't ever face anyone again.'

'Why?'

I sit up and the world spins. Patting the bedside, I find the water and painkillers and swallow them down, briefly wondering how they got there. 'You obviously know why, Aria.'

She dons her most innocent expression but doesn't fool me. 'Max brought you home,' she says, 'and put you to bed, big deal.'

'Then how do you know about the kiss?'

'Well…' She grins and her eyes glint. 'I stumbled back from a late dinner with some nomads just as Max walked out of your van touching his lips and murmuring something about you. Methinks the man is smitten.'

I close my eyes. 'I probably bit him or hurt him in my efforts TO THROW MYSELF AT HIM. Espresso martinis should be outlawed.'

'I don't think so,' she says more seriously. 'I think whatever happened, he was being a true gentleman and knew maybe you'd imbibed one too many a martini and escorted you home safe and sound. You can't fault a man who does that.'

'No, I can't.'

'So?'

'I don't think that's the reason.'

'Then what?'

'I don't think I'm his type somehow. From what I can piece together.' *Kill me, universe!* 'I had this epiphany, this sudden intense urge to kiss him and it was magnificent in my drunken haze, and then he abruptly stopped. Pulled away from me. *Reeled*, even. Gah, and to be honest, he isn't my type at all!'

She stares me down as though she doesn't believe me, and I vow to never make that mistake again.

'I'm going to shower,' I say.

'I'll cook up that breakfast then.'

'Thanks.'

When she leaves, I notice a note under the other pillow. Oh, god, don't tell me he had time to scribe a Dear John letter!

Rosie,
   I hope you didn't mind me taking the liberty of undressing you…

WHAT! I peek under the blanket and find myself wearing only my underwear.

After the altercation in the mud I thought it best that you didn't sleep in that grime, but I want you to know I didn't peep. OK, I peeped once or twice, but can you blame me? Mostly though I squinted as to keep your modesty in check. Thank you for a great night. I won't forget dancing with you under the moonlight…
   Max

I throw myself back under the blankets and hide. *An altercation in the mud?* He's seen me practically naked. I will never be able to face him and his leonine looks again. That's it, I'll leave, I'll drive Poppy right out of this field. I'll say I've been called back to London…

And then I remember. Poppy is broken! Dammit all to hell and back!

CHAPTER TWENTY-TWO

The day is interminable. As the painkillers wear off the crowds thicken and I am the sole resident of struggle town. On a happier note I sold out of cupcakes within the first hour, so maybe simplicity is best in the land of festivals.

Aria as usual has left her little bookshop on a hope and a breeze that people are honest and pay for what they take and comes to help me serve, so I can whip up another few batches of scones.

She's got the boggle-eyed attention of the queue, regaling them with antics various Van Lifers have gotten up to in the past. They're so rapt I bet there's a few more nomads on the road before the season is out. Once again I send up thanks for Aria; without her I'd be making a stellar mess of my life, well, more of a mess than I already am.

Just when I'm about to dash off to find some more aspirin, the daylight disappears and that can only mean one thing. Max. I pretend to be totally focused on my scone batter, and hope he goes away, but a blush goes from my head and travels all the way to my toes. I'm not going to think of anything I might have said. Or the fact he's seen me in my barely-there underwear! And anyway, he shouldn't have peeped, it's beyond rude, it's an invasion of—

'Rosie,' he says.

I stir the batter as though my life depends on it. As if I'm performing surgery. As if—

'Rosie!'

The queue goes quiet and I know all eyes are on him. The Max effect, dammit.

'ROSIE!'

I turn, mock surprise on my face. 'Oh, Max, hi! Sorry, I was a million miles away.'

He gives me a *yeah right* look, but doesn't call me up on it. 'The mechanic is going to come and check over Poppy later tonight. Is that cool?'

'Peachy, thanks.'

The women in the queue are (not surprisingly) staring at Max, mouths agape, and I'm sure I catch a few of them frowning when they wrench their eyes from him to me, as if thinking he is way out of my league. Urgh. And didn't he practically say so last night? Pulling away when I kissed him? At the memory, my face flushes and I go back to my scone batter praying he'll vanish, but no, he wants to see my mortification, the masochist.

'When you get a minute can we talk?'

'I don't think so, Max.'

Annoyance flashes across his face. 'Why not?'

Why, oh why, do I have to have so many witnesses to this! 'You've been a great friend, a great support when Poppy broke down, but I think we're just two different people, Max.'

A rueful grin replaces his annoyance. 'Is this about last night?'

Even Aria stops serving to listen more closely. She then does the unthinkable and holds a finger up to her lips so the queue hushes too.

'I don't know what you mean?' I want to curl up in a ball and sleep for a decade.

'Undressing you.'

There are audible gasps and if I could reach him I'd kick him.

'I don't think now is the time or place,' I say huffily.

'Don't mind us,' says a pretty brunette, as she pushes up her sunnies. 'We're in no hurry.'

I clamp my lips tight while I think of an excuse. 'I fell in the mud,' I explain hastily, to save my reputation.

'We *wrestled* in the mud,' he says more emphatically. 'You insisted.'

Note to self: alcohol is now off limits. For the rest of my natural-born life.

I let out a faux giggle as if I'm just a carefree, laid back wanderer, but it actually burns my throat it's so hard to get out. 'It's important to let out your inner child every once in a while.'

'So why are you giving him the cold shoulder?' The brunette asks.

'*Moi?*' I say touching my chest, and managing to get scone batter all over my shirt. When I break into French I know that's a bad sign. I'm about to turn robot and I will myself to act normal. *Sane.*

The brunette stares me down. 'Yeah, you. He's obviously interested in you. Aren't you?' she turns and asks Max.

Aria pipes up. 'I'd say he definitely is, this is your textbook enemies to lovers trope.'

Before he replies I say sharply, 'Ah, no, you're wrong there, that's what reading too many romance books does to a girl, gives you false expectations—'

Aria says, 'That is unequivocally incorrect. And there's no such thing as reading too many romance books.'

The brunette smirks at me. 'Well?' she says to Max, seemingly not intimidated by his powerful presence at all. 'Do you like the girl or what?'

Max is unexpectedly ruffled, he shuffles from foot to foot. 'Well, she kissed me, it's true…'

'Stop!' I hold a hand up, no way am I letting him reject me in front of so many witnesses. 'I kissed him, yes, but I'd had a very long and arduous day, a very *stressful* day, a very *long* day.'

'You've already said long.'

I shoot her daggers. 'An emotional rollercoaster of a day and then I drank three espresso martinis.'

'Six,' Max coughs into his hand.

'*Four* espresso martinis on an empty stomach and I acted on some stupid impulse.'

'So you're not into him? *Him*?' The girl points to Max, her voice incredulous.

'I'm sure he's got legions of fans, sadly I am not one of them.'

'I'll happily volunteer,' she says and gives Max the eye. Suddenly I feel homicidal for some reason.

Max gives her a saucy smile before he turns to me and says, 'I'll be back later, Rosie, to check out your parts.'

'You... you...'

He lifts a brow. 'Mechanical parts.'

I promptly close my mouth as everyone in the queue titters. Will this day ever end?

***

Day one of the Fringe Festival is done and I ache to fall into bed, but the mechanic Josh is fiddling around with Poppy and thinks he may have to tow her into town to use his hoist. If that's the case, I'm going to be homeless for a day or two, not to mention unable to bake and make any money to help pay for the repairs.

'No can do, Rosie,' Josh says rubbing his grease-stained hands on a rag. 'I'll have to work on Poppy in the garage. I'll work as fast as I can, but with waiting on parts and all it might take a week or so.'

A week! Homeless and jobless for a week!

And what about Ollie arriving tomorrow? He is going to be looking for the fuchsia pink van in the sea of hundreds and it's not going to be here. I'll have to email him and hope he has Wi-Fi wherever he is.

'OK, Josh, and what do you think about cost, any idea yet?'

He shrugs. 'Hard to say, won't know until I get the parts in.'

'OK, can you keep me in the loop?' My cheeks flame. 'I've only got so much money saved, you see. If it's any more than that, I'll… I'll…' What? Borrow the money – from who? How could I let myself get in such a predicament? 'Have to sort something else out.'

'Sure thing,' he says, giving me the ghost of a smile. 'Hopefully it won't be exorbitant. You just never know with these old engines.'

'I appreciate the help.'

'I'll call Lars and sort the tow.'

He wanders off, phone pressed against his ear, and I walk glumly over to Aria's little bookshop. 'Bad news?' she says when she sees my face.

'He has to have Poppy towed and it might take a week, depending on where he can source the parts.'

'Shoot. A week without your kitchen.'

'Without sales.'

'And then you'll have the mechanical bill on top of all that. Why don't you cook in here?'

I gaze around the little bookshop. There is a kitchen buried under all the books, but could I work in such a chaotic mess? I'm liable to burn the place down with books scattered everywhere. I'd have to declutter or I couldn't cope, which is not fair on Aria.

'Maybe,' I say hesitantly. 'It could work.'

'Of course it will!' she says brightly. 'Let's start moving things around, so you've got some space.'

'Thanks, Aria.' I know she also likes her own space at times, we all do, so it's very generous of her to give that up for an entire week, which reminds me. 'Oh god, where will I sleep?'

She grins.

'Don't you dare say in Max's van!'

'Why not! He's got the biggest van around and you know what they say, big van equals...'

'No!' I cover my ears.

'Lots of space. Get your mind out of the gutter!'

'No, absolutely no way. Nope.'

She shrugs airily. 'I'd say bunk in with me, but as you can see there's no room.'

Aria's bed, if you can call it that, is one big pile of books with the thinnest strip left to sleep in. How she can sleep without worrying the pile will fall and topple on her head suffocating her is beyond me.

'Maybe someone has a tent I can borrow?'

'Let's just ask Max.'

'No!'

Before I can say anything she's out the door dashing across the grass to Max's van.

That minx!

I run after her – well, it's more of a canter, then I take a quick rest break, and hobble forth.

When I catch up to them, Max is nodding and Aria wears a smug grin on her face.

'Thanks, Max you've saved our bacon, well our *faux* bacon, anyway... Rosie, Max says it's fine if you bunk in with him. He does have a *spare* bed and all.'

Steam comes out of my nose, I'm sure of it. 'That won't be necessary,' I say. 'I'll borrow a tent off someone, I'll be fine, alone, at night, in the cold, with the friendly wolf pack...' Oh god, I'm going to die!

Max frowns. 'Rosie, you're not going to die.'

I crinkle my brow, how is he reading my mind?

'Just bunk in with me. And I promise—', cue the eye sparkle, '—I won't throw my pelt of fur on the floor, you'll be safe as houses with me.'

I fold my arms. 'You just have to keep bringing it up, don't you?'

'All in good fun, roomie.'

'Roomie!' I turn on my heel and stride off back to Poppy to get my things before Lars arrives. Will I be safe as houses with Max? There's really no other option, I suppose. Max is the only one with a spare bed that I know of, and I don't fancy bunking in a van with someone else I hardly know. I could sleep sitting up in Aria's van but she is a night owl, and I'm more of an early sleeper. At least in Max's van I will have my own side of the van, and he will have his.

Back inside Poppy, I pack a few essentials, and my laptop. And then I stop. What about Ollie's impending visit? I can't exactly welcome him into Max's van to share an almond milk latte, can I? After the kissing fiasco with Max, Ollie seems more suited to me. We'll drink sparkling water and discuss Yeats... Not an espresso martini in sight!

I open my laptop and email him.

Hi Ollie,

What fun would it be having a drama-free day? Poor Poppy is getting carted off to van hospital to get her engine fixed. Sadly that means I'm homeless and kitchen-less for the week, but never fear! If you look for Aria's van, The Little Bookshop of Happy Ever After, I'll be baking in there as best I can. I hope you get this message in time and don't hunt around for a fuchsia pink van that's absent!

See you soon!
Rosie

I don't want Ollie to think I've vanished! If he can't find me will he think I got cold feet? That I disappeared because I'm nervous? Surely if I spread the word around he'll eventually ask a Van Lifer who will steer him to me if he doesn't get the email in time.

He usually doesn't have his own Wi-Fi, which is the same for a lot of the Van Lifers who rely on public Wi-Fi when they can – partly a money saving measure, and partly to be less connected, and more attuned to the world around them.

How will I spread the word and fast, with all the work I have to do? Aria!

I go back to the little bookshop and fill her in on my predicament. As expected she jumps up. 'I'll tell everyone to expect a tall, dark and handsome stranger, shall I?'

I frown. 'Well, I don't know how tall he is. And he's not dark, he's actually a little pale in his profile pic, I mean it could be the lighting, but yes a handsome stranger.'

'Well, that narrows it down,' she jokes. 'What else, Rosie? What makes him stand out?'

Hmm. 'Nothing really. That's the appeal, I suppose. He's got those dependable eyes, and that sweet smile that conjures lazy Sunday picnics in his arms, while he reads you a passage of poetry. The boy-next-door who grew into a good man, a man who arrives on time, and brings flowers.'

'You're getting all that from his profile pic?'

I nod.

'Well, it's not helping. I can't say all that to the other stall holders, now can I? What else?'

'Slightly wavy brown hair, brown eyes, and a stage or two before you'd call him athletic, but not weedy either.'

'Right. Let me see what I can do. Do you need help bringing your things from Poppy?'

'No, I can manage. I've got enough cakes baked to last me through tomorrow, so I'll just use your kitchen to whip up milkshakes and make pots of tea and some scones for cream teas if I'm desperate.'

'You *can* use the oven, it's not that bad,' she says.

It's a black charred mess. Whatever she cooked in there last turned to charcoal and she didn't bother removing it. I could scrub it, I want to scrub it, but the hangover from hell still lingers. 'OK, thanks.'

'Right, well rest up and I'll get the message passed along. You should have an early night, no? Get ready for a busy day tomorrow.'

'I could sleep for a week.'

She gives me a quick hug. 'Well, off you go. We'll get up extra early to prepare.'

'OK, thanks for everything, Aria.'

With a wave she's off and running to spread the word about Ollie, and I just hope he asks around when he arrives tomorrow. I'd feel awful if he came all this way and thought I'd disappeared.

I head to Max's van and knock, there's no answer so I tentatively poke my head inside. There's a note propped up against the kettle.

Make yourself at home. There're some zucchini zoodles with walnut 'Volognese' in the fridge...

Is that his substitute version of spaghetti Bolognese? After the meal I cooked for him I am tempted to try it. I'll never tell Max of course, but I enjoyed the vegan meals more than I imagined. Who knew a raw dessert could be so tasty?

I'll be in later, or if you're lonely you can find me at The Wandering Yogi, getting all loose and limber.

Namaste

I laugh and throw the note down. Is he really doing yoga? I can't see him folding his gigantic frame into all those tricky positions, somehow.

My brain is dizzy with fatigue so I drop my backpack on a seat and make my way to a single bed he's folded out in preparation for me. I've never been so excited to slip into PJs and climb into bed. Even a strange bed in a bustling city, sharing with a man who has seen me half naked, is no hindrance as I lay my head on the pillow, noting the peppermint smell of the freshly washed sheets and fall into a deep slumber.

CHAPTER TWENTY-THREE

The next day I awaken with the birds who are quickly drowned out by the sounds of a blender, blitzing something to smithereens. Groaning, I pull the pillow over my face but it's quickly wrenched away and Max appears over me, holding out a glass filled with seaweed-green liquid.

'Breakfast, Mademoiselle?'

'I don't drink my food,' I say, rolling my eyes.

'As my *guest*, I think it's only fair you drink my superfoods smoothie, don't you?' He stares down at me and I try to ignore just how alive he looks first thing in the morning, how awake and sparkly his eyes are, when it usually takes me a fair amount of tea and a good pep talk to will myself back into the world for another day despite being an early waker myself. Max is the epitome of bright-eyed and bushy tailed.

I tut and take the proffered glass. 'This looks suspiciously like lawn clippings.'

'There's nothing wrong with a little wheatgrass…'

I take a sip.

'And if you don't have any wheatgrass on hand, suburban grass will do just fine.'

I splutter green smoothie all over myself. 'What!'

'Joke.'

'You *are* evil.'

'I try.'

'This is payback for me winning the bet, isn't it?'

He shrugs and laughs. 'Yeah.'

'Well, it's actually pretty damn good,' I say, wondering how blended wheat grass can taste so sweet.

'You're coming around to my way of life, right?'

'Wrong.'

He tries to stare me down.

'I'm not turning vegan.'

I return his stare. He can't do the eye flash thing and have any effect over me, and better he learns that… But *golly*, it's so hot and cramped in here, I need a cold shower, I need… *something*. He smells like wind and rain, like he's been outside, soaking up the atmosphere into every pore, every olive-skinned, tattooed part of him. Just how far do those tattoos go? My eyes trail the length of him…

'Are you OK?'

'Yes, why?'

'You've gone all misty-eyed.'

I shake myself back to the now. 'You've probably poisoned me.' Or else I was in some kind of weird fantasy land. What exactly is in this smoothie? 'Maybe I'm allergic to grass?'

'Well,' Max says, shaking his head as if I'm an unsolvable mystery. 'The day is but young, shall we start it with a bit of the downward dog?'

'You wish.'

'I do wish.'

I narrow my eyes. Is he flirting? He just cannot help himself. He's got to turn on the charm, even though he's made it abundantly clear I am not even kissable in his eyes.

'If there's nothing else?' I say a little archly as his previous rejection at the Vintage Cocktail Bar spools like a movie reel in my mind again. 'I'll borrow your shower and then head to Aria's, I have Ollie meeting me today, you see...'

'Ollie?' He feigns confusion.

I wrench the covers back and stand and stretch. 'Yes, Ollie, gorgeous photographer, fellow traveller and all-round poetic soul. Dreamy eyes. That Ollie. Remember?'

'Can't say I do. Dreamy eyes? Nope.'

'Ah, well, maybe I'll introduce you today?' I don't know why I'm toying with him like this, probably to take the sting out of Max's disinterest. It's pathetic but it makes me feel better at any rate.

'Sure, I'd like to shake his hand, why not?'

I picture Max crushing the bones in poor Ollie's delicate photographer's hand and wince.

'OK, I'm going to take that shower now, unless you want to go first?'

'You go, holler if you need me to wash your back.'

'You're incorrigible.'

'Thanks.' He grins.

***

In Aria's little bookshop, we sit and chat over steaming cups of blood orange tisane. My new blend of orange zest, green apple, papaya and hibiscus. 'What do you think?'

'This is lovely,' Aria says, nodding her approval.

'It's got a punchy mouthfeel, right?' Making blends of tea in my downtime had proven to be a lot more fun than I expected, getting the balance between flavours right and concocting unique blends.

'It's got to be called *The Great Gatsby* tea. It reminds me of his sprawling garden, the manicured beds, all that glamour...'

'I'll have to re-read the book and decide what to write on the cards.'

'I've got a copy around here somewhere,' she says, gazing around the various piles. She always figures it out though, like she can sense where a certain novel is among the disorder.

As if we willed it, filmy sunlight filters into Aria's little van, catching dust motes as if they're pirouetting. The day about to begin, I pull myself from the old wrinkled leather chair and grab my apron. 'I'd better get sorted.'

Aria has her nose pressed in a book while I stir, whisk and bang around the tiny space.

'Are you nervous, is that what this is?' She peers over the cover of her book.

'What?'

'All that bosom heaving, hand fluttering, mumbling?'

'Oh, sorry. It's just if I don't sell enough cream teas I have no idea how I'll pay for the repairs for Poppy. I have a horrible feeling the bill is going to be more than I imagine.'

'Oh, that. I thought you were nervous about Ollie.'

'Now you've reminded me!'

She laughs. And the day soon begins in earnest and I don't have time to worry about anything other than how quickly my hands fly over the bench and replenishing teapots and chatting away to keep the queue smiling as they wait.

After the lunch rush, I tidy the tables out front, snatching up mugs and plates and dashing back inside to wash them. I go back and give the tables a wipe down, and worry once again that everything seems covered in dust no matter how much I clean it. But there's no time to scrub everything properly, as the next wave of festival-goers will hit soon, and I need to prepare for them.

My phone rings and I snatch it up, hoping it's Ollie. 'Hello?'

'Hey, Rosie, its Josh the mechanic.'

I'd half expected to hear Ollie's voice for the first time, and wondered if it would be as smooth and velvety as I imagined.

'Hey, Josh. How's Poppy?'

He clucks his tongue. 'The repairs themselves aren't that much trouble,' he says. 'It's sourcing the parts at a reasonable price for the old girl.' He goes on to describe the intricacies of the mechanical work undertaken and I *hmm* and *ahh* as if I know what he means but it boils down to: it's going to be expensive and more so if I want the parts sooner rather than later.

'I understand,' I say. 'I think the best course of action, despite it being more expensive, is to get the parts you need express shipped otherwise I'll be stuck here once the festival is over, waiting for Poppy and unable to work. But just how much are we looking at price wise, you think?'

He rattles off a figure.

After one lonely chest-clutching moment I compose myself. 'Right. I'd better sell up a storm today!'

'OK, I'll get it done and call you if anything changes.'

I gulp. I hope nothing else crops up. 'Thanks again.'

As I hang up I realise I need to find another way to make money. I can't count on food alone when things like this happen. Isn't the side hustle the way of the world these days? Aria wanders over, book in one hand, teapot in the other. 'Was it Ollie?'

I fill her in on Poppy's progress and explain my idea.

She taps a finger to her chin. 'Yes, yes, you can't always rely on people being hungry, especially when the competition increases and there's pop-up food vans from one end to the other.'

I groan. 'A lifetime of planning and I've ended up here.'

She gives me a dazzling smile. 'And what better place to be, my pretty.'

As I gaze around me at the people meandering along the walkway between the vans, I see her point. This is a whole new way of living, of making each moment count, and I am grateful for the chance to do it. But she of the contingency plan, would really have preferred the safety net of more savings. What if Poppy breaks down continually? I'll be hard pushed to survive. It's a scary thought.

'Right, what can I sell, other than food?'

She picks up a chipped teapot to pour our tea, it's once bright cobalt a faded cornflower and it hits me, it's so obvious I slap my forehead. 'TEAPOTS!'

Aria jumps in fright.

'Sorry! I could sell teapots, maybe not at festivals because I can't quite see people lugging them around, but what if we set up an online shop? I can sell my tea blends, a range of unique teapots, you could even pair them up with books that match!'

Aria shakes her head. 'Why didn't we think of that sooner? '

I laugh, and a rush of energy races through me. 'OK, so I can make more blends easily enough but where will I find some unique teapots? We want them to be handcrafted, and utterly beguiling.'

Aria lifts a finger. 'Ah, Nola would know!'

Lovely ageless Nola. 'Great idea.'

Aria smacks my shoulder. 'Go see her now, if it gets busy I'll call you – or if you-know-who shows up.'

Before she can tease me, I head off to Nola's, spurred by the thought of a new income stream, money I hope I can squirrel away for rainy days, Max's foundation and problems with Poppy.

Nola's van, *Wandering Star*, is a few rows away, and catches the weak sunlight, her dream catchers blowing gently back and forth in the wind.

'There you are!' she says as if she's been waiting for me. Before I can respond she's gathered me into her arms, she smells like sandalwood and sunshine.

'Hey, erm, Nola.' I'm struck suddenly shy. Like her son, Nola has a presence that puts me on the back foot for some reason and the old Rosie, the robotic one, threatens to make a return.

'Max has been keeping me in the loop on all your adventures – sounds like you've had a blast, these last few weeks.'

Oh god, had Max told his *mother* about my inebriated kiss? He wouldn't, would he?

198

'He says you've been baking up a storm and have been popular among the crowds, which is a great sign so early on in your journey.'

I search her face for any clues she knows more, but all I see her is open and honest smile. 'Yeah, it's been a baptism of fire, but every day I'm learning more. Max has been very helpful, very supportive.'

She waves me away as if that's just Max. 'He's always there to lend a hand, just like so many people have done for us.'

'I'm actually staying in his van at the moment. Poppy is in for repairs.'

'I know,' she says and winks. 'I know everything, that boy sure can't keep a secret.'

I groan. 'Oh god, everything?'

'Everything.'

'Espresso martinis…?'

'Are a great party starter, but what happened after? Max seems to think you're in a relationship with some other guy?'

'Well, I'm not in a relationship per se. I've been corresponding with Oliver from the forum.' I shrug.

'Oliver?' she frowns.

'A photographer.'

'Haven't stumbled across him as yet, I don't think.'

'He's down to earth, dependable…' Why am I rattling off his attributes to Nola of all people?

'Max isn't the heartbreaker he gets pegged for, you know.'

'Is that a mother's wishful thinking?' I try and make light of it to Nola. But I want to believe her, believe in Max, but he does have a tendency to pull away, to leave and I never quite know where I stand. I don't want to make a fool of myself, or risk my heart getting broken again so soon.

She smiles. 'That's what it sounds like, right? But he's a good boy, is respectful towards women. Those rumours that circulate about him get my goat, and I truly don't know why they start.

199

But enough about all that, that's not why you came here is it?'

'No, that's not why I'm here.' I smile, glad for the subject change. 'Aria suggested you might know where I can find some unique teapots to sell until I can find a designer of my own.'

Her eyes brighten. 'Spencer can make them! If you give him a design he can make them out of ceramic. I'm sure we can find a kiln, somewhere. He's an artist, he can use almost any medium.'

'Great! How long would that take do you think?'

'I guess it depends on the design, how intricate they are, how long it takes him to make the moulds for them. But in the interim you could ask Mai Ling from Precious Porcelain. She cultivates the most stunning pieces. I'm sure she'd sell to you at wholesale so you could still make a tidy profit.'

'Thank you!' The world is opening up to me as I try to blunder my way in! 'And just how intricate could my ideas be for Spencer, do you think?'

'The sky is the limit, my darling.'

I give her a megawatt smile. 'I'll be back!'

'Mai is a few rows behind you, her shop is all blue!'

I wave my thanks as I dash to find Mai, my ideas coming quick and fast. Having teapots and house-made tea blends ready to go, would be great gift ideas. Teapots shaped like bookshelves, cupcakes, flowers, unicorns, the list is endless…

I find her sweet indigo blue van, strung with blue bunting that shivers in the breeze. On a table out front is display of pretty porcelain pieces, Asian in style, waiting for the right buyer. I spy a teapot, and then another, and hope we can work out a deal so we both make money. I introduce myself and she nods solemnly, and then continues shuffling about watering her pot plants. Her little set-up is so homely, like she's here for the duration and not a few days. 'Nola suggested I visit,' I say and explain my needs, all the while wondering why the woman's face is so inscrutable. It's almost as if she's forgotten I'm there. 'So, have you got any teapots you'd like to part with?'

'It depends,' she says. 'Come into the van, the light is better there.'

O-kaaay. I follow Mai's tiny frame into her van. It's sparse, minimalist and very clean.

'Sit.' She points to a stool, and turns on a bright light overhead. Am I about to get interrogated? Will she pull out a pad like detectives do and ask my whereabouts on a certain night? The thought makes giggles rise which I swallow back as quickly as I can, sensing whatever this is, is serious for Mai.

I duly sit.

'Keep still.'

Just how well does Nola know this woman? What if she hypnotises me, or something equally irrational? Goose bumps prickle my skin.

With pursed mouth she stares intently at my face, as if reading every line, every nuance. I fight the urge to shrink against such scrutiny and silently panic about what it might mean. What if she's a closet plastic surgeon and thinks I need work done? Or some sort of body snatcher? Or...

'Right, that's done.'

'What exactly did you do?' I tentatively ask.

'Mien Shiang.'

'Which is...?'

'The ancient Chinese art of face reading. If we're going to work with each other I need to know what kind of person you are, your character, how you'll behave.'

Golly. 'I see.'

'Your features are part of the twelve categories or "houses". First I check your "Fude Gong" or Fortune House.'

The hair on my arms stand on end.

'You've worked very hard, but had little reward, and that's because people have taken advantage of you, and you weren't aware of it at the time. You've had bad relationships, stemming from your childhood and your lack of confidence. Again, recently you were hurt in your personal life by someone you loved.'

I don't dare breathe. How can she know all of this? Sure, there's gossip about any new nomad but they don't know my past, only what I've cared to share which is virtually nothing. She studies other areas of my face, taking her time, leaning close. Is she checking my other 'houses'?

'Your father had an illness, it wasn't his fault, and the people who tormented you about him will one day realise their error. That is not for you to hold onto, you must make peace with that. You must let it go.'

The air in my lungs leaves with a *whoosh* and I can't think of what to say. Just how can I let my past go so easily? If I don't hold the reins tight the same thing might happen to me, right? Life could spiral out of control like it did for dad when mum left. One minute he was fine, and then slowly but surely he replaced her presence for *things*. Stupid things, like old newspapers, and pizza boxes, bits of ribbon, worn car tyres.

The once immaculate house was suddenly a storage compound and eyesore, and we were the laughing stock of our small village. Dad stopped leaving the house, started muttering to himself. And I tried so hard to fix it, to fix him, until he ordered me out for throwing away his things. It was only later, a specialist explained that it wasn't as easy as tidying and hauling everything to a skip bin; it ran far deeper than that.

Dad died of a heart attack a few years ago before I could really make amends, and that guilt has followed me ever since. A stray tear falls down my cheek, and more build like a wave about to break.

It has always been my shameful secret, my part in Dad's downfall, and how my embarrassment forced me to help him which actually did more damage than good. 'It's just that I can't forget it, it's always there, always in the back of my mind.'

'Only because you hold on to it, as if you'll find some atonement blaming yourself, and that will never happen. You were a child, then a teenager, and did only what you thought was right. There's no malice in that. No need to alter the course of your own life in order to rectify the issues of others. And you will alter your path, if you continue to hang onto it.'

'So what, I just pretend it didn't happen?' Incredulity seeps out of every word. It's all well and good saying move past it, but quite another actually doing that. My dad deserved better, didn't he?

Ever patient Mai says, 'You meditate over it, and by that I mean, clear your mind from time to time, and let those thoughts and feelings come and then absolve yourself. Remember the child you were, not the adult you became.'

I think back to when it began, my messy pigtails, my unironed clothes. The angst, the fear, the sudden knowing that my parents were flawed. How I grew from girl to woman and realised I couldn't fix it, I couldn't stay. How alone I had been.

Could I forgive myself, or at least try to? How much easier would life be?

'You have money troubles now, and you will, off and on. Your journey won't be easy, but it will be worth it. Be careful of falling in love, he isn't who you think he is. Don't trust so easily.'

I slump. I knew Max wasn't to be trusted, but it's not like I love the guy is it? People have obviously warned me for a reason, and I knew deep down, anyway.

'Don't be morose,' she says. 'There's lots of good coming your way. You have to find the right path, be aware of the fork in the road.'

'Thanks, Mai.'

'And I can see you're trustworthy, a good character, so we may go into business together.'

I beam, relieved at least one thing is going right.

'Take whichever teapots you like and when you sell them you may pay me my share.'

The offer is so generous I feel tears prick the back of my eyes. 'I really appreciate this.'

She waves me away. And I leave with a box full of delicate porcelain teapots and a mind that is spinning.

CHAPTER TWENTY-FOUR

Later that evening, after tidying Aria's tiny kitchen I count the takings for the day. My cupcakes had sold out and I discounted my cream teas as the day had worn on to recoup as much money as I could for Poppy's repairs. My profit margin had been less, but all I cared about was having enough money for the mechanic. Still, as I fold the pounds into piles, I have a fair way to go.

With a sigh I head back to Max's and pull the curtain between us closed, even though he's not in. After my chat with Mai I feel lighter about my past.

But can you ever really forgive yourself when the person in question isn't here anymore? I think of my poor dad, and how I tried so hard to help him, when all I had to do was listen, to care. It's not like we never saw each other again, I visited every Christmas, up until his death, but our visits were strained. He watched me hawk-like as though at any moment I'd spring to action and throw away his things. I felt like we never really ironed our relationship out.

I was only seventeen when he insisted I leave, a baby really. I'd grown up so sheltered. Dad had called an old school friend who worked in a restaurant in London and that's how I become a part-time pot scrubber at Époque, while completing my formal training.

And I'd felt so adrift, so I worked nonstop. London was just so very far away, as if Dad orchestrated that on purpose, so he could live his sad, reclusive, cluttered life in private. It's all so messy and complicated to dwell on so I push it all to the back of my mind, and lock it away for later.

Instead I think of the now. Ollie hasn't shown up so I take up my laptop and email him hoping he hasn't spent the better part of the day looking for me, that he's just been waylaid. He could have seen me and bolted, right? Changed his mind about visiting me altogether? Any number of things. Normally I'd make a list of reasons why, but today I don't. Instead, like a *real* grown up, a woman who lives in the *real* world, I email him and ask.

Dear Ollie,

I missed you today. Not sure if you got my earlier message about Poppy or not, probably tricky without Wi-Fi! Anyway, I hope you didn't waste the day searching for me, because we didn't see you! And if you ran out of time to get here, I understand that too.

It's been a crazy, busy, tumultuous festival! Life changing in a way, or maybe eye opening is a better way to describe it.

I hesitate about confiding in him about what Mai said, I know he'd get it, but it's probably information overload by email. So I leave it out.

While it was hectic, the festival-goers were patient, the weekend had a good vibe about it.

If you're still about or haven't changed your mind *wink* I'd love to catch up. I'm still waiting on parts for Poppy, so I'll be here for a day or two more at least.

I've been staying in Max's…

I think of Mai's warning about Max and then delete any mention of him. It's got nothing to do with Ollie anyway. And why waste my time talking about where I'm sleeping?

Hope to hear from you soon,
Rosie x

CHAPTER TWENTY-FIVE

'She's ready to rock and roll,' the mechanic chortles down the phone line.

'Already?'

'Yeah, love, I worked through and got it done so you wouldn't be stuck here. I'll wash up and drop her back in ten minutes or so.'

'Wow, thank you. I really appreciate it.' My voice is full of wonder. 'And what's the damage?' I cross my fingers, and hope and pray my savings will cover this latest fiasco.

'Erm, well, see…'

I close my eyes. It's horrendous, it's sky high, I'm going to need to beg, borrow and steal to pay for the repairs. How mortifying.

'It's OK, you can tell me. I know the parts weren't cheap.'

'Actually they were, and it didn't take me long to fix her, so we'll leave it at that, eh?'

I frown. 'You just said you worked through to get it done.'

'Did I? I'm an old man, forgetful, like.'

'What's really going on?'

There's a sigh and then silence.

'Well?' I probe.

'Can't you just say thanks and be done with it?'

'Thanks, but why is it free? Has someone paid for the repairs?'

He mumbles, 'I told him, I said women are like bloodhounds, they sniff out secrets like nobody's business.'

'Told who?' And then it dawns on me. 'Max paid you?'

'Eh?'

'Don't try the old and doddery act with me.'

'Blimey. He made me swear not to tell you.'

'How much was it?'

He mumbles.

'What?'

'Seven hundred and fifty pounds, give or take a penny or two.'

'SEVEN HUNDRED AND FIFTY POUNDS!?'

'Steady on, most of that were for the parts, missus.'

My heart bonks painfully inside my chest. 'It's not the bill, it's him paying that much money out of his own pocket. I can't imagine what he was thinking.'

'He was helping a mate, is all.'

I soften, and then stiffen when I remember what Mai said: don't trust so easily. This is probably how he sweetens women up, and then boom, garners their trust and leaves them in ruins.

'Thanks, I'll make sure I pay him it all back with interest. And thank you for working so hard for so long to get it done.'

'No worries, spread the word to your friends, will ya? I'm mobile so can get about the countryside.'

'I sure will.'

We hang up and I leave to find Max.

He's sitting around a campfire, guitar in hands, seemingly soaking up the adoring gaze of Mellie, a twenty-something who makes her own jewellery. I quash the sudden need to roll my eyes.

'There she is,' he says, grinning up at me, strumming the guitar like a pro. I find it endlessly fascinating that there's nothing the man can't do.

'A word please, Max,' I say and Mellie pouts. '*If* you can drag yourself away.'

He registers the irritation in my tone. Unwinding the guitar strap he hands the instrument to Mellie who looks at him like all of her Christmases have come at once.

'What's up?' he says following me away from the group.

'Why'd you pay for Poppy's repairs?'

The smile disappears. 'He told you?'

'It wasn't hard to guess.'

His face clouds. 'I know you needed a hand, and you'd never ask for one, so I paid and that's all there is to it. It's only money, Rosie.'

'It's only money?' I clench my jaw. 'I don't need a hand.' I hate feeling like I can't take care of myself!'

'So you had enough to pay the bill?'

I fumble with a response. 'Not exactly but I was working on it.' What kind of person am I? Did I have any hope of being able to pay in full? What would I have done if Max hadn't paid?

'Just accept it for what it is, Rosie. A hand up when you need one, OK? We've all been there, we've all had someone step in when things were tight, that's what's so amazing about this nomadic community. But instead you stomp over and demand to know why someone is being nice to you – you look for hidden intentions when there're none there.'

I go to speak but he holds up a palm. 'Don't deny it, I can read it on your face. I know what you were thinking, that you'd owe me and I'd expect you to fall into bed with me and that was my ploy, right?'

I hope guilt doesn't shine in my eyes, but I'm fairly certain it does.

'I know the rumours, I hear the gossip, but you can't always believe everything you hear, right?'

'Depends who's doing the talking, I suppose.'

He smiles and shakes his mane of hair. 'So I guess we're not bunking together tonight, then?'

'We didn't *bunk* together, Max, before you start rumours!'

'Close enough.'

'Troublemaker.'

'You know it.'

'Look, thanks, Max. For putting me up, for sorting out Poppy's bill. I'll get the money back to you by the end of the week.'

'No rush. Save yourself a little nest egg, and then worry about paying me back.'

'Oh, no I don't want to owe anyone, it doesn't seem right.' In fact it screams bad management.

'Up to you.'

'I'll go grab my things from your van, and leave the key inside.'

'Sure, see you later.'

With a wave he's back in front of Mellie's adoring gaze, and I'm forgotten. That's what I wanted, wasn't it? To slide from his gaze, his flirtatious banter? I stomp away, my chest tight and get my things from his van, tidy the space and leave the key.

When I get back to our area, Poppy is back sitting pretty next to Aria's little bookshop. I've never been so happy to see anything in my life. I'm indelibly attached to Poppy and I've missed her so. She's the key to my freedom, and also my privacy. I simply cannot wait to get into my own bed, and be alone. It's funny how you take your own space for granted until it's gone. This fishbowl way in which we live is so hectic, that I didn't realise how much I needed to close the curtains at night and be alone with my thoughts and the occasional creak and groan from Poppy.

'She's back!' Aria jumps from the step of her van and joins me. 'He left me the keys and the report on what work he carried out. He apologised for not staying to find you but he had to get back to work.'

'That's so sweet of him. I've never been so happy to see a vehicle in all my life.'

She smiles. 'That's not a vehicle, it's Poppy, rejuvenated after a makeover! Let's be honest we all need a little attention every now and then.'

'We sure do and doesn't she look all the better for it.' He'd given Poppy a scrub, she'd come back polished to a shine.

'So no Ollie?'

'Nope. No sign of him. I emailed him though and asked.'

She makes an 'O' with her mouth. 'Look at you, you're not the same girl I met a few months ago.'

I contemplate it. 'No, I'm not, I guess. And I want to love someone, I want to prove to myself I'm capable of loving and being loved, but so far, I'm not having any luck. Do you think I'm holding back too much? Or am I just not the lovable sort? Maybe I'm trying to rush?'

'Sweetie, you're completely lovable! But I think you're in two minds yourself, aren't you? One minute you're terrified of sharing a drink with Ollie, the next you're doubting his feelings, and you haven't even met him. It's not a matter of rushing, it's more a matter of truly knowing how you feel, and you won't know that, until you meet him in person. What if the chemistry is all wrong?'

'You're right. It's just I feel like I know him, or know his sort, and we're so alike, and that's never happened to me before. I'm usually the odd one in the group, you know? The person on the edge, trying to make sense of everyone else. And Ollie is the same. But what if he's taken one look at me and left?' The words are hollow though as I think of Max, who is unlike me in a lot of ways, but makes my heart race all the same.

She puts a hand to her chest. 'You know, Rosie, you always seem to think *you* have to change, you think you have to improve yourself, to be like everyone else, to fit in, but can't you see you're perfect just the way you are? If Ollie left without saying a word – and I highly doubt it – then that says more about him, than you.'

Are they just words of encouragement from one friend to

another or are they based on truth? For as long as I can remember my faults were always front and centre in my life, always well known, always a hindrance, and something I felt held me back. But the way Aria talks they make me special, just like Max said.

This whole journey I'd undertaken to learn how to assimilate, to blend in, find my feet socially. Whatever Aria's motivation, her sentiment makes me a little teary – what was happening to that composed, controlled chef from London?

She laughs. 'Just be *you*. And I bet Ollie got a flat tyre, or got held up, like we know happens all the damn time when you least want it to. There's no way he'd see you and run, no one would. Go chill out in Poppy and I'll start carting your stuff over.'

'Thanks, Aria. I'm all over the place because I just had a run-in with Max. Urgh. Honestly I don't quite know what's wrong with me lately. He paid for Poppy's repairs and I thought he had an ulterior motive so I stormed over there...' My words bubble and hiss out of me in one long rush.

'Slow down, Rosie. Tell me what exactly what happened.'

So I do. I go right back and tell her all about Mai and her predictions, about Max paying for Poppy, and Mellie sitting next to him as if he were the sun, the stars and the moon all rolled into one.

'Darling, you're overwhelmed. I get why you're hesitant about Max, but I still think why not see what happens? You don't have to commit to Ollie *or* him! I know you're a relationship girl, but sometimes you've got to kiss a few frogs first, you know?'

I consider it. 'No, Max probably is the heartbreaker everyone pegs him for and I don't want to tie myself up with someone who will leave when something better comes along. Been there, done that. Have the apron.' This provokes a smile. 'It does bother me, though, because I did develop feelings for him... but at the end of the day he's still a lovely guy and I'd like to be friends with him.'

'Oh, Rosie.' She hugs me tight. 'I can see why you're so confused.

213

The best remedy is keeping busy and it will sort itself out. Go see to Poppy and we can meet up later for proper chat?'

'Good plan!' It's life changing having someone to talk to, someone who truly listens and understands, particularly a girl as special as Aria who never makes me feel silly for needing to do things my own way.

I go to my van with my backpack and sort the clothes I need to wash. It's so strange how living inside such a small space seemed impossible at first and now it seems downright palatial. How much does a person really need? A few clothes for each season, books, cookware, kitchen accoutrements, a computer, maps and notepads, a medical kit, toiletries and that's about it.

I think back on my life of hastily-bought purchases, the must-have denim, impulse buys of make-up I've never worn, décor for the flat I couldn't really afford, and have since donated, expensive jewellery I could never wear while working, electronics that are now outmoded, so many things I've wasted my hard-earned money on thinking it would fill the gap, the void inside of me. And now I see with such life-altering clarity, that all those material things did the exact opposite of fulfilling me, they held me back, kept me in debt, kept me working to maintain a lifestyle that didn't satisfy me at all.

With so much less, I have so much more.

The real gift, as I'm coming to learn, is the people in your life, the friendships you nurture, the people you give your heart to. That can't be bought. The sudden realisation reminds me of Max, and how he paid for Poppy, with no strings attached.

It strikes me I have so much to learn about this messy crazy thing called life, but it's as though a light has been switched on, and I see with so much clarity that I've been chasing the wrong dreams.

I've been so caught up in what might happen, that I haven't thought about what might *not* happen – and that's seeing the world in all its glory, the hidden lakes, the magic trees, the rocky paths no one has wandered down for decades, hearing a birdsong symphony just for one, watching the majesty of sunrise and discerning each hue of orange without rushing to the next thing.

It's about appreciating this moment, this one right here…

Poor Max had tried to help me and I'd thrown it in his face because I'm so used to every favour coming at a price. Time to get my big girl boots on and apologise.

CHAPTER TWENTY-SIX

Night closes in and I walk under the cover of darkness to Max's van. Stars sparkle overhead, guiding the way. The atmosphere is subdued in the campground tonight, lots of nomads packed up early and left for other locations to beat the traffic.

As I approach I hear raucous laughter coming from the inside of Max's van. His deep baritone joins in. Are he and Mellie tangled together? I shouldn't intrude, should I? I'd hate to see them barely clothed, his broad shoulders bare, tribal tattoos snaking along his arms and over his chest…

I knock decisively. Hard. So hard my fist hurts. Time is of the essence, isn't it? I don't have all night to stand and listen to them canoodle, which I'm sure they are.

I hear a groan, and then some muffled talking and finally Max wrenches the door open, his face dark at the interruption, no doubt.

'I'm not disturbing you, am I? I ask. Hurt leaks out and I colour in mortification.

'Not at all, do you want to come in?'

Mellie peers over his shoulder, and I see she's wrapped in a blanket. 'Hiya.'

I can hardly form words to reply.

'Umm, hello there.' Cue the robot. I have to get away, but my feet are rooted to the spot.

Max frowns as if he can't work out why I'm there. 'Come on in. You know Mellie.'

'I *feel* like I'm intruding.'

'No,' she says tightly. 'You just caught us by surprise, that's all.' As she wriggles inside the throw I see she's just wearing the teeniest tiniest bralette underneath. Oh, dammit, they were canoodling. The thought makes my gut roil.

'Oh, you're half naked! Maybe I should go?'

Max grips my shoulders, like he's done so many times over the last few months when he's tried to comfort me. Does he grip her shoulders like that? 'Mellie wanted to show me her new tattoo,' he said.

Of all the tricks!

She bounces around as if she's a cheerleader or something. 'The *om* symbolises the source of life for the entire universe, but in reality the *om* is a vibration, a sound... profound, huh? We are all part of this great big cosmos.'

I frown. 'I don't get it.'

Her lips press together.

Max laughs. 'I don't either, but that's the beauty of tattoos, they're meaningful in their own unique ways.'

Mellie looks downright murderous.

'Perhaps you should put your jumper back on. Aren't you cold?'

Anger flashes in her eyes. 'I was just leaving, actually.' She snatches up her jumper, drops the blanket and slides it on. Who doesn't wear a T-shirt under their jumper in this weather?

'Bye!' I say.

She gives me the side eye as she leaves and slams the door behind her.

'She seems angry.'

Max laughs again and shakes his head. 'I wonder why?'

'Why?' I ask. 'Because I didn't understand the significance of her tattoo? So sue me!'

'My Rosie is a Pandora's box of surprises.'

My Rosie?

'Umm, yeah,' I manage.

'So what do I owe the pleasure of your company this time?'

'I wanted to thank you for paying for Poppy's repairs.'

'No need, you already did.'

'Yes, but I didn't mean it, this time I mean it.'

A line appears between his eyes. 'O-kaaay.'

I sit down on the little sofa. It smells like Max, that peppery, earthy fragrance of his. 'I thought you were angling for something untoward, and now I see my folly.'

'Your folly?'

'Yes, my folly.'

'Right.'

'So, thank you and like I said, I will pay you back as soon as I can.'

'I'm good,' he says. 'You just worry about getting on an even keel, first.'

'OK, I will. But without you, I truly don't know what I would have done, and I felt really stupid, really inadequate, and now I see that this is part of growing as a person, and dealing with one day at a time.'

He cocks his head. 'You're so different to everyone, Rosie.'

Here we go.

'I'm well aware of that, but shouldn't we celebrate our differences?'

The hands appear on my shoulders again, like he's trying to ground himself. 'What I mean, Rosie, is you're not like anyone I've met before. I find you downright fascinating and I love the way your mind works. It's your differences that make you special.'

'Is that some kind of line?' Foot in mouth disease returns with a vengeance.

218

He throws his head back and laughs, and I have an urge to trace a finger along his jaw and feel the reverberation of his laugh. Maybe that's the *om* we were talking about…? What would Max's vibration feel like? These long days are making me cuckoo!

The vibration!

The what!

'I'll have to work on my delivery, I guess. You bring out the soppy in me, Rosie. And I don't quite know why.'

He may have not met anyone like me before, I sure as hell as haven't met anyone quite like him! The muscle man vegan yogi who helps out people in a bind. What a contradiction he is!

'I might have got you all wrong,' I say more to myself.

He sits down and pats the sofa for me to join him and we fall into silence. Warmth radiates off him, my body sizzles being so close. I have this overwhelming desire to curl into him, to wrap my arms around his big, tough, frame, but Mai's warning comes racing back. I'd be a fool to pursue something when I've been told it will end up breaking my heart. Or am I a fool to believe a face-reading eccentric like her? But it's not just Mai who's warned me away, is it?

I jump up, and my hasty exit sends him sprawling sideways, surprise dashes across his features.

'I left a pot on the stove!' I say and leave before he can woo me into a false sense of security. As I run back to Poppy my heart races, and not only from exertion. The best course of action is to stay away from Max. It would be self-sabotage to try my luck with a man like him, no matter what my lonely heart feels.

When I get back to the van my laptop flashes with a new email. Ollie. A more reserved type, a better bet, if I truly am to risk falling in love again. Someone safe who *doesn't* set my world on fire…

I open the email.

Dearest Rosie,

I'm so sorry I missed you! I didn't get either of your messages until just now. I was out of range and couldn't email to let you know that I'd been approached by a local for a last-minute job and finances in mind, I had to accept. Their wedding photographer had come down with some god-awful lurgy and they were desperate to find a stand-in. I couldn't say no, imagining them without any photographs of their most special day...

I hope you'll forgive me. I've been so worried that you wasted a day waiting for a no-show. If you're still keen (and I hope you are!) I'd love to meet you wherever you are next? I have to edit those photographs before I move on but that will only take a day or two.

Please respond and put a fellow out of misery!

Ollie x

Pushing the thought of Max to the side is the best way forward. Ollie's the safer choice, and I know it.

Hi Ollie,

Please don't be sorry! I'm glad you didn't spend the day searching for a fuchsia pink van that wasn't here. And I completely understand about taking work when it's available, and by the sounds of it, you made a couple very happy indeed. A wedding isn't truly a wedding without photographs as precious keepsakes, is it?

And of course, I'd love to see you for a drink still. I'll be in Edinburgh for the next little while. There's a range of fairs and foodie markets to attend, and a lot of us are going to camp together for those.

And then we're off to the end of summer Lindisfarne Music Festival on the Northumberland Coast.

What a great schedule, eh? I can see why people fall in love with the idea of wandering. Who wouldn't want this life? The minor annoyances, are just that – minor. It makes me think of my previous life, and how stiffly I held on to it, as if by letting go I'd lose control, and here you can't be like that. It's not sink or swim, because if you do flounder someone will haul you out. It's been a bit of a revelation and something I'm still processing, I guess.

Look at me all deep and meaningful, all mystical! But it has been refreshing to lighten up, not hold so tight, if that makes sense, while remaining true to myself. I thought I had to change, to develop a new alter ego, but Aria told me I'm perfect as I am. Maybe I was just in the wrong environment before where I always felt inadequate, or like I wasn't enough.

Lots to think about at any rate! I'd love to grab that drink, but no pressure.

Rosie xx

While I pretend not to wait for a reply, I potter around Poppy. Dust. Sort. Stash my washing in a bag. Losing access to a washing machine is strangely one of the hardest parts of travelling as silly as it sounds. Finding laundromats is tricky sometimes and I've had to learn to adjust to the fact I might not be able to wash my clothes properly as often or as quickly as I'd like. Handwashing works to a degree but only if I'm in a pinch.

Finally, my emails pings.

Dear Rosie,

I'd love to visit you at Lindisfarne. That will give me enough time to edit these pics and do a little mechanical work on the van that desperately needs doing! Thank you for being so understanding about the photography job.

As you can imagine work is sporadic so I have to take what I can find, especially something as lucrative as a wedding, although I did it at bargain rates for the poor couple as they'd already paid the other guy, and weren't sure how the refund was going to go. Still, it all ended well and as you say, they have some beautiful snapshots to remember their day.

It sounds as though you've got the travelling bug, Rosie! Welcome to the club! I'm glad to hear it, because it can go both ways depending on the person and what they're searching for... and we're all searching for something, even if we don't admit it. Do you remember your first lot of emails to me? Full of uncertainty, of fear? How far your mindset has changed already! It's like a drug this way of living, and the more time you spend seeking those answers, the more certain you'll be that there is no better lifestyle, no matter what wobbles you encounter along the way.

I remember too being surprised how inclusive everyone was. Coming from a finance background (yes, cue the sad music: was once a number cruncher, go figure!) where it was every man and woman for themselves – that race up the corporate ladder, the desire to get the bonus, the promotion, ready to hip and shoulder anyone in my path – the travelling community was a nice surprise. I'd have thought with everyone selling this and that, there'd be a layer of competitiveness under the surface, but there just isn't. It's almost as though they figure if they miss a sale one day, they'll get one the next and what will be will be. At first I put it all down to this sort of lackadaisical nature as if they were living in dreamland, but then I realised it was much deeper than that. And I'd judged them unfairly, these people who'd invited me around their camp fires and shared their wine, like I was a long-lost cousin.

It's a learning curve, this thing called life.

See you soon.

Ollie x

Finally, I'll meet the man behind the words. The *right* sort of man. A trustworthy man, and see if there's any chemistry between us. I want to be in love, I want to share those momentous sunsets hand in hand with a guy. Re-plan when my future children will arrive. Am I naïve hoping it's Ollie? Or worse, acting desperate?

The weekend catches up with me and I yawn so long my jaw clicks. I tumble into bed in Poppy sure I've never felt a mattress as comfortable *and* comforting in my entire life.

CHAPTER TWENTY-SEVEN

'Your smile looks like it could swallow you whole,' Aria says, wandering over, chipped coffee mug in hand, still wearing her PJs.

'Oh?' I say, only half listening. I'd been thinking of Max, but I don't want her to latch on to that, I don't want to think of him any more than I already do.

'And why is that?' She tilts her head, and waves her hands in the air, splashing coffee all over the place.

'Ollie is going to meet me at the Lindisfarne Festival in a few weeks.'

'So where was he?'

'Held up with work.'

'Hmm.'

'What's the hmm supposed to mean.'

'What about Max?'

'What about him?'

Frowning she says, 'I heard Mellie is not too happy with you, after your little performance.'

'*My* performance? She was the one performing, she had her little act all rehearsed. "Oh, let's compare tattoos, Max, but I'll have to get naked to show you mine." Insert airy, flirtatious giggle. It was sickening. And *so* obvious.'

Aria narrows her eyes. 'Why do you care? I thought you'd decided not to risk anything with Max?'

I swallow hard. 'I know, I'm so confused. But out of the two men Ollie is clearly the safer bet. Yeah, so he's not disarming like Max, but he's more likely to be around in ten years, right?'

'How can you know that?'

I shake my head. 'Virtually everyone has warned me away from him, including Mai.'

Her face softens. 'Aww you really do like Max, don't you?'

I turn away.

'I enjoyed teasing him about you because I didn't think you cared, but do you do. You do care! What's stopping you following your heart? I just don't get it.'

I cross my arms. 'Trust. I don't want to get hurt again, Aria.'

'And you feel like you can trust a guy you've *never* met over Max?'

I throw my hands into the air. 'Wouldn't you?'

CHAPTER TWENTY-EIGHT

My whole body vibrates as the music festival goes up a notch every hour or so. The gnarly whine of an electric guitar makes my brain shake. Silly me had presumed it'd be some cruisy folk music festival, peace, love and all that stuff, and instead there's some incessant screaming, some downright butchering of words that makes the singer sounds as though he's in the death throes. Still, the acts have been mixed and I hope soon some cruisy folk band will replace the current singer, who I imagine will need a big glass of water to calm his throat.

'Here's your apple crumble with an extra serve of cream.'

The customer in front of me yells back, 'I didn't order apple crumble, I said I can't hear you when you mumble!'

I can't hear a bloody thing and I've got critics as customers now? There's a lot to be said for remaining anonymous in a commercial kitchen! I paste on smile but I can tell by the steeliness of her gaze that it's more a grimace. 'What. Can. I. Get. For. You?' I enunciate slowly and loudly so she can hear me.

'Apple crumble,' she says with a sly grin. 'No cream, watching my waistline.' She pats her non-existent hips and it's all I can do not to scream.

'Sure, coming right up!' I slice another piece of apple crumble, one not marred by a whole serve of hand-whipped Chantilly cream. 'Anything else?'

'Be humble.'

Did she say be humble? 'What?'

'JUST THE CRUMBLE!'

I pass the plate over and take her money, hoping the musicians take a break soon. I can't hear myself think, let alone what the patrons are trying to order.

A drumming solo begins and my head threatens to explode.

'Need a hand?' Max saunters over, shirtless, drawing the admiring gazes of *every single person who ever lived*. Isn't he cold?

'No!' Just what I need, a shirtless, heroic, steaming hot Max bumping me hip to hip as he helps, just as Ollie arrives. 'And I think it's against some sort of health code to be half naked in the kitchen, just speaking out loud here.'

He laughs, and his eyes crinkle up.

'Let me help, you've got a queue a mile long.'

'You'd deign to sell sugary food?'

'As long as I don't have to eat it.'

The queue grows longer still and my impatience rolls off the waiting crowd, I can tell by their frosty-eyed glares and their hands-on-hips belligerence. When will this day end?

Max jumps into Poppy, and I almost *boing* upwards at the shift in weight.

'What can I get you?' he asks a girl wearing black lipstick.

'Depends what you're selling?' she purrs. I mean, really! My hackles rise.

'How about a piece of chocolate mud cake that you can get down and dirty with?'

He just can't help himself, can he?

'In that case I'll take two.'

I serve beside him, cranking out orders as quick as my hands can fly.

When we get a two-minute lull, I ask, 'Why aren't you working in your van?'

He feigns nonchalance. 'Sold out, already. In record time too.'

'Don't you get tired of being adored?'

'It's my charisma.'

'You're teasing me.'

'You make it so easy.'

'Thanks for your help, oh humble one, but I think I'm OK now.'

'You don't look it.' He presses a finger to my brow, and slowly draws it across. 'Headache, I can tell by the way you're squinting.'

His touch sends a bolt through me, probably because it takes me by surprise. 'You need a break. Want me to keep serving and you go lie down in the dark for a while?'

'Gosh, that sounds amazing but I'm waiting on Ollie…'

His eyes flash. 'That guy from the forum? Wasn't he supposed to turn up a few weeks ago?'

'He didn't get my message in time. No Wi-Fi. But we've become really good… friends.'

'A *friend* you've met over the internet.' Sarcasm leaches from every word.

'It's the way the world works these days, Max.' I hate the way he cheapens it, as though what Ollie and I have is lesser just because we met online. Is he jealous?

He shakes his head. 'Well, you're all caught up now,' he says and lopes off. What is up with him? Guys like Max hate when someone else is in the spotlight; they want everyone to admire them, to fawn over them. Well, I'm not that girl.

Max is right about one thing. I have a screaming headache and if I get another rude customer I think I'll curl into a ball and weep, so I pull the serving awning closed, and decide to break for a while. Like Max, I've almost sold out. The difference is, I plan to replenish my stock so I can squirrel more money away

228

for what I owe him, and hopefully have some left for my own expenses going forward.

I leave a note tacked to the awning for Ollie saying to call me if he arrives, and I go inside and throw myself into bed. A power nap will be just the ticket and a cure for the throbbing in my brain. Before I shut my eyes I check my emails and there's one from the man himself, Ollie.

Dear Rosie,

I've just stopped off for some lunch and to fill up my fridge with some staples, then I'll refuel and head over to the music festival. If all goes according to plan I should be there before nightfall.

Maybe we can swap our tea for a glass of wine?

Ollie x

He's on his way! I close the curtains, set my alarm for an hour from now, sling on an eye mask, and fall against the pillow, into a restless sleep.

***

A few hours later, the crowd gets thicker as more campers arrive. The pop-up food vans are quiet in the lull between lunch and dinner, and it gives me time to prepare food for boozy stomachs. Beef and Guinness pies, pork and fennel sausage rolls with home-made tomato chutney. Hotdogs layered with onions, bacon, American cheddar, and all the accoutrements! Quick and easy comfort food for the attendees who'd probably been waiting weeks for the experience. Sleep has done me the world of good, and cooking without the added pressure of serving at the same time has calmed me.

As evening approaches, I dash to Aria's van to check how she's going. She's smiling away chatting to some guy about rom-coms of all the things. He's a studious, spectacle-wearing, beige chinos type of guy, who is sweet looking in a bumbling sort of way.

They don't notice me, and I gauge he's been here for quite some time, by the coffee mugs strewn around where they sit. Aria cannot use the same cup twice when she's making coffee for her customers, it's like she gets bamboozled, and starts over with a fresh mug, chipped as they all are.

The man fumbles and blushes when Aria discusses her favourite kissing scene in a book she's just read. My inner matchmaker (who knew I had one of those!) senses an opportunity. While Aria has sworn off love, that doesn't mean she has to spend every night alone in the arms of dashing *fictional* hero. She can socialise, can't she?

'Sorry to interrupt,' I say as if I'm extremely busy, and fraught. 'It's just I've had second thoughts about meeting Ollie on my own, he could be anyone after all, will you come and have a drink say at 9 p.m.? I'll close up shop just before then.'

She shoots me an understanding look. 'Sure, Rosie, of course, and then I can make myself scarce once you're settled in and talking ten to the dozen.'

I beam. 'Thank you. But it will seem odd if it's just you, it'll be too obvious that I'm nervous, so bring your friend.' I turn to him, 'Sorry, I didn't catch your name?'

Colour races from his neck upwards. 'Jonathan.'

'Great Jonathan, see you at nine, eh? You're really helping me out of a spot of bother! Must dash, cakes in the oven!'

I spin on my heel but not before I catch the wide-eyed look of shock on Aria's face. She is going to kill me! What have I done? It's only a drink, right? Hasn't she been harping on at me like that? I supress nervous laughter, and head back to the safety of Poppy and the rowdy festival-goers.

***

As nine o'clock creeps closer, I'm almost dead on my feet, not just from working a long day, but all the edgy tension that's gone with it. I tidy the kitchen, wipe down the table and fluff the cushions on the bench seats. Will four people even fit around Poppy's tiny dining room table? I unpack my 'office' – the chair that holds all of my paperwork – and put that at the head of the table so at least one person won't be squished alongside another, that person being me. I don't want to be pressed up against Ollie, not yet, not until I've decided it there's anything there, if it's worth pursuing.

There's a light tap at the door, and Aria steps inside and glowers at me. I pretend I don't notice and envelop her in a hug. 'Hello, lovely! Welcome, welcome. Come on in Jonathan, make yourself comfortable. Oh, not there,' I say as he goes for the safe seat. 'On the other side, yes, perfect.'

'I'll grab the wine, won't be a sec.' Instead I pick up my phone and check if there's any contact from Ollie. Nothing, as I'd expect. He's probably trying to find me amidst all the vans, tents, and festival-goers and screeching music. Really, I should have given him some direction as to where to find me.

Plonking down the phone I grab a bottle of red and some glasses.

'So, Jonathan, you're a music festival fan then?'

He lets out a jumpy laugh, more like a cough. 'No, actually, not at all. A friend had a spare ticket so I tagged along… and then he stumbled across his ex-girlfriend, and I thought I'd escape the fireworks between them, seems there's a lot of unfinished business between the pair.'

I laugh but it must be too loud, too maniacal because Aria narrows her eyes. Where is Ollie? Aria has her arms folded tight across her chest and hasn't even picked up her wine glass – very rare indeed. I might have pushed her too far…

Finally there's a knock on the door. Ollie! As anxious as I am about meeting him at least he will defuse the tension in the room.

We've talked so much this last week, it almost feels like I'm meeting an old friend. Maybe I'm finally learning how to adult.

Flushed with the thought, I open the van door. 'Welcome! Come in, oh – Max.'

'You look disappointed.'

'I was expecting someone else.'

'Your internet person?'

I huff. 'His name is Ollie.'

'You *think* his name is Ollie.'

'What is that supposed to mean?'

Aria, still obviously dark about my little set-up for her, creeps up behind me, all sweetness and light, but I can practically feel revenge radiating from her. 'Max!' she says in a sugary voice. 'Please do come on in! I'm sure we've got some preservative-free wine here!'

It's my turn to glower at her, but I can't exactly argue, can I?

'Love to,' he says, smirking at me as he waits for me to move, which I reluctantly do, knowing he'll just barrel me over otherwise.

'We don't have preservative-free wine, how ridiculous is that!' I say, and push Aria sideways as she tries to steal the safe stool.

'It's not at all!' Aria says. 'I've been reading up on the merits of such a thing, and it's fascinating, actually.'

I frown at her. Suddenly she's a fan of Max? Unlikely.

Max slides into the booth, managing to shake the table and the glass cloche full of cake. Golly, I wonder if he'll be pinioned there for the duration.

'I'm Max,' he says and shakes Jonathan's hand.

'Jonathan, nice to meet you.'

'So where is the mystery man, then?'

I roll my eyes. 'What's it to you, Max?'

'You seem very taken with a man you've never met, that's all. It's strikes me as dangerous.'

'Not this again.'

'Just watching out for you.'

'Thanks, I'll let you know if I need any protection,' I say, and then blush to the roots of my hair when I see they've misinterpreted what I've said. I hastily add, 'Not protection as in…' *Kill me.* '… You know, protection as in you, erm, standing guard like some obnoxious overbearing…'

Aria butts in. 'He's only got your best interests at heart, darling. Really, you should be thankful you have a man like Max onside.' She beams prettily up at him. What is this? Poor Jonathan stares at his wine glass as if it's the most fascinating object he's ever seen.

'Well, I'm an adult, thank you, and I'm fairly sure I can look after myself. Ah, speaking of which…' I dash to my bedside table and take a roll of pounds I've bound with a rubber band. It's not quite what I owe but it's a start. 'Here's part of what I owe you.'

'You sure?' he says, and the hostility ebbs away.

I nod. 'I'm good.'

He pockets the money without counting it.

We fall into chatter, the earlier mood morphing into a more relaxed vibe, and I pour more wine, laced with preservatives, which Max drinks happily enough. When the bottle is empty, I go to replenish it, surreptitiously checking my phone and find a message from Ollie.

Rosie,
  Family emergency – can't make it to you. Be in touch when
I can.
  Sorry.
  O x

My heart sinks. Is Max right? Is Ollie leading me on?

I go back to the trio sitting around the little table in Poppy. Jonathan is telling a lame joke that has Aria clutching her belly and Max grinning like a madman. I paste on a smile and try to join in, but I don't quite manage to focus long enough to hear them. They don't seem to notice, so I let my mind drift. Am I crazy for hoping a man on the internet could be the next great love of my life? At this moment it certainly seems so. Max asks where the mystery man is but I pretend not to hear and change the subject.

As midnight comes and goes, Aria says her goodbye and Jonathan promises to escort her safely back to her van which is sweet since it's all of two metres away.

That leaves me and Max staring at each other over the table.

'So…?' he says.

'Then there were two.'

'Sorry if I came across as gruff. I worry about you, that's all.'

'Why though, Max?'

Do I detect a faint blush in his cheeks?

'Because you're… my friend.'

'Well, I'm a big girl, Max and I can look after myself.'

'Be that as it may, I can't wait to meet this Ollie character.'

'Why is that?' I have this sudden vision of Max shaking him by the collar demanding to know every last detail about the guy. Max would frighten the life out of the toughest of men if he wanted to.

'I don't like the sound of him, that's all.'

I scoff. 'You don't know a thing about him!'

'That's what I'm worried about.'

I rub my face with my hands. 'I'm tired, Max. I think I'll call it a night.'

'I'm only across the way if you need me.' He's dead serious, as if Ollie will arrive in the middle of the night wielding an axe or something.

'You're starting to sound like me, Max. Thinking there's a serial killer at every turn.'

'When it comes to you, I'm not taking the chance.'

'That's very noble of you, really. But I'm fine and when Ollie arrives I'd rather you didn't scare him off.'

He shakes his head and leaves. Why doesn't he say what he really means?

CHAPTER TWENTY-NINE

The next day Aria comes over before the sun is up with two coffee mugs in hand and hands me one.

I grab two throw rugs and we sit at one of the tables outside and cocoon ourselves in the fabric, curling our hands around the steaming cups of coffee. The early mornings are chilly and my favourite part of the day, watching the inky sky swirl into hues of magenta, amber and orange as the sun rises and fights the grey.

Sheepishly I say, 'Sorry about trying to play matchmaker.'

She half grins. 'It's OK, but I don't exactly want to be matched,' she says and takes a sip. 'It's far too soon for me.'

A tiny thrill runs through me at the realisation she's gone from saying never to maybe someday. That sounds like progress to me but I don't mention it. 'Jonathan seemed so lovely though – he could be a great friend?'

She clucks her tongue. 'Too complicated. He tried to kiss me goodnight, only a chaste peck on the cheek, but it felt like too much, you know? Besides, he's a city dweller, so even friendship is unlikely. He was sweet though, a word nerd and all.'

A downside to being a Van Lifer is saying goodbye to people like Jonathan, people you have a connection with but probably won't see again. These days there's so many ways to communicate, but would you pursue every person you meet? No, and after a while the light dims as that person is slowly forgotten, the connection broken as new people take their place.

Maybe in some respects we are limiting ourselves with this travel caper. Perhaps, though, if it's meant to be with Jonathan, it will be when the time is right. We have to believe that true love always finds a way, right?

'What happened with Ollie? You might have fooled the guys last night, but you didn't fool me with your hangdog eyes.'

I run a hand through my hair and exhale. 'He was on his way, had stopped to grab lunch and refuel and then next minute there's a family emergency and he's not coming.' I explain how brief his message was.

'So what do you think?'

I shrug. 'I believe him, no one would lie about such a thing, and even though we haven't met face to face, I know him, know what sort of man he is. But I'm disappointed he didn't arrive. And I hope whatever the emergency is, it's nothing too serious.'

'Yes, I hope it's only minor. Where do his family live?'

'I have no idea.'

'Did you reply so he knows you're not mad?'

'No, I should, shouldn't I? And it wasn't a case of being mad, it was giving him space. Last thing you want in a crisis is someone constantly messaging you.'

'Still, it would be worse if he checked and there was nothing from you.'

'Yes, you're right.'

I take my phone from my pocket, and reply.

Dear Ollie,
   So sorry to hear this. Hope it's not too serious. We'll meet eventually, but until then take care.
   Rosie x

237

A week passes and there's no word from Ollie. I begin to worry. Should I be offering my support as a friend? Reaching out in case he's in a dark place? I don't want to intrude, but maybe he needs a shoulder and what if there's no one offering? I'm torn over whether to contact him or not.

The season is wrapping up as the full force of winter hits, and nomads are off to other exotic climes. Nola and Spencer are Barcelona-bound, Mai is off to Portugal, and Aria and I have been discussing the possibility of a long road trip snaking from France to Italy, and Spain.

It seems such an audacious plan, the potential for catastrophe so great, but she urges me to consider it, and I do. I really do. In my home country though, I feel so safe. If anything happened I could pick up the phone and speak in my native tongue, I could go to hospital if I were sick, call the police, an ambulance, a tow truck. But I know I'd adapt elsewhere too – I have here, haven't I?

We park down a side street, ready for the parade, to be followed up by the Alnwick Food Festival. There are a few familiar faces but I don't see Max's van anywhere. He left before us but as far as I know he was following the same route as we were.

My phone buzzes as I jump from Poppy. Aria looks over so I point to my phone, she nods and gestures to a group of people she wants to say hello to, so we go our separate ways.

'Hello?'

'Rosie?' asks a slightly tinny voice.

'Speaking.'

'It's Ollie.'

My breath leaves me in a whoosh. 'Ollie, hi!'

We've never spoken despite exchanging numbers, and I am lost for words, unsure on how to act, what to say.

'Is this a good time?' His voice sounds so far away, like he's in a tunnel.

'Yes, yes. How's things with you? I didn't want to intrude.'

There's a weighted pause, and I sense I'm going to regret doubting him before he continues: 'Well, the thing is—', there's a muffled sound as though he's covering the phone as he tries to what… compose himself? '—the thing is…' I can hear pain in every syllable. 'My mum passed away. I didn't get there on time. It was her heart.'

I cover my face with my free hand. 'Oh, Ollie, I'm so very sorry.' I scramble for the right words, but all that springs to mind are platitudes. 'Really, really sorry.' *Just stop.* Her heart, just like it was for my dad.

'Thank you, Rosie.'

There's another aching silence and I wrack my brain to think of something supportive to say. 'I'm terribly sorry.' Words just won't come.

'I appreciate that. I'm still hoping we'll have that drink.' His voice drops, and I strain to make out what he's saying. 'The funeral was yesterday.' His voice breaks and I wish I was there to give him a great big hug. 'It was so moving, such a tribute to the wonderful woman she was. Leading up to the funeral there was so much to organise, people to call, arrangements to be made, you sort of run on autopilot. You know people say the funeral is goodbye, closure, life come full circle, but it doesn't feel like that Rosie, it feels unbelievable that she's gone. Now the guests have left, and friends and family have flown or driven home and I'm here by myself, completely heartbroken. I don't think it's really sunk in until now and I don't quite know what to do with myself.'

The street becomes a riot of noise as more vans pull up so I head back into the quiet of Poppy. 'Ollie, I know exactly how you feel, and I know that probably doesn't mean much right now, but I do empathise, and I can only tell you it will get better, but it takes time. The absolute best thing you can do is keep yourself busy, it doesn't cure the pain in your heart or your soul, but it helps you get through each day.'

When Dad died my pain had been so great, I wondered if I'd ever get over it. The guilt woke me up at all hours of the night as if I deserved the punishment. And clearing out his little cottage took me *months*. I'd needed six skip bins just for the rubbish, before I could sort any of his belongings out. It had been such a lonely devastating time.

'I guess that's what I'll do then,' he said, resigned. 'I'll have to sort out Mum's affairs, decide what to do with her cottage, her things…'

For me there'd been a real need to get Dad's place cleaned and sold; I didn't want to stay in my village any longer than necessary. The locals had come to me with pitying eyes and empty condolences but none of them were there when he'd truly needed a friend, when I needed friends. The same people who wandered over with casseroles were the ones who let their children mock me at school and make my life hell, and it had been impossible to push that to the side even all those years later. It wasn't so much holding a grudge, it was that same hurt rising up and clouding my mind. That and my own demons about Dad, my own part in his sorry story.

'Take your time with it, Ollie. When you go through her things it will bring back so many memories…' I'd found old photographs buried under dusty boxes, me with no front teeth sitting on Mum's lap laughing uproariously about who knows what, dad standing off to the side, giving me that look parents do, one steeped in pride. Another of Mum and Dad on the beach at Cornwall, Mum's white-blonde hair so similar to mine, Dad clasping her hand, and staring out to sea. They'd been so in love once, so devoted, I still don't know where it all went wrong.

'I will, I will. I spent a few hours this morning going through her desk. I found a stack of old diaries which hurt so badly to read. It had all her hopes and dreams for me, my achievements, the worry I caused her, the teenage lies she caught me out on, ones I thought I'd gotten away with…' He lets out a hollow laugh.

We are so similar, Ollie and I. I grew up without a mum and he grew up without his dad, and then we'd both lost our remaining parent, our one tenuous link to this world. When my dad died I remember thinking that if anything serious ever happened to me, there wasn't one person in the world who'd really care. Not one person would mourn me. And that's when I set about finding love, and Callum had wandered into my path.

'Precious mementos, even with her catching you out on your white lies! I would have loved to know the inner workings of my own dad's mind. Imagine that. What a gift she left you, Ollie. Something tangible you can always turn to when you're feeling blue.'

'You're right, Rosie. When I read her words, I "hear" her voice, it's almost as if she's reading to me.'

'Will you keep her cottage?' Part of me asked for selfish reasons. Would this loss stop him from travelling, would he resume a normal life, live in his mum's place and go back to nine-to-five?

'For the foreseeable future. I can't imagine ever selling it, another family living here, but maybe things will change.'

'Yes, best not to make any rash decisions.'

'It would be so easy to move right back in but I think that'd be taking a step backwards, you know? Mum wrote that she loved hearing about my adventures, thought it was commendable to go against the grain, live life on my terms, so I'll definitely continue my travels, probably with a renewed sense of purpose.'

'She sounds like she was a really lovely lady.'

He chokes up. 'She was. The best.'

'Oh, Ollie. Please do reach out if you ever need to chat, I really mean it. I don't care if it's ten past midnight…'

'Thanks, Rosie, for everything.'

We say our goodbyes, and I hang up, my mind a flutter of emotions. I worry about Ollie, his grief, the sudden loneliness when he's lost his one surviving parent, his anchor to this world.

The street comes alive. People are getting ready for the morning parade, there's children running around their high-pitched giggles punctuating the air. The street party is a celebration of multiculturalism: native songs, food, national dress, I can't wait to set up with a bird's-eye view of the parade. Already the atmosphere has a joyful quality to it, but a small part of me feels guilty being excited about the day, when Ollie is sitting elsewhere head in hands, grieving.

Aria runs over, her cheeks rosy red from exertion. She's got quite the bloom about her and looks almost ethereal in the soft light. 'We've got clearance to move our vans to the roadside, just before the corner!' she says animatedly. 'We'll be able to watch the parade, and we'll have a good position for the rest of the street party.'

'I'll follow you.'

Once we're parked side by side, I carry a few tables and chairs out front and set them up. We can only fit a handful because crowds are expected to be three of four deep down the length of the street, but at least we'll have a few handy if someone needs to rest their legs.

When we're all set up, I fling on my apron and get baking. Today I'm highlighting the same comfort foods from the past that I love baking so much. Scotch eggs, beef and ale pies, Cornish pasties, bread and butter pudding, simple rib sticker foods that are easy to make, wholesome and a nod to our ancestors.

Soon more vans pull up alongside us and before long the most delectable scents waft out, making my mouth water. I detect, cumin, cinnamon, cayenne from the Indian street food vendor next door – chicken tikka masala skewers, maybe? Onion bhajis being fried! On Aria's left is a Greek pop-up, and they're laughing and singing as they prepare. Across the street is red and white Napoli pizza van with what looks like a husband-and-wife team throwing pizza dough into the air, stretching the bases. I sense a full belly in my future, and hope I have time to duck out and sample all the tasty morsels on offer.

For the next couple of hours I get my bake on, all thought disappears and I do what I love best. Aria steps into the van, hands full of beautifully written cards for the tea blends.

'Oh, thank you!'

'My pleasure! I'll get the tea bagged up while you finish there.'

'I'm done so I'll make us some tea and we can do that together.' With a pot of *The Great Gatsby* tea brewing, I sit next to Aria and help string the labels on.

'So who was on the phone. Your face went white for a moment there and I was worried it was something serious.'

I sigh, remembering the call. 'It was Ollie.' I fill her in on the sad story and watch as the light slowly leaches from her eyes.

'Oh, that poor man. And to think he was so close but didn't quite get there in time to say goodbye.'

'Isn't it tragic? And I feel *so* bad having doubted him. I get this real sense we were meant to meet, though, you know? We're so similar, and we've both lost our folks, and it feels like I can be a real comfort to him as time goes on… Or am I crazy thinking that way?'

She tilts her head. 'You two are eerily similar. And sometimes the universe puts someone right in our path when we most need them, and it sounds to me like he could really use a friend like you, right now.'

I nod, sipping my tea, missing my dad suddenly. Wishing as always that things were different.

Aria senses my mood shift, and gives my arm a pat. 'Come on, lovie. We've got work to do, eh? When we stop for a break, you can send Ollie a message and tell him you're thinking of him, yeah?'

'Yeah, good plan.'

Slowly people begin to wander up and down the street to find a position for the parade. Soon all we see is the tops of heads as the crowd thickens, the sound of laughter, music, and the scent of onion bhajis filling the air. It's impossible not to smile; a real sense of joy hovers unseen and before long I'm singing Greek songs I don't know the words to and smiling so hard my face aches for hours afterwards.

If this is real life, then I never want it to end. It occurs to me I haven't thought about Callum in aeons, and even though he pops into my mind now, it doesn't hurt quite so much. It's more just a dull ache, the memory of a different time of my life that didn't work out.

Later we're in the little bookshop, feet up, glass of wine in hand, reminiscing about the day. How much fun it'd been, how much food we'd eaten, from samosas, to stuffed vine leaves, arancini balls, rice paper rolls, and all topped off with my very own knickerbocker glories.

'I don't think I'll be able to move from here,' I say.

'Me either.'

'It seemed like a good idea at the time.'

'Why do you never feel full, and then bang, too full? It's seems unfair there's no warning.'

I laugh. Aria with her tiny frame, and voracious appetite, the girl must have had the world's fastest metabolism, or hollow legs and I'd hate her for it, if I didn't love her so much. I just had to think about food and *click*, another centimetre on my hips.

Food is such a celebration, a way to express your love that my figure doesn't ever enter the equation. So I'm curvy, who cares? A lot of love went into these hips of mine.

A knock at the door startles us and we both jump in fright. Wine sloshes up and out of my glass, running down the side of my wrist.

'Don't answer it!' I hiss.

'Why?' Aria laughs.

244

'Because it's almost ten o'clock and we're down some lonely laneway in the back of nowhere! It could be anyone! A serial...'

'Yeah, yeah, let's just see who it is and if it's a serial killer I'll take him down with a bundle of vintage Mills and Boon books to the head, and you hog tie him with your scarf!'

'What? I'm not *wearing* a scarf!' Before I can debate the method of a bundle of vintage Mills and Boon books actually having enough force to take him down the knock becomes more insistent.

'Girls?'

I almost flop with relief at the sound of Max's voice. There's no way a bundle of books would ever knock him out, but thankfully he's not a threat so we don't have to test it out. He'd texted me earlier to ask where we were, but he's missed the parade so why is he here now?

Aria opens the door to Max's thunderous face. 'What's wrong?' she asks.

He steps into the van bringing the cool night air with him.

'It's your friend, Rosie. It's Ollie.'

'What about him? Is he OK?' Max doesn't know Ollie, does he?

I've never seen Max so angry, his eyes are dark with fury. 'Have you met him yet?'

'No,' I say trying to keep defensiveness from my voice. 'What's it to you?'

Max goes to speak and then hesitates.

'Well?' I say. 'This is just crazy, Max. You can't come stomping in here...'

'Ollie isn't who he says he is.' Max's face colours as if he's embarrassed.

'What?' I eventually manage.

'He's not who he says he is. I checked him out Rosie. If he's a photographer, why aren't there any contact details on his website? No phone number, no email, no contact form? How does he get work then? And those photos of his, if you do a

245

reverse search on Google, you'll see they're stolen, they're not his photographs. His profile picture is not him, it's been stolen from someone else too.'

It's like the air has been sucked from the room. We stand, wide-eyed and silent.

'No!' I say, and feel the blood drain from my face.

Max slumps, as if sharing the secret has exhausted him. 'I'm so sorry, Rosie. You're the victim of a catfish.'

'A catfish?'

Aria quietly explains what the term means. *Someone who poses as another person online.*

'Max, you're wrong! You're so wrong about this. There must be some explanation for the photographs, and his business. The profile picture…' My words peter off as I recall our conversation earlier that day. There's just no way he lied about that, you couldn't fake that emotion. 'His mother died quite suddenly and he's going through a horrendous time. Maybe that's why there's no contact details on his website, he doesn't want to be bothered right now.' I know Ollie, I know what we've talked about is real, Max is grasping at straws, why I don't know.

'His mother did die, but years ago, Rosie. The man posing as Ollie isn't your age, he's much, *much* older.'

I swallow panic, remembering the tinniness of Ollie's voice on the phone, how it sounded as though he was in a tunnel. Was he trying to disguise the way he sounded? No, he would never do that.

'You know who he is then?' Aria asks Max, her face pale.

Max nods. I can't bear to hear any more, I push quickly past Max and run back to the safety of Poppy. It cannot be true! It can't be.

Tears sting my eyes as I lock the door, ignoring Aria's plaintive voice to come back and look into it together. If it's true and I'm the world's biggest fool I don't need an audience to witness my shame.

The break in my heart, the one that's just healed over, twinges. I should never have left London, I should never have pushed myself to be an extrovert, to make friends, worse – to try and find love.

I snatch up my phone and text Ollie on the number he called me on.

Do you fancy a visitor?

I'll know, won't I, by how he responds. But I wait an age, and get nothing. He could be asleep, he is grieving, after all. He could be panicking. He could be watching me.

How did Max suspect such a thing? How did he find out for sure?

Ollie's explanations for his absence were legitimate, they seemed believable, all sorts happens on the road, it's unpredictable at the best of times.

I think of all our similarities. He couldn't have known me, he couldn't have known what I liked and made himself the same, could he? And then I remember making friends with him on Facebook. We like the same music. The same books. Food. Locations. I open my account and check what I've written in the Interests tab, and see with a heavy heart that once upon a time, I filled out my interests, and it's all right there for anyone to see. That and a quick Google search of my full name, which he had after I friended him, and he'd have enough information to make me think we were so alike, treading the same path.

But why? Why would someone do something so evil, so hurtful? What did he hope to achieve? Surely I'd have become suspicious when he kept cancelling on me. A shiver runs through me, I trusted a complete stranger and he could be anyone. How could I be so utterly stupid? Had I been *that* desperate for affection?

Fully clothed, I fall into bed, and pull a pillow over my face. I hope I'll wake up and this is all a horrible dream. That Ollie is in fact that trusty-eyed, boy next door and not a figment of some lunatic's imagination. I'm probably in danger, he's probably a criminal, but I'm too heartsore to care. I fall into a turbulent sleep.

CHAPTER THIRTY

The next day, I'm up early, showered and dressed before I check my phone. There's a message from Ollie. Or whoever he is.

Hey Rosie, I'd love to see you.

My heart lifts.

But not while I'm like this. First impressions and all that. I'm sure you understand. O x

I think of Mai's prediction and realise with a sinking gut that she was referring to Ollie, not to Max!

Something in me hardens and a new sense of determination fills me. I go to Aria.

'Rosie! How are you feeling?'

I push past her. 'We need to find him ourselves. I need to confront him.'

'So you think Max is right? Ollie is a catfish?' her face pinches.

'That is the most ridiculous term I've ever heard, but yes, all signs lead me to believe that well might be the case, and if so I want to know why, I want to make him face up to what he's done, and I just hope he isn't a black belt in Brazilian Jujitsu or anything.'

'OK, so where do we begin?'

'Well, let's see if his mum has an obituary. That it will give us a location. Maybe he is at her place? Where else can we start?'

'We could ask Max? From what he said last night, I'm fairly sure he knows exactly who Ollie is.'

'No, no, I don't want Max involved. I don't want anything to do with him.'

She touches my arm. 'Max is not the bad guy here.'

'He couldn't wait to tell me I'd been catfished, could he? Couldn't wait to see my embarrassment.'

Her pretty face falls. 'It wasn't like that at all, Rosie. He was concerned, he really cares about you.'

I brush the words aside. 'Let's just do it ourselves.'

She nods and grabs her laptop. 'What did he say his last name was?'

'Hartman.' But it dawns on me. 'He wouldn't have used his real name would he? And didn't Max say his mum died a long time ago? There probably is no obituary. We're looking for a needle in a haystack here.'

'Unless Ollie is real? There might be one, it's worth a shot?' With a shrug she types it into the search engine. Nothing comes up. 'No death notice or obituary in the last six months with that name. Right, so Ollie rang you yesterday, right?' she asks.

'Or whoever he is, yeah.'

'What's the number? Let's do a reverse search on it.'

'Can you do that?'

'Technology is a wonderful thing, well, sometimes...' She blushes. Technology got me into this mess, after all, but I can't focus on that now.

I read her the number and she searches for listings. 'It's a long shot,' she says. 'It could be private... but nope, here he is.' She turns the computer to me.

'M. Miller. 42 Swanbourne Way, Durham.'

I gasp. 'Oh holy moly, that's not far from here.'

Aria's eyes are as wide as saucers. 'Do we need weapons?'

The serious look on her face suddenly strikes me as funny and I burst into laughter which eases the tension. 'What have you got in mind?'

'Chopsticks? A fork?'

'Let's not take any weapons. Let's just be fierce in body and mind.'

'Good plan.'

'OK, so what do we say? Like he's obviously going to deny he's Ollie, right? He's...' I look back at the computer. 'M. Miller. What, Michael, Matthew, Mason...?'

'Of course he's going to deny it. So we need the element of surprise.' She fingers her chin, deep in thought. 'Got it! Right, so we drive to that address and just hope it's current. Then we hide out front, behind a shrub, or some such. Then you text him and say something really lovey dovey, like I didn't want to intrude but there's a gift outside for you. Hope you like it! He's going to freak out, right, because you aren't supposed to know his address. He'll go outside to check if there's something there. And then boom he comes out and there we are! That proves he got the text, he isn't Ollie, and we catch him in the act.'

'It's genius.'

'I read a lot of crime novels before I became obsessed with romance.'

We pack up our vans, and I lock up Poppy, giving her a tap goodbye and promise I'll be back soon. We'd decided to drive there in Aria's more inconspicuous (not vibrant fuchsia) van and park at a nature reserve around the corner and walk the rest of the way.

On the drive there I tamp down the nerves by reminding myself just how angry I am.

'Do you think he's got a number of girls on the hook?' I ask Aria.

She grimaces. 'Probably. That's what they do, isn't it? Live in a world of make-believe.'

'I still don't understand why someone would do it. What do they get out of it?'

She shakes her head. 'I guess it's a lack of self-confidence thing. They probably hate their life, the way they look or something so can create this whole new online persona and have people fall in love with the *idea* of them, girls who normally wouldn't give them the time of day.'

'It's sad, that. Isn't it? Pitiful.'

'They find a way in, some vulnerability, and it goes from there.'

I think of how we met, how it didn't take long for Ollie to find his angle. 'I'm such a fool.'

'You're not a fool at all. These people are master manipulators, it's what they do. And it happens more often than you know. These days we live in an online world so much of the time, it's easy to believe someone who seems so genuine especially when they do their research on a person, makes it so much easier for them.'

'Yeah,' I say, wondering how I was so easily convinced by him.

We find the nature reserve and park up. I take a deep centring breath, and try to control the shake in my hands.

'You sure you want to do this?' Aria asks.

I swallow hard. 'I'm sure.'

We creep around the corner, counting off the numbers of each ordinary village house. 'That's his, number 42,' I say. 'The one with the red car.' Mercifully, I see a bushy plant that is big enough for us to hide behind and still get a good view of him as he leaves the house.

'Get the text ready, and then we'll walk over and send it when we're in position.'

Ollie, I didn't want to intrude at this sad time, so I've left you a gift outside your front door. Rosie

Of course there is no gift but he'll have to come outside to investigate.

'Put a kiss,' she says. 'Make it real.'

I add an X and we walk quietly to our spot.

'Here goes,' I whisper, and press send.

Aria clutches my arm and I stand on tiptoes when I see the door creaks open a touch. And then it closes. She puts a finger to her lips and I nod. Blood thunders in my ears. Is he going to come out or not? After a full five minutes or so which feels more like an hour, the door is wrenched open and a man wearing a tracksuit appears. He must be sixty! He drops his gaze to the porch looking for a gift that's not there, and then heads down to the letterbox.

We step out from our hiding spot and surprise him, my pulse racing at the idea of confrontation.

'Hi *Ollie*,' I say caustically. The guy is old enough to be my father!

His mouth opens and closes, and he finally finds his voice. 'I'm sorry, I think you have the wrong…'

'Don't make it worse, M. Miller!' Aria says, glaring at him.

'What *is* your name?' I ask.

'If you'll excuse me,' he says and turns away. I grab his elbow.

'Not so fast.' I almost grin as the line is so movie-like, the situation seems so unreal it's almost hysteria inducing. 'Why'd you do it?'

When he doesn't respond Aria takes her phone from her pocket. 'I'm sure the police would love to ask you themselves.'

'Call the police, love. Be my guest. I have no idea what you're on about, yeah? They'll only tell you you've got your facts wrong and remove you from *private* property.'

I try to discern if his is the voice I heard on the phone but it's impossible to tell. For a moment my confidence wanes. He holds his hands out like he's got nothing to hide. I turn to Aria but she isn't convinced by him. 'Sure, then tell me your name and I can confirm it with the police.'

'I'm sorry but I'm not giving out my private details…' He smiles but it doesn't reach his eyes.

'Fine. I'll get the police here! I bet they'd like to see every email you've ever sent to Rosie! All your texts. Your fake blog. I bet we could even ask the other moderators of the Van Lifers forum to check who else you've been messaging!'

Her words must hit home as fear flashes in his widened eyes. 'OK, OK, don't call the police, please. I'll tell you everything but don't call them. I haven't actually done anything wrong, have I? Except fallen in love with a beautiful girl.'

My stomach churns. 'Except committing a cyber-crime, you mean?' Surely catfishing is a crime, but I really have no idea and hope to bluff him to confess.

'So, why?' Aria prods.

His face crumples and he looks like an old, frail man. It's hard to reconcile that this is Ollie, that this is the man who wrote me such beautiful emails. It's sickening and sad and many mixed emotions flare. Starting at his weathered face, his lonely sunken eyes, I feel pity for him.

'Because who doesn't want a beautiful girl like Rosie in their life?' he says quietly. 'She makes me feel alive, passionate, like I matter. I've never been married, never had kids. I feel like I missed the boat in life, and then I found her, and I felt like I wasn't alone anymore.'

'Cut the crap,' Aria says. 'This isn't the first time you've done this.'

At that his hangdog expression changes into something more malevolent. God, I almost believed him again! Thank god Aria is with me.

'So?'

'So you think it's OK to stalk people online, find out every last detail about them and then betray them by pretending to be someone you're not?'

'What if I do?' He is belligerent all of a sudden and I feel a prickle of fear. This man could be more dangerous than we thought.

Aria toys with her phone and shrugs.

'Rosie here never got hurt, did she? So what if she poured her heart out to me, I didn't actually *do* anything to her, did I? Except be the guy she so desperately needed in her life. Sent her passages from some other guy's blog, bloody hell she really liked all that mushy talk.' He makes air quotes. '"*When I'm sitting in the van as the sun retreats for another day casting an orange glow across the sky, I feel so alive ...*" Come on, Rosie. You fell for lovey dovey idiocy?'

He stole the words that spoke to me on a deeper level? They didn't come from him, there is some beautiful poetic genuine soul out there, and M. Miller just copied and pasted those words knowing it's what I wanted to hear. Anger makes my vision cloud.

'Umm, hello? You're old enough to be her father and you're setting up "dates" to meet her. She shared private information with someone she thought she could trust. What did you hope to get out of it?'

'Photos.'

'What do you mean?'

'I hoped we'd get closer and start sending pics, and one thing would lead to another...'

Nausea rises up at just thinking about what kind of photos he means.

'You're sick.' Aria spits.

'You can't blame a guy for trying.'

'Ah, yeah you can. It's immoral, illegal and it's just plain creepy.'

He's clearly disturbed. The desire to flee is huge, but for some inexplicable reason Aria doesn't move. I tug her arm to let her know it's time to go. I'm vacillating between fear and queasiness and the overwhelming feeling of being duped, actually falling for a con from this deluded individual.

The sound of a motorbike roaring along drowns out his reply and then I see him. Max, on someone's bike. He looks like a demi god roaring towards us, his leonine locks blowing out from under his helmet.

'Did you tell him?' I ask Aria.

'I sure did. Back up.'

Oh holy mother of smoke. 'Max isn't going to kill him, is he?'

Max parks the bike, steps off and handles his helmet all in one swift move. Standing to his full height, his feline eyes are fierce, and if I didn't know him better I'd be terrified. Rage radiates off him.

'This the guy?' he growls.

'This is him.' Aria grins.

'Max, don't hurt him!' I say.

Before we can say any more M. Miller lets out a high-pitched scream and runs back to the house, stumbling and falling before eventually slamming the door shut with a bang.

Max laughs.

'I'm not going to hurt him; I'm a pacifist remember? I just wanted to scare him a little.'

Aria grins. 'It was my idea.'

'Why did you tell Max we were coming here?'

'Safety precaution. What if M. Miller was the serial killer you're always going on about?'

The stress leaves my body as I know I'm safe. Max is here, Aria is here, and I'm with good people who have my best interests at heart.

'You'll still have to go the police,' Max says. 'File a report so they look into this guy. Other girls might not be so lucky as you.'

'Yeah,' I shiver. 'Never in a million years would I have thought he wasn't real.'

'What made you suspicious?' Aria asks Max.

'No one would stand Rosie up on a date. No one.'

I blush to the roots of my hair, sure he's lying. He's trying to bolster my ego after I shared confidences with a 60-year-old sociopath on the internet. But I hadn't been in love with Ollie, had I? I just been open to the idea of meeting him. If I were honest the person who makes my pulse race stands in front of me, his hair blowing in the wind, his fierce gaze trained on me.

'Let's head back.' I say, taking Max's hand and giving it a thank you squeeze. I know I need to sort the catfish mess out but right now I want to get as far away from M. Miller's house as possible.

'If you don't mind, Aria, I'd like Rosie to ride with me?'

'Go for it,' she says and winks at me when his back is turned.

'But…but…' I splutter. A motorbike!

'Trust me, Rosie, and hold me tight.'

He hands me a helmet which I clip on, and then I swing my leg over the back of the motorbike, hugging into Max as tight as I can so I don't fly off the back of the bike as he roars away. I can feel the heat of him through his shirt, and lean into him under the guise of motorbike safety.

Hugging Max is a security all of its own. While we roar along quiet streets heading back to camp, my mind wanders back to the sweet encounters I've shared with Max. He always put my needs first. I resisted it, thinking he had ulterior motives, but that was the same old fear popping up. Callum told me to find someone who set my world on fire, and at the time I'd thought it was a cop-out a way to get out the door faster, but he was right. I'd never felt that pull with anyone, the way I do with Max.

Max lights me up from the inside out, makes me hope and dream about what could be, if I only I trust in him, in *myself*. Shouldn't I throw caution to the wind and live my truth, the very thing that's in my heart? You can't plan who you're going to fall in love with, you just have to believe Cupid knows who's best.

Max.

When we get back to camp, he pulls up alongside Poppy.

'We have to talk,' he says, more a demand than a statement.

'OK.' Is this where he says goodbye, tells me not to be such a damn fool again?

Inside, I make tea, and sit and wait him out as he paces the van like he's about to give me bad news. But, if I believe in my feelings then I have to voice them no matter what he says to me. Honesty, going forward, always. It's the only way.

'Max sit down, you'll wear out the vinyl.'

He runs a hand through his hair and grins at me. 'Sorry, I'm nervous.'

The moment of truth. 'Just say it, Max I can handle it.'

'Rosie, I don't want to scare you off, especially after what happened today.'

'OK...?' I stare at the contradiction that is Max: big and burly, tattooed, wild and free, but with a heart of gold, who'd do anything to make someone else's life easier. Happier. My fun-loving vegan who wants to make the world a better place, starting with himself. It's hard not to well up thinking how close we are here, on the cusp of admitting how we feel, and it could all be taken away from me if he's decided he doesn't feel the same way.

'Rosie, there's no easy way to say this, so I'm just going to say it. I fell in love with you right around the time you parked in my spot, and it's only grown from there. I kept leaving, because I figured you didn't feel the same because this Ollie guy kept cropping up in conversations and you acted as though you weren't that keen...'

All those times he disappeared weren't because he didn't care about saying goodbye? He wasn't giving me the cold shoulder. How much I've misread Max.

'And then I hear more and more about this Ollie guy, and I know it in my heart somehow that it's not right, something is off about the whole situation. I had to protect you as much as you hate the idea of that.'

258

Goose bumps prickle my skin. Max's protective instincts were right and I fought him every step of the way.

He scrubs his face with his hand. 'I'd do anything for you. I want, I *need*, you in my life. You make me feel like bouncing out of bed in the mornings, like running up mountains and screaming to the world I've met this crazy, eccentric, girl who manically cleans, and bakes with too much sugar, who fits into my arms as if she were made for them, who giggles after too much wine, who argues just to have the last word and I can't see straight for wanting to love you with all of me, Rosie.'

It's as if my every wish has been granted, the love in my heart that threatens to burst out. My legs are like jelly and yet, I stand and stare into Max's eyes and see my own reflected back. 'Well, why didn't you say so earlier?'

'And get the last word in? Is that even possible with you, Rosie?'

I laugh, and lean into him. 'Never!' As I relax into his arms, I feel like I'm exactly where I'm meant to be. 'Maybe we had to wait for the stars to align, or maybe we just had to learn about each other first, but either way I'm completely besotted with you, Max.'

'So what now?' he asks.

He means the future, I can tell by the question in his eyes. 'What do you want?'

'I want to follow the sun and see where the breeze blows us. How does that sound?'

A little too vague for me. I go to speak but he puts a finger to my lips. 'But I know you, Rosie, I know you need a plan in place. So with that in mind, I'd like to see where our relationship goes, and if you still love me in a year or so, I'd like to marry you. Plan our future children.'

I slap my forehead. 'I mentioned our future children?'

'You sleep talk.'

Oh golly, what had I said when I bunked in Max's van when Poppy was in for repairs? I have a vision of our children with tangled curls, and wise owl faces running free in meadows, while we lay tangled in each other's arms, watching them from afar, living life on our terms.

'We can settle down, or stay on the road, it will be your call. I'll be happy wherever you are, Rosie.'

I can schedule our lives to the last millisecond and that will be fine by him. I don't have to change who I am, I don't have to fit into any mould, I just have to be who I am and I am enough for him. 'I'll be happy wherever you are too, Max.'

I envisage Max and I stargazing under the moonlight. Us getting lost in foreign locals, drinking cheap warm beer, and finding lost laneways where I grab his hand and lean him up against a crumbling brick wall and steal a kiss. Speaking of which...

'This is the part of a romance novel where you'd lean down and kiss me.'

'But this isn't a romance novel.'

'Who says? Kiss me and then we'll know for sure.'

All the pieces click into place as Max lifts me into his arms where I fit perfectly like the last piece of a puzzle. He presses his lips hard against mine, and makes me dizzy with desire as I recognise he's the one, *the one* I've been waiting for my entire life, and I just didn't know it. There's no spark, instead there's great big fireworks in every colour of the rainbow. Eventually we draw back for breath.

'So...' he says, his saucy smile makes my legs wobble.

'Kiss me again.' *And again. And again.*

Maybe you can't fall in love over the internet but you can fall in love after a kiss.

ACKNOWLEDGEMENTS

The beautiful bohemian Nola is named in honour of Peggy Sheppard's Nana, Nola Bell Shannon. I hope I've done her justice Peggy!

Dear Reader,

Thank you for shutting out the real world and diving into the land of fiction for a while. I hope you've journeyed far and wide and had an incredible adventure from the comfort of your own home.

Without you I wouldn't be able to spend my days talking to my invisible friends who become so real to me I name drop them in conversations with my family who all think I'm a little batty at the best of times... so thanks again!

My sincerest hope is that you connected with my characters and laughed and cried and cheered them on (even the baddies who I hope redeemed themselves in the end) and that they also became your friends too.

I'd love to connect with you! Find me on Facebook @RebeccaRaisinAuthor or on Twitter @Jaxandwillsmum. I'm a bibliophile from way back so you'll find me chatting about books and romance but I'm also obsessed with travel, wine and food!

Reviews are worth their weight in gold to authors so if the book touched you and left you feeling 'happy ever after' please consider sharing your thoughts and I'll send you cyber hugs in return!

Follow my publisher @HQDigitalUK for book news, giveaways, and lots of FriYAY fun!

Love,
Rebecca x

Dear Reader,

Thank you so much for taking the time to read this book – we hope you enjoyed it! If you did, we'd be so appreciative if you left a review.

Here at HQ Digital we are dedicated to publishing fiction that will keep you turning the pages into the early hours. We publish a variety of genres, from heartwarming romance, to thrilling crime and sweeping historical fiction.

To find out more about our books, enter competitions and discover exclusive content, please join our community of readers by following us at:

🐦 *@HQDigitalUK*

f *facebook.com/HQDigitalUK*

Are you a budding writer? We're also looking for authors to join the HQ Digital family! Please submit your manuscript to:

HQDigital@harpercollins.co.uk.

Hope to hear from you soon!

Turn the page for an extract from Rebecca Raisin's
enchanting *Celebrations and Confetti at Cedarwood Lodge...*

CHAPTER ONE

Staring up at the imposing structure with its weathered facade, I had a terrible premonition that I'd made a mistake. A huge one. But, I reasoned, clawing back rising panic, I had *always* wanted to buy the 100-year-old abandoned lodge. It had been put up for sale recently, and I'd jumped at the chance. The old place had good sturdy bones; it was solid, despite the desertion of its caretakers aeons ago.

Even though I'd always dreamed about owning Cedarwood Lodge I hadn't expected for it to happen so soon. But it had, and I'd fallen madly in love with the place as it stood, shutters broken, doors in need of paint, ivy creeping through broken panes of glass, and cascading roses growing wild and free around the porch balustrades. Here was a place untouched for decades and I had a chance to bring it back to its former glory.

The September sky shifted from foggy wisps of gray to country blue as dawn arrived in the small New Hampshire town of Evergreen. A sputtering car swung into the long, winding driveway and I turned to watch my oldest friend Micah leap from his battered hatchback.

We'd been best friends since childhood, and though we'd drifted apart as adults he was the first person I called when I bought Cedarwood Lodge – I offered him the job of maintenance manager which he'd accepted with a *'Hell yeah.'*

'You look exactly the same, Micah,' I said, reaching up for a hug. 'You haven't aged a bit.' He'd filled out, no longer the lanky teenager I'd left behind, but aside from that he was the same old Micah with the same affable smile.

'It's the daily hikes up the bluff. That thin mountain air does wonders for my skin.' He waggled his eyebrows. 'We've got a lot of catching up to do. I almost fell over when you called. Lucky for you I was between jobs…'

'Lucky for me, all right.'

I couldn't believe it'd been so long – when was the last time we had properly caught up, five years ago, six? Time ticked by so fast while I'd been away.

'You're different,' he said, gesturing to my outfit and my usual flyaway curls restrained with a clip. 'A little more polished.'

I grinned. 'Denim cut offs and messy hair didn't quite cut it in Manhattan.'

'What? Crazy city folk.' He clucked his tongue.

'Right?' I joked. 'How's Veronica?' I expected him to gush about his long-term girlfriend. Instead, his lips turned down for the briefest second, before he masked it with a smile.

'Veronica? There's a blast from the past. I haven't seen her for two and a bit years now. She was like you, Clio, left town and didn't look back.'

Surprise knocked me sideways that she'd left town, left Micah.

'Sorry, Micah. I thought…' *Way to go, Clio!*

He touched my shoulder, giving me time to wrench the meta-phorical foot from my mouth. 'It's OK.' He let out a half laugh. 'One day she just decided that this place was too small for her big dreams. This town, it isn't for everyone.'

An awkward silence hung between us. What kind of friend had I been to him? If I'd have known I would have come home for a visit to comfort him, make sure he was OK. Shame colored

270

my cheeks, and in reality, I realized if he had called me I probably would have played the *too busy* card.

I knew Micah inside out, and sensed he was downplaying the split. I could see by the set of his jaw that the conversation was closed. A part of me deflated – if they couldn't make it, what hope did any of us have? They'd been *the* perfect couple.

I tried desperately to think of a subject that would get us back on an even keel. 'Look at that view, Micah. Tell me I'm not imagining it – this place *is* magical, right?'

'Magic to its very core.' He flashed a grin, reminding me of the playful guy he was in high school. The one who transcended cliques and was friends with everyone. 'And soon you'll have the banging of hammers and the whine of drills to contend with, so soak up the serenity while you can.'

Work was set to start today – with plumbers, electricians, glaziers and carpenters arriving. Once they'd completed their jobs, painters would come in to pretty the place up. A project manager called Kai would be here soon to oversee it all while I concentrated on the business and event side of things. Micah would float between us all and make sure things ran smoothly.

'Who'd have thought I'd end up back here, the proud and slightly nervous owner of Cedarwood Lodge?' I scrunched up my nose, my earlier doubts creeping back in. What had I done? I planned *parties*, not renovations! I *hired* places for events, I didn't buy them! Sometimes my audacity at buying Cedarwood Lodge scared me silly. It was such a huge gamble.

With a smile Micah said softly, 'Never in a million years would I have thought you'd come back from the bright lights of the big city. Seems once people get a taste for it, Evergreen pales into insignificance. But I'm so glad you did. Remember when we were kids and hung out here? Even back then you talked about the parties you'd host, colors you'd paint the place. Ten years old and you predicted Cedarwood would be yours, *and* you were right.'

The memories brought out a rash of goose bumps.

Cedarwood had been our own private playground. We'd run breathless through the overgrown grounds, peeked into dusty windows and imagined the scenes that might have taken place there before it was abandoned.

The lodge had been closed ever since we could remember and while stories had been whispered around town about the previous owners, we'd been too young to understand.

'It feels good to be home,' I said, meaning it. At that moment Manhattan seemed light years away. 'I didn't realize how much I missed you until I saw your goofy face.'

'Oh, that hurt, that hurt a lot. *Goofy*? Don't think that just because *you've* come back all New York-ified that I've forgotten the girl with the uneven pig tails and a mouth full of metal? The one who wore leg warmers as a fashion statement!' He raised a brow, challenging me.

I stifled a laugh. He was right. I had been a fashion *don't* when I was a teenager, but things quickly changed when I met Amory – my best friend in New York – who showed me how to dress to impress.

Would I regress, being back home? Go back to sweats and trainers? In my tailored suits and perilously high heels, I felt as though I slipped on a different persona.

In the so-called 'city that never sleeps' it had been crucial to be assertive, ambitious, and one step ahead of the game. It had taken me years to build up my client list and I worked so damn hard for it. Maybe the old adage was true: you can take the girl out of Evergreen but you can't take Evergreen out of the girl, because here I was, home again.

I shielded my eyes from the rising sun. In the distance the mountain range was a riot of autumnal color, reds, ochres, dusty orange, and saffron yellow – the leaves on the hardwood trees clinging on for one more day.

'I hope I don't mess things up, Micah. This is my last chance. So many things could go wrong,' I said seriously. I could lose everything. The place could remain silent, might never be filled with the tapping of high heel shoes, the popping of champagne corks and peals of laughter. I couldn't go back to Manhattan, that door was firmly closed. 'What if after all the work is done no one hires the place?'

'Hey…' he said, gently rubbing my arm. 'That's not the Clio I know. Where's the girl who left town screeching about setting the world ablaze?' He gave me a playful shove. 'Where's she gone?'

Up until a few months ago I'd been brimming with confidence, sure of my place in the world. But then I'd messed up – being too honest with a bride, misunderstanding her nerves for something else entirely. It had shaken me up, and made me question myself and my ambitions. Maybe I'd just been lucky before, but that bride kicked my legs out from under me, and I hadn't quite managed to get back up yet.

'She's. Right. Here.' I rallied, pasting on a smile.

'Is that supposed to be a smile or a grimace?'

I flashed a sillier grin, regressing back to my teenage self and finding it refreshing. 'God, it's good to see you, Micah.' He was the one person I could be myself with. There was no point pretending because he knew the real me.

'Evergreen was never quite the same without you.'

During our teenage years we'd spent weekends dreaming of a life outside of here. I guess we always thought the grass was greener elsewhere, and for a small town girl, it was. It was so damn green it glowed, and I wished things had turned out differently. At least I had Cedarwood as a consolation prize.

Micah grinned. 'Hey,' he checked his watch. 'Where's your mom? I thought she'd be here.'

I shrugged. 'I have no idea. When I rang again she made some flimsy excuse. I honestly thought she'd be bursting to see the inside of the lodge after all these years. But I guess she'll get here when she gets here.'

My first day back in Evergreen I had driven straight to Mom's place to surprise her with the news about buying Cedarwood Lodge. It had been almost impossible to keep it secret but I'd wanted to tell her face to face and had guilelessly expected shrieks of joy. Instead she paled to a ghostly white, as if I had told her something shocking. We'd never been super close, but still, I'd expected a smile, a word of encouragement, a *welcome home* hug.

Up until last winter Mom had owned an inn in the center of Evergreen, so I'd also been hoping for a bit of guidance. In my heart of hearts I hoped buying the lodge would bring us closer together, but I guessed hoping didn't make it so.

Micah smiled but it didn't reach his eyes. 'She's probably just tying things up so she can concentrate properly once she gets here.' He pulled me into one of his breath-stealing bear hugs to comfort me, because we both knew it was more than that.

'Yeah,' I said, pulling away. Mom was retired now, so it wasn't as if she had anything keeping her away *per se*. Maybe she just needed to get used to the idea that her taking-the-world-by-storm daughter was back home… *without* actually having exactly taken the world by storm. Was she disappointed in me? It was hard to tell.

'First things first,' Micah said, dragging me back to reality. 'Let's check out your bedroom and see if I can make it a little more comfortable like you asked.'

Stepping into the warmth of the lodge, I snuck a glance over my shoulder to watch Micah's reaction, and sure enough he was wide-eyed just like I'd been at seeing the place for the first time. Faded sunlight caught the crystals in the chandeliers and cast prisms of color around the room. I breathed in the scent of long-forgotten memories before leading Micah up the spiral stairs to the suite that was to become my home for the foreseeable future.

I swung open the heavy oak door. The suite needed a little TLC, though the stone fireplace and view to the mountains made up for it.

'Right,' he said, surveying the scene. 'This shouldn't take too long, just needs a few nips and tucks and a lick of paint here and there.'

I smiled at Micah's assurances that it wasn't a big job, as I was eager to make the suite my own, and snuggle in bed with the mountains a stunning backdrop to my dreams. In the basement I'd found an antique bed with an elaborate bedhead which I repainted champagne white. Dragging it upstairs had been a feat, but one I managed with only a few scrapes and bruises. Once the room had a facelift with paint, some luxurious bedding, and new décor, it would feel more like me, more like home.

He opened the creaky bathroom door, exposing the old claw foot tub and a marble vanity – the perfect room to relax in with a book and a rose-scented bubble bath after a long day.

'I can fix the broken tiles, and redo the grout.'

I nodded eagerly. While the lodge was ancient, the bathrooms were still functional, and would only need some modern accoutrements to get them up to code. Some proper exhaust fans, and new lighting, maybe heat lights for winter... my list kept on growing. 'Great!'

I grabbed Micah's arm, eager to show him the view from the landing at the top of the stairs and ask his advice on what to do with the space. The mountain range was visible from every window on the east side of the lodge and I wanted people to be able to soak it up in comfort. The reflection of the trees shimmied on the surface of the lake, and it was easy to lose an hour staring outside at such elemental beauty – it was spellbinding.

Our tour was interrupted by the rumble of engines roaring along the main road.

'Can you hear that?' I asked, dropping his arm, and dashing closer to the window to get a glimpse of them arriving.

'That, my friend, is the sound of progress. Time to get your overalls on, Clio!' He gave my high heels a pointed look and was rewarded with an eye roll. 'Let's meet them out front!'

We flew down the stairs and on to the porch to watch the

procession arrive. Cars and trucks turned into the driveway in convoy. Some were loaded with supplies, others bare except for hard-hatted drivers with determined expressions.

Anticipation sizzled through me. It was really happening! This beautiful timeworn lodge was about to be transformed back into its glorious self.

My old life was behind me. Here – in the town I grew up, in the abandoned lodge I played by as a child – people would fall in love, they'd marry, they'd have families and then they'd return to Cedarwood and celebrate once more...

CHAPTER TWO

A few weeks later, ignoring a head throb from the ever-present noise, I gave myself a silent pep talk. *You can do this! All you have to do is paint them a charming picture of what will be.* I buttoned up my navy blue blazer, straightened the seam of my crisp linen trousers and slipped on red heels, the ones Micah teased me relentlessly over.

With the buzz of a drill nearby, I picked up my paperwork and iPad, which had a 3D presentation loaded and ready to play. Eventually I'd have an office in a suite off the lobby but right now it was still too frenetic with workers for me to concentrate, so in the interim I'd set up a temporary office in the front parlor, a room once used for pre-dinner aperitifs.

The couple's car churned up the gravel and my heart rate increased. They'd called the night before and enquired about hiring the ballroom for their fiftieth wedding anniversary. It had taken all of my might to keep my voice level and act like I'd hired out the ballroom a hundred times already. But it bode well, having interest in Cedarwood at this early stage.

I peeked out of the newly replaced window and watched Edgar help his wife Imelda into a wheelchair. *Damn it!* There were no ramps in place. I made a mental note to check we had mobility aids on the list. Cedarwood had to be accessible to everyone.

With a broad smile in place, I hurried outside to greet them.

'Welcome to Cedarwood!' I said too brightly, my nerves jangling to the surface as I half jogged toward them, mentally assessing the area for a plank of wood, or something to use as a ramp... when the heel of my stiletto got caught in a hole in the deck. With a calm smile that belied the drumming of my heart, I attempted to wrench my heel out, trying to appear casual, but it wouldn't budge. Damn it! With one last heave, the heel came free but momentum sent me flying forward with a screech. *Oh, god!* I flew precariously into the air, taking great leaps to avoid a tray of paint and a scattering of drill bits. *Please*, I silently willed the universe, *don't let me upend the paint all over her!* With a hop, skip, and a jump to avoid everything, I ended up on my knees by the woman's lap, my pulse thrumming in my ears.

Note to self: make sure walkways are cleared at all times.

Sweat broke out on my forehead despite the chilly autumn day. Red-faced and righting myself, I held out a hand and said breezily, 'I'm Clio. And as you can see, I've been falling over myself to meet you.' *Kill me.* Thank god I hadn't taken her out. I could already imagine the story getting Chinese-whispered around town: *Did you hear Clio Winters tried to murder her first client, and it was little old Imelda no less!*

Imelda chuckled and shook my hand. 'Aren't you as pretty as a picture? I hope you didn't ruin those heels, do you think they come in my size? My life flashed before my eyes but all I could think was, I need a pair of those dancing shoes for the party...' her eyes twinkled mischievously.

Admonishing myself silently for being a klutz, I dared a quick peek at my trousers; they had somehow remained intact – however, from the pain radiating upwards, my knees hadn't fared as well. 'I'm sure they'd have your size and I think the leopard print would suit you...'

She cocked her head as if contemplating. 'I might just have to find some for the party, what do you say, Edgar?' She craned her neck and smiled benignly at her husband.

'They most certainly *look* like dancing shoes… Could be a new type of work boot, what would I know?' He glanced at the hole in the deck, and then my heels and raised his eyes to the heavens. I tried to hide a smile and remain professional, but a giggle escaped, it couldn't be helped, I liked them both instantly.

I stepped forward and shook Edgar's hand. The speech I'd prepared had flown straight out of my head as I'd toppled into Imelda's personal space, but I sensed my spiel would have been too formal, too stuffy for these people. Game face on, I cleared my throat and tried to regroup.

Right. *Explain yourself, and don't fall over!* 'As you can see, Cedarwood is getting a bit of a make-over. It's a work site at the moment, but soon…'

'It's just as gorgeous as ever,' Imelda said, her eyes shining. 'Can we take a look through?'

'It's a little noisy what with the…'

'Noise schmoise,' she said, waving me away. 'We don't mind that, do we Edgar?'

I gulped. What if something fell on them, or Edgar tripped and broke a leg? I'd planned on showing them the ballroom from the adjoining outdoor deck and showing my presentation. Not opening myself up for a health and safety lawsuit on the first day.

'We're as tough as old boots even if we look a little fragile, don't you worry about us.' Imelda said.

If we walked slowly, and carefully, surely it would be OK for a few minutes? Though I'd managed to fall over already…

'So sorry that we're not fully equipped at the moment. Let me help you lift the chair,' I said, praying I didn't get a finger caught in the wheel spokes and drop her, or something equally idiotic.

'Help with the chair would be mighty kind,' Edgar said and moved to one side while I took the other. We hefted the surprisingly light Imelda up.

With my back holding open the oak door, Edgar wheeled Imelda into the lobby, the scent of wet paint heavy in the air. Drop sheets were scattered across the floor to catch spills and the sounds of work echoed around the lodge.

'It might look like a big mess at the moment, but trust me there's a method to the madness. We have a strict schedule in place.' It was hard to envisage what the lodge *would* look like with groups of laborers in clusters, drilling, hammering, filing, and edging. Tools were scattered, buckets were littered here and there. Bags of rubbish sat awaiting removal. The couple followed my noisy tread, the wood underfoot making a weird kind of song depending on where we stepped. *Squeak, ping, pop, ahh.*

Imelda shook her head as if she was mesmerized, 'I'm sure you've got a handle on it all.' We continued through the expanse of the lobby with its thick American oak pillars, and dusty chandeliers swaying in the breeze, their crystals clinking gently like a song, prisms of colored light dancing on the walls. The stone fireplace needed a little love, its mantle was missing, but still a fire crackled in the grate, adding to the ambience.

Firelight shimmered across the room. Even in its disorderly state the lodge radiated a type of warmth, a feeling of relaxation and expectation of what might be…

'As you can see I'm trying to keep as much of it original as I can.' I wanted the lodge to keep its old-world charm. 'The overall look will remain as it was all those years ago.'

'That's music to my ears,' Imelda said, beaming. 'We worried the lodge might've been purchased by a huge consortium and turned into some modern monolith. I'm so glad that's not the case.'

We continued to a small salon. I just managed to narrowly avoid kicking over a bucket full of cleaning equipment. The room was musty, with old brocade curtains clinging to their rusty rails. 'Edgar, don't you remember, we used to play charades in here,' Imelda said, reaching up to grasp her husband's hand.

'You've stayed here before?' I asked, a shiver of excitement running through me. They'd stayed at Cedarwood in its heyday? No one I'd known had actually been *inside* the lodge as it had been closed down for so long.

Edgar turned Imelda's chair to face me. 'We got married here,' she said dreamily.

I gasped. 'You did? That's incredible!' No wonder they'd been so eager to see the place as it was – warts and all – and could imagine what it would look like in the future.

Her face broke into a smile and I could see the bright-eyed young girl she'd been. 'Coming up to fifty years ago I was a blushing bride of 25 years old. Edgar was 26. We found each other late in life, or what was deemed late back then. All our friends were already married and had a bunch of babies. We fell in love but there were only a few weeks before Edgar was shipped off to the war.'

'I can't believe this!' My pulse thrummed knowing their story ended in Happy Ever After, because here they stood. 'What a story, and to have you return to the lodge…' I wanted to hug them, but held myself in check. 'How long were you away, Edgar?' I shuddered, thinking of the young man – as he then was – being thrust into such a dangerous wartime situation.

He gave Imelda a meaningful glance and said, 'Two years, four months, and one day,' he blushed. 'Or thereabouts. Thankfully, or not so thankfully depending how you see it, I was shot in the foot and sent home. Never ended up making it back to my platoon though…'

A ray of sunlight landed on Imelda like a soft spotlight. 'Yes, I was lucky and got to keep him safe at home with me.'

They recollected the war, and how they missed each other fiercely for the two and a bit years he was away. The talked about the letters they wrote and all the promises they vowed to keep as soon as he returned home.

'Did you keep those promises?' I asked.

'We did,' he said. 'You just don't have an inkling when you're young how fast those years flick by. Though I'm sure there's been plenty of days Imelda has wanted to walk off into the sunset with someone else,' he laughed.

Imelda considered it. 'Once or twice I wanted to put your head in the oven, I can't lie.'

He nodded. 'See? Luckily our oven is electric. And we made it through fifty years with lots of talking, lots of *communicating* as you young folks call it.' He chortled. 'When we heard this place had itself a new owner, we knew it was a chance to throw one hell of a party. We like the idea of coming back to where we began.'

They exchanged a glance, a private message in their rheumy eyes. Whatever happened in my life I vowed right then to wait for the perfect man, I wouldn't compromise. I wanted the fairy tale that I saw before me. Even if I ran into my old gang of friends in Evergreen and I was the only one still single. Still utterly without *The One* at thirty-three. Now was not the time to dwell on it. It didn't matter. Love couldn't be rushed. *Focus, Clio, this isn't about you.*

'I promise if you have the party at Cedarwood there'll be lots of celebrations, and confetti. It will be an ode to your life together, the love you share. I'll make it as special as it so deserves to be.'

Imelda gestured for me to lean close and gave me a tight hug. 'What do you mean *if*... We came here to tell you to get the ball rolling... We aren't spring chickens anymore. The only problem I envisage is time. You see, we want to celebrate on our wedding day, makes sense of course, but that's only six weeks away... you think you can do it?' She gazed around the lodge, like she was imagining the place as it once was.

Could we get the ballroom and entrance done in six short weeks? There was the garden to consider, guest bathrooms, safety measures... But their faces... they looked so awed by the lodge, how could I say no? 'Sure,' I said, voice brimming with confidence for the first time since I'd arrived. 'We can do it.'

She gave me a grateful smile. 'I better find those high heels then. Maybe I'll get the leopard print *and* the red, you just never know when a gal might need a pair of fancy shoes.'

'It pays to be organized.' I winked. 'And I'm truly honored you're going to have the party here.' My mind spun with ideas, questions, solutions, and we hadn't even started yet.

'It's like the circle of life, we started here, and it will end here...' Imelda was a romantic, I sensed a likeminded soul.

I said, 'Would you like to continue to the ballroom?'

Edgar pushed the wheelchair slowly forward. 'Sure, let's see it.'

Imelda smiled, and fussed with a rug on her lap. 'If I close my eyes I can still recall the excitement in that young girl's heart, feel the butterflies floating in her belly at the thought that handsome young man was going to be her husband. I really didn't believe you'd show up, Edgar. Isn't that the silliest thing?'

Edgar went to reply but stopped as Imelda's hand went to her throat, and her face paled. She let out a small groan, and scrunched her eyes closed.

I dropped to my knees and gazed into her face, but her eyes stayed tightly shut, screwed up in pain. 'Imelda? Are you OK?' Panic seized me, but Edgar appeared resigned but calm.

Edgar rubbed her shoulder, 'She's OK. She'll be right in a moment.' His voice was soft with acceptance at whatever it was causing her pain. He opened a bag hanging on the back of the wheelchair and rummaged around, taking out a pillbox and a bottle of water. 'We could fight a war, financial troubles, and everything in between, but we can't fight time,' he said, sadly.

It was a full minute before Imelda returned to us, 'Sorry,' she said, giving my hand a pat. 'Another spell I take it?'

Edgar stooped forward and handed her two pills and the bottle of water. She took them with trembling hands and drank, before saying, 'The mind is willing, but the body just won't listen sometimes. Don't you worry, pet. It's OK. Nothing is going to stop me from having a party at Cedarwood Lodge. Nothing.' She stuck her chin forward, resolute.

Once Imelda's color returned to normal they peeked into the ballroom with cries of delight. 'I'm so glad you're not fussing with it,' she said. 'It's like something out of an F. Scott Fitzgerald novel.'

'I know,' I said, her description apt. 'Have you thought about themes, colors? Cuisines? I can show…'

She cut me off. 'You're the expert,' Imelda said. 'All I ask is that the room is bright and cheerful, think colorful bunting, and streamers cascading down. I know it doesn't sound like much, but I'd love for it to look just like we had it all those years ago.'

An hour later, after firming up more details, we said our goodbyes and I told them to visit any time so they could see the lodge being shaped back into the beauty of its halcyon days.

Hopefully it would return them to their wedding night and their hearts and souls would be young again, with their whole life ahead of them.

I couldn't wait to call Amory and tell her every little thing. And to see if my name was still making the gossip page…

CHAPTER THREE

'Clio, they sound amazing! So they've booked the party?' Amory shrieked as I sat down with a laugh at my desk, ignoring piles of invoices that needed to be paid.

'They did! And get this: they didn't want to see color swatches and menus, or a song list. They said I was the expert and just make it bright and colorful. Only kicker is I have to get everything finished and organized in six weeks.'

'You can do it, that's what you're good at. Deadlines.' She let out a laugh. 'You lucky thing not having to consult with them every five minutes – why can't they all be like that?'

Our clients in New York were pernickety to say the least. Bridezillas were plentiful, and the women weren't opposed to throwing tantrums a 5-year-old would be proud of, but I always rolled with it. It came with the territory to receive phone calls at two a.m. from a blushing bride-to-be, sobbing about centerpieces or tiaras. That's what separated the good party planners from the bad. My job was to say *yes*, always.

I could fix anything, especially under pressure.

But then I had opened my big mouth.

Shaking myself out of reverie I said, 'I'm sure the next clients won't be so easy.' In the background phones buzzed and drawers banged. Office life. I felt a pang for it. We lapsed into silence as I debated whether to ask.

'Darling about…' she hesitated and I steeled myself. Amory always knew what I was thinking without me having to say a word.

'Don't tell me. They're still talking about it? Still?' It had been months. Months since I'd packed up my desk and hidden in my shoebox sized apartment until the sale of Cedarwood had settled. Surely they'd moved on to newer scandals by now? I'd been avoiding the online gossip sites for months in case I saw my own name trapped in a headline once more.

The previous headlines were still burned into my retinas *Party planner to the A-listers tells reality star bride to run from celebrity groom!*

Amory let out a nervous laugh. 'Well…'

I groaned and cupped my face. 'Tell me. I can handle it.'

She took an audible intake of breath before she launched into the whole sorry story. 'It seems it's ramping up. She's saying you had a thing for the groom, and that's why you did what you did. Because you were after him and his… money.'

I let out a squeal of protest. '*She didn't!*'

'She did.'

'But that's not true!' I wailed. Outside the sun sank low, coloring the sky saffron.

Her voice came back a hissed whisper. '*I* know it's not true. But you've really underestimated her. She's set on ruining your reputation to save hers.'

'But my reputation is *already* ruined! Why does she have to continue with it?' The whole sordid thing was so unfair, and I kicked myself for believing in the blushing bride-to-be when she'd poured her heart out to me minutes before she was supposed to walk down the aisle. I was appalled by her confession – how could she marry someone she didn't love when her heart belonged to another? With the clock ticking I advised her to run, get out

286

of that church before she made a huge mistake because I believed her tale of woe and didn't want to see her waste her life with the wrong man! And it turned out to be the stupidest thing I'd ever done.

Really, I should have known. It was Dealing with Brides 101. Never, *ever* advise them. Wedding day jitters and cold feet can make a person say the craziest things. It was my job to reassure them, not tell them to run! And these were not your average Manhattanites. He was a millionaire movie star, for god's sake.

'She's vindictive.'

'I can understand why she'd try and save face. What she told me was pretty damning, but to turn it around like that...' I was bewildered by it. I had only met the groom twice and one of those times was on the aborted wedding day when I had to tell him she'd taken flight. *Because of my advice... stupid, stupid, stupid.*

Amory clucked her tongue. 'It's a simple case of: you know too much. She's got to make you the villain, so nothing rubs off on her. It wouldn't take a genius to unearth her real story ... but it's juicier with you cast as the crazed, infatuated wedding planner.'

It was so damn ridiculous I could only sigh. Something like this would only happen in New York. 'She's so bloody cunning. I wish I'd shared my side of the story earlier. But it's too late, no one would believe me now.'

'She's called Flirty McFlirtison for a reason,' Amory said sadly.

I couldn't help but giggle. Amory had disliked the reality star bride Monica intensely and given her the nickname. It had been tricky to mask our true feelings around her because she'd been the client from hell, unless a man happened to walk by and then she'd bat her lashes, leaving us shaking our heads.

I should have known never to trust her. The day after the wedding Flirty started doing some major damage control and piling the blame on me. Once the news broke, no bride would go near me with a ten foot pole.

'Jesus, Amory, I thought it would've all blown over by now,' I said, slumping in my chair and gazing out at the beautiful explosion of color as the sun sank below the mountains.

'Here's an interesting twist... it's come out that he had her sign a watertight pre-nup the night *before* the wedding, so that's why she did a runner. You were just the perfect scapegoat. She's denying that of course.'

I groaned. 'Celebrities. I will never understand them.'

Still, even after all the A-list weddings I'd planned, I believed true love conquered all. Nothing would take away the pleasure I got out of organizing nuptials between two people who were *truly* smitten, even if they were on the never-heard-of-you list. Monica was driven by greed – she was just a reality TV starlet whose show was cancelled after one season, but she still craved the limelight and would do anything she could to get tabloid attention. I was unlucky to get caught up in her schemes.

'Celebrities,' she agreed. 'You don't know how lucky you are, Clio. Granted it wasn't an ideal exit from the agency but look where it's taken you! I'm *wildly* envious. In time you'll see it was the best decision you've ever made, and you'll think of us scrabbling after every high-profile party with pity.'

This was Amory's way, to silver line every cloud. 'I hope you're right. Otherwise I've bought a lodge on a whim because of what happened. In Evergreen. A town with a population of five hundred and three people!'

'That's the spirit!' she shouted and I could just see her swinging in her office chair, throwing her head back and laughing, as if I was sitting across from her. 'Now turn off Bonnie Tyler, please, I can almost hear your sobs from here – leave Bonnie for the broken hearted. And get back to work. You're the boss now, darling, so square those shoulders and own it.'

She knew me so well, even what my choice of music meant.

Once I hung up, I turned the volume up and listened to Bonnie's gravelly voice, not sobbing... not quite.

After all, what did *I* have to cry about? My reputation in New York was ruined. I'd invested every last dollar into a rundown lodge in a small town. There was nothing to worry about!

When I did something, like mess up my life, I did it right. And that included listening to music and crying like it was an Olympic sport. Who cares if *they* said I loved some random celebrity and ruined his marriage? It would be yesterday's news eventually, right? And being blacklisted by every New York event planning agency? Pffft. Big deal. I'd make my own success. In a town with five-oh-three people. Easy.

Oh, god, what had I done?

The next book from Rebecca Raisin is coming in 2019!